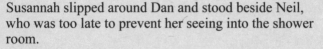
---- ★ ----

Susannah slipped around Dan and stood beside Neil, who was too late to prevent her seeing into the shower room.

"Oh, God." She gagged. "It's him...."

"Get out," Dan told the man, who fled.

"Don't move," he instructed the trembling kid, who probably couldn't.

I'd used the moment to grab my daughter and see the body on the shower floor. The young man had one bloodied eye, and a bruise the size of Nebraska on the same side of his face. But whatever had caused the bruises hadn't killed him. The victim was wearing a thin length of chain tightly wound around his neck, the links digging into his tanned throat. The handsome young man was no longer.

I'd only been to two horse shows, and had stumbled over a dead body each time. That made my average for involvement in murder one hundred percent. I wondered how I went about trading it in for a zero.

---- ★ ----

Previously published Worldwide Mystery title by
KATHLEEN DELANEY

DYING FOR A CHANGE

GIVE FIRST PLACE TO MURDER

KATHLEEN DELANEY

TORONTO • NEW YORK • LONDON
AMSTERDAM • PARIS • SYDNEY • HAMBURG
STOCKHOLM • ATHENS • TOKYO • MILAN
MADRID • WARSAW • BUDAPEST • AUCKLAND

Recycling programs
for this product may
not exist in your area.

GIVE FIRST PLACE TO MURDER

A Worldwide Mystery/December 2012

First published by PublishAmerica.com

ISBN-13: 978-0-373-26828-3

Printed in U.S.A.

Acknowledgments

This book is gratefully dedicated to my children and their partners, Jeff and Kris Penick, Dave and Nancy Koppang, Shannon O'Connell and Laura Koppang, Eric and Linda Koppang, and Lynne Koppang, and to my brother and sister-in-law, Mike and Mary Delaney. Their constant support, help, and belief in me keep me going in the toughest of times.

ONE

HIS HEAD WAS SLUMPED to one side, his mouth slightly open, his brown eyes unseeing. Small streams of blood cascaded down from the prongs of the pitchfork protruding from his chest to pool over the front of his jeans. His body slumped against a bale of hay, wedged between it and an open trunk of some kind.

The door of the feed room had closed behind me, and the room was dim. Almost against my will I took a step closer, not believing what my eyes told me.

I clutched the red plaid horse blanket to my mouth to keep from screaming, letting the overpowering smell of horse blot out other smells I didn't want to identify. My stomach was doing back flips, and I wasn't going anywhere until some feeling returned to my legs. There was no sound in the room. Gradually, I became conscious of a buzzing noise. A fly landed on the pitchfork, boldly walked up the still shirtfront, made a short hop and perched on the boy's nose. I gagged, and backed as far as the door. I was counting on it to hold me up. I wasn't certain my legs could.

Some semblance of rational thought started to edge out shock and horror. Murder. Someone had been murdered! Brutally, horribly murdered, in a feed room, at an Arabian horse show at our county fair. Impossible. Only I was looking at the victim. Another thought, even more unwelcome, pushed its way in. Where there was a murder, there was a murderer.

"Mom!" The voice broke through my paralysis. "Mom, what are you doing in there?"

Susannah. Coming this way. She would open the door, and she would see…she might be in danger, the murderer might…not if I could help it. Willing my legs to do their job, I stumbled out the door, slammed it quickly behind me and rammed home the bolt.

Susannah grabbed the horse blanket I'd been asked to get with a muttered, "What took you so long?" She flung it over the back of a magnificent horse that danced at the end of a lead rope held by a morose-looking man with a Pancho Villa mustache.

I stood, numb, watching her fumble with the straps. What should I do? A casual "by the way, there's a dead body in the feed room" wasn't going to cut it. On the other hand, if I started screaming, which is what I felt like doing, I'd cause an instant riot. There were people milling around all over the place. Someone would open that damn door and destroy whatever evidence—what was the matter with me! Police. I had to get the police. And fast. But how did I do that without letting everyone at the horse show, especially my nineteen-year-old daughter, Susannah, know there'd been a murder? There was no doubt in my mind that if I blurted out the horrible news she'd be the first one in the door. That was one sight I'd just as soon spare her. Right now, the only thing separating her from that gruesome sight was a flimsy door and a mother thinking about having hysterics. Stay calm, I cautioned myself, just stay calm.

"Are you all right?" Susannah asked. "You look kind of funny."

"I'm fine. Just fine," I told her, swallowing hard. I needed to tell somebody, get some help. My friend, Pat. I needed her. She'd been standing in the barn aisle when

I went into that feed room, but now she was nowhere in sight. I gritted my teeth.

"Where's Rusty?" Susannah asked. She straightened up and looked around. "He's supposed to be doing this. Why Bryce hired a low life like him…"

"Rusty'll turn up. The important thing is, we won." Irma Long, owner of the horse Susannah was struggling to blanket, appeared. A blue ribbon fluttered in her bony hand. The horse snorted and backed away, evidently not impressed he'd won it. Irma laughed.

"Congratulations," I found myself saying. "He's beautiful." Inside, a scream was forming again and I was having a hard time keeping it contained. Where was Pat? More to the point, where was the person who had pushed the pitchfork through that boy?

"I'm still walking on clouds," Irma said, gazing reverently at her blue ribbon. "You'd think I'd never owned a horse who'd won before, but I've never bred one like this. Last Challenge. A great name for a great horse."

She grinned at the horse and the walnut-brown man who held him, then turned to me. "I'm so glad you came, Ellen." She crossed her arms over her skinny chest and hugged herself. "I'm so happy, so excited, I could take off and fly. It's been a wonderful morning."

I smiled weakly.

"First horse show and he wins. Pretty good. There. I got it." Susannah finished buckling the blanket around the horse's chest and stood back to admire him. "I'll bet he wins the championship too."

Irma beamed some more. "Ellen," she said, "have you met my ranch manager, Chovalo Gutierrez? Chovalo, this is Susannah's mother, Ellen McKenzie. She's also my real estate agent."

I nodded, so did Chovalo. He looked at me from

under the brim of a large black sombrero, reminding me of all the Grade B Westerns I'd watched so enthusiastically while growing up. The bad guys always wore big black hats.

Irma looked like she was all set to chat on. I dug my fingernails into my hands, not hearing her words. If I could just get away, I could call the police on my cell phone.

A couple came down the barn aisle, shouting congratulations. I backed a few steps and immediately dug into my purse. No phone. Where was it? I'd left it in the car. Damn! Where was Pat? I had to find Pat. She had one. We'd use hers to phone.

"Did you know Irma's horse is going to be shown again in some kind of championship?" Pat Bennington was right behind me.

I jumped at least a mile. "Where did you come from?" I almost snapped. "I've been looking for you."

"I went to the ladies' room," she said, a little defensively. "What's the matter? You look like you've seen a ghost."

"You're close." I clutched her arm. "Oh, dear God. Where is he going with that horse?"

"Who?" Pat looked around. "What horse?"

"Him," I said. "Where's he taking Irma's horse?"

Chovalo led Last Challenge down the row of stalls, toward the closed feed room door. Surely he wouldn't open the door. Would he? I took a step toward them.

"He's putting him in that open stall. Isn't that where the horse is supposed to go?" Pat gave me a confused look.

"Yes." I sighed with relief as Chovalo and the horse disappeared into a stall a few doors away from the feed room. "Pat, something awful has happened. I need you…"

"I know we said we'd leave right after Irma's horse was shown," Pat said, not listening to me, "but I'd like to stay, wouldn't you?"

I didn't think we had much choice. "Pat." I grabbed her arm, pulling her out of earshot of the people still gathered around Irma and her trainer, Bryce Ellis.

"Ellen McKenzie, what are you doing?"

I ignored it and tightened my grip on her arm. "Give me your cell phone. Quick."

"My…why?"

"There's a dead body in that feed room. I need to phone the police."

"A dead…what?" She was paying attention to me now.

"Someone's been murdered. Pat, I saw the body when I went to get that horse blanket."

It was the quiver in my voice that convinced her. I watched all the color drain out of her face and then rush back again. Finally she said, "Ellen, is this some kind of joke?"

"I wish it was. I think it's Rusty, that groom Susannah's been looking for. He's in the feed room with a pitchfork stuck through his middle. Give me the phone. I need to call Dan. Now."

"I didn't bring it. My God. A pitchfork?"

"You didn't bring it? Why not? You should always have your cell…"

"I didn't know there was going to be a murder." She looked at me defensively. "Where's yours?"

"In the car."

She didn't say anything. She didn't have to. The look she gave me was enough.

"Sorry. I'm a little uptight."

"Yeah. Now what do we do."

"You go phone. There's a bank of pay phones by the fair entrance. Get Dan. Tell him to come quietly. No sirens or screeching tires."

"I'm supposed to tell the Chief of Police to come quietly to a murder. Are you serious?"

"Try," I urged. "And for God's sake, hurry."

"What are you going to do?"

"I'm going to keep everyone, especially Susannah, out of that room and say a few prayers whoever impaled that kid doesn't decide to come back."

Pat took a long look at the closed feed room door, a shorter one at me and left. I started down the row of stalls. Chovalo came out of Challenge's stall, carrying something. He closed the bottom then the top door behind him and walked away from me.

I almost called out to him. Standing guard in front of that door was not something I wanted to do. What if the murderer came back? What would I do? Chovalo looked pretty intimidating. Not too many people would try to push past him, and surely any prudent murderer would think twice before... But what if Chovalo was the murderer? No. He couldn't be. Oh? How did I know that? I didn't know him, or the dead kid. I'd better keep my mouth and the door shut until Dan and his troops arrived.

What would I do if he went toward the feed room? He was almost there, he was...no, he went into the open door of the room next to it. I froze, waiting. Almost immediately he returned, empty-handed. He came toward me, nodding politely as he passed. He paused when he got to Irma and Susannah.

"We have a little time." He gestured toward the show

ring. "Bryce has gone to show Señor Manning's filly. Perhaps we should watch the class?"

"Let's." Irma picked up her program and stood up. "Come on, Susannah. Ellen, are you coming?"

"No, no," I said hurriedly. "You go along. I'll stay here and, ah, enjoy the sun."

"Where's Pat?" Susannah peered past me, searching the barn aisle. "I've hardly seen her. Isn't she enjoying the show?"

"Of course. She's, ah, I'm waiting for her. We'll be along." I sank down on a deck chair and tried to look casual.

Susannah seemed doubtful, but followed Irma and Chovalo toward the show ring. Shouts, whistles and cheers filled the air. Susannah walked a little faster. I got up, took a deep breath and wondered if Pat had found Dan.

My old playmate, Dan Dunham. He'd been better than a brother; he'd been my best friend the entire time we were growing up next door to each other. Although more than twenty years had passed since we both had left Santa Louisa, we were back, both once more single, me a recent divorcée, Dan a not-so-recent widower. We had spent the last six months renewing our old friendship and edging our way toward a new one. Actually, a little more than edging. Dan had once again established a presence in my life, a reliable, solid-as-a-rock presence. There were times that made me a little nervous, but not now. A rock was exactly what I needed.

I couldn't see Pat anywhere. The Arabian horse show we had been watching was only one part of the county fair, and the phones were by the main gate. It might take her a while. In the meantime, there were people and horses everywhere. People leading horses, people riding horses, groups of people standing around talking about them. A small girl passed me, leading a large white horse hung with leather straps and ropes. It followed her patiently, not seeming to heed her urging. Most of this activity was in the main aisle, headed toward or away from the show ring. Irma's side barn aisle was quiet. No telling how long that would last. Someone was certain to want to go into that feed room, soon. I needed to get down there and stand guard and I wasn't letting anyone in until Dan and the cops got there. Fervently hoping no one would try, I turned abruptly. That's when I ran into him.

TWO

"AVAST THERE. You've got to watch where you place your keel."

I found myself staring up at a real live parrot-carrying pirate. Blond curls fell to his shoulders from under a battered black hat hitched up on the side. There was a patch over one eye, a bird on his shoulder, another on the hat. One more hung upside down from the arm that reached out to steady me. The visible eye was faded blue. An enormous blond mustache hid the rest of the face.

"Shiver me timbers," he shouted. "You gave us a start."

He let go, looked me up and down and strode off, laughing. It sounded like ho, ho, ho, but it couldn't have been, any more than the pistol hanging from the thick black belt could be real, or the dagger stuck so prominently in the high black boot could be sharp. I stared after him, momentarily paralyzed. The parrot on his hat turned for one last look, cocked his head and squawked.

"Where on earth did he come from?" I said out loud. There was no one around to answer. It wasn't until the pirate and his parrots rounded the end of the barn aisle and disappeared that I roused myself. "What an idiot you are, Ellen McKenzie," I continued, cross with myself for being so jumpy. "He's one of the roving fair entertainers. Did you think he was the murderer?" Still, it was odd he was so far from the main part of the fair. But it was the feed room I needed to worry about and right now. Susannah was back. She led a horse past me, toward its closed door.

"Susannah." I caught up with her and tried to edge past her. "Where are you going?"

"I'm getting Mariah ready for her class." Susannah looked at me curiously as I flattened myself against the feed room door. She walked the pretty, delicate-looking horse into the open door of the room next to it, turned it around and snapped the chains that hung from each side of the room onto the halter. I looked into the largest, brownest eyes I had ever seen. My hand went out without conscious thought to stroke the thin white stripe that ran down the middle of the brown face.

"Cute, isn't she?" Susannah ran her hand softly down the horse's neck. "I think she's my favorite. Maybe because she's so easy."

The horse nuzzled my palm, probably looking for carrots or something, but all I could think of was teeth. Big teeth. I jerked my hand behind my back, and the horse threw her head up, startled.

"Mom, what are you doing? You scared her."

"She scared me first. Susannah, get out from behind that horse before you get kicked."

"Don't be silly. She doesn't have room to kick me even if she wanted. Her class is coming up soon and I've got to get her ready. I hope I'm doing this right. I've never done it before."

Susannah's voice became a little muffled as she disappeared with a large comb into a cloud of tail.

"Susannah, get out of there," I ordered. "Why are you doing that, anyway?"

"Because no one can find Rusty."

The horse pricked her ears at me, but Susannah paid no attention. She kept combing.

"Wait until I get my hands on that little rat." She re-emerged brushing tail hairs away from her face. "He knew Bryce hired him because this is only my second horse show ever. I'm supposed to be doing all the paperwork, not grooming. I'll kill him."

That brought me back to reality. I glanced at the feed room door, then stood stock-still, watching Susannah, wondering what I should do.

"Bryce'll be back soon." She moved from the tail around to the horse's side and started doing something to the legs. "He gets on my nerves with his prima-donna act, but he can sure show a horse. Oh, I hope Challenge wins the championship. Then he'd really be on his way."

On his way where, I wondered, but wasn't in the mood to ask. I was too busy wondering if I had time for a nervous breakdown. Where was Pat? Where were the police? I took a quick look at the feed room door. The bolt was still in place. No one had tried to go in, but that wouldn't last much longer. Where was Dan?

Chovalo appeared in the doorway, nodded to me gravely, picked up a brush and started to go over the mare with it.

"She looks pretty good." Irma's voice, directly behind me, almost sent me to the ceiling. "What do you think, Chovalo? Does she have a chance to win?" Irma gave me a quizzical look, but her attention was on the horse.

"She probably will not win, but I think she will receive a ribbon. Bryce will get all she has to give." Chovalo looked past Irma and studied me for a moment. I leaned against the doorjamb, trying to appear nonchalant. He looked a little puzzled, but said nothing. Instead, he started to gently rub oil into the horse's soft muzzle and over her eyelids, letting the black skin show through. I watched him, thinking that, from his tone of voice, he wasn't a member of Bryce's fan club.

"There. She needs only the final brushing before she goes into the ring." He looked over at Susannah. "Now we will give the rest of the horses a little lunch and make sure that they have water. Rusty should be doing this, but as he is not here..." He let the statement hang in the air. Susannah took it up immediately.

"Shall I do hay while you do water?"

Chovalo smiled for the first time I had seen, although it was hard to tell under that abundant mustache, and nodded to her. She headed for the feed room door. I flung myself in front of it.

"You can't go in there."

"Why not? Come on, Mom. We don't have much time." She tried to push past me.

"No." This time I almost screamed it.

"Ellen. What on earth is the matter with you?" Irma's voice was full of surprise and a little irritation. "Please move. I'll help too."

I stood my ground, trying frantically to figure out how not to tell them what was in the room until the police arrived.

"Mom?" Susannah was staring at me, her eyes questioning, wondering if she should be alarmed.

Chovalo hadn't said a thing, but there was a stillness building around him as he watched.

I gave up. "You can't go in because Rusty's in there."

"Is that all!" said Susannah, relief evident. "Let me at him. I've been dying to get my hands on that lazy little no-good."

I winced at this unfortunate choice of words and plowed on. "He's dead. The police are on their way."

"Dead?" Susannah said.

"Dead!" Irma echoed.

"The police?" said Chovalo.

I nodded.

"But…" Susannah had reached for the bolt holding the feed room door closed. She abruptly snatched her hand back.

"How…?" Irma stared from me to the door, then back to me.

Chovalo seemed to melt back into the stall beside the mare. I was sure he picked up a bucket and put something into it, but I was distracted by the sound of a car coming fast down the barn aisle, a squeal of brakes and the slam of a door. Dan Dunham. The Marines had landed.

Dan paused, stared at each of us in turn, reserving the longest stare for me, then walked toward us. Pat climbed out of the passenger seat and followed him.

"Ellen's there, guarding the door."

"I can see that." Dan's tone would have frozen ice.

I had started to smile with relief at the sight of him, but could feel it fade. He looked downright unfriendly, and I had no idea why.

"I understand that you have a body." His syntax made me give a little nervous laugh.

"Most people do." The words were out before I could stop them. Instantly, I knew it was a mistake. Dan was in no mood for grammar and even less for nervous jokes. Everything about him bristled, even his neat little mustache. Sure were a lot of mustaches around here today, I thought irrelevantly.

No one else said anything, so finally I pointed at the closed feed room door. "He's in there."

"And you found him." Dan was addressing me. It

wasn't exactly a question and his tone wasn't entirely acid free.

"You don't have to sound like I did it on purpose," I told him, stung. "Not having seen that would have been fine with me."

"Did you touch anything?" The expression on Dan's face was as frosty as his tone.

"The door when I went in. And the horse blanket thing. If I'd known there was a body in there, I would have been more careful." What was the matter with him? I'd had a terrible morning and had been counting on Dan, but all I was getting was this brusque official behavior. Where was my friend, where was my comfort, where was my rock?

By now, two other black-and-whites had arrived, spilling uniformed officers into the barn aisle. A fire truck pulled slowly toward us, the paramedics right behind them. An unmarked car, with our town's only two plainclothes officers, stopped behind Dan's.

"Ricker." Dan turned toward one of the men. "Start taping this place off. Get all these people out of here. Is there someplace you can all go? Out of our way?"

This was addressed to all of us, but Susannah, still ashen-faced, answered. "There are some deck chairs up there, at the end of the barn aisle."

"Good. Go there, all of you, and stay there. I'll be up to talk to you. Soon. Gary?" Dan motioned to one of the uniformed officers. "Let's take a look."

He eased the door open without touching the handle and slid in. Gary, smooth-faced and eager, tugged at his gun belt, smiled shyly at me and followed.

All the rest of our group obediently trooped down toward the deck chairs, but I hung back. It didn't take long to get a reaction.

"Jesus Christ," came Dan's voice, uncharacteristically awed.

Gary said nothing. He appeared at the door, his hand over his mouth, his eyes wild. I pointed down the barn aisle toward the bathrooms, and he ran off.

Dan followed him out, looking a little whiter and a lot less angry. "You saw that?" he asked.

I nodded.

"Not very pretty." That held the first trace of humanity I'd heard since he arrived. "Who was he?"

"Some kid who worked for Bryce Ellis, Irma's horse trainer. I think his name was Rusty."

"Rusty what?"

"No idea. Ask Susannah. Or Irma." I could be brusque too.

Dan looked down at me for a moment. "Let's do that."

We walked back to the group without speaking. Irma sat in one of the deck chairs, Susannah stood beside her. Pat had pulled her chair a little way back toward the barn, out of the way and in the shade. Chovalo was nowhere to be seen.

Dan didn't glance at Susannah or Pat, but addressed Irma gently. "The boy in there, he worked for your trainer, Bryce Ellis?"

"I guess so." Irma's face had a gray tinge and her wrinkled hand shook a little. "He only started this morning. Bryce hadn't told me he'd hired him. How did he—why would someone—are you sure it's Rusty?"

"All things we're trying to find out. Now, stay here and I'll be back to talk to you soon. All of you. Right here." Dan had been polite to Irma, but that vanished as he pointed to the one remaining empty deck chair while glaring meaningfully at me. I dropped into it. He turned on his heel and strode back down the barn aisle.

"What's the matter with him?" Pat asked.

I shrugged. I had an idea, but wasn't sure I wanted to talk about it.

"What's going on?" Bryce had returned, a short, chunky girl hanging on his arm. "Why are all these police cars here? And that ambulance. Is someone hurt?"

"Someone's murdered your friend Rusty," Susannah told him grimly.

"Murdered! What do you mean, murdered!" Bryce handed the girl his show whip and started to remove his gloves. Now he stopped, a glove dangling from his hand, to stare at Susannah.

"She couldn't make it much clearer." Irma sat up straighter, color once again in her cheeks. "He's dead and in my feed room. How did you come to hire him, anyway?"

It was Bryce's turn to look gray. "He was available and besides, you know…" He looked down at the glove, finished removing it and crunched both of them in his hand.

"Bryce needed somebody." The girl once more tried to cling to Bryce's arm, but he absentmindedly brushed her off. "He hasn't had anyone to help him since Miguel died. I volunteered, but you wouldn't let me." She thrust her chin out and the expression in her pale blue eyes was sullen.

"I'm aware of how much help Bryce has, Stephanie," Irma said. "That is not the issue."

Bryce turned to look down the barn aisle, slapping his gloves against his leg, staring at all the activity. Not only had the coroner's car arrived, so had half the show grounds. There were people everywhere, staring, gawking, asking questions that went unanswered. A uniformed officer I didn't recognize dragged out several sawhorses, from where I had no idea, and yellow tape was being strung up across the barn aisle below where we waited. Another officer was trying to clear the area, asking people to move along, without much success. A loudspeaker blared, "Class forty-two, four-year-old mares, you're next." It was a lot more effective than the policeman. People drifted away toward the grandstand, still casting curious glances at the activity behind the yellow tape. A man dressed in show clothes was arguing with the officer, yelling that he had to get past, his horse was down that aisle and he was going to miss his class. The officer looked at him blankly. "This is a crime scene, mister. Your horse will have to wait." The man uttered a four-letter word, actually several of them, and ran off, evidently looking for some higher authority.

"That's Mariah's class," Susannah said forlornly.

Irma looked at her, then down the barn aisle. "Yes" was all she said.

"These horse show people take this stuff seriously," I murmured to Pat, as I moved my chair closer to hers.

"In more ways than one," she agreed. "I told you going anywhere at eight o'clock on a Saturday morning could be hazardous to our health."

"It's been hazardous all right, but not to us. Unless you count fright, trauma and damn near nervous collapse."

Pat examined me carefully over the top of her dark glasses. "Not to mention anger igniting a touch of righteous indignation."

I knew she was referring to Dan, his peculiar behavior and my reaction to it.

"What are they doing down there?" I changed the subject to one less personal. "There's the ambulance, and that car says 'coroner.' I wonder how long before they remove the body?"

"I've no idea. Why is that man brushing the door?"

I peered down the barn aisle. A man in a light tan suit was squatting in front of the feed room door, doing something with tape and a fine brush. "Fingerprints." I hadn't spent the last six months with the Chief of Police for nothing.

It wasn't the police activity that held Pat's attention. It was the girl beside Bryce. "Who is she?" Pat echoed my low tone.

"Never saw her before."

"Sturdy type." She examined the girl thoughtfully. "Do you suppose she's his girlfriend?"

I was briefly amused. Neil, Pat's son, had arranged this summer job for Susannah. They had been like a couple of magnets since the day they met, with our complete approval. Was Pat wondering if Susannah's exposure to the beautiful Bryce was a good idea? I didn't think Neil, or Pat, had a thing to worry about, but I took another look at the girl.

"She doesn't exactly seem his type." The baggy tee shirt, somewhat rumpled khaki shorts, athletic socks and running shoes did nothing to flatten a little too much tummy, or to define a missing waistline. No makeup softened her fair complexion, now freshly sunburned. She was quite a contrast to the strikingly handsome Bryce Ellis, with his carefully styled wavy dark hair, long lashes that framed large deep brown eyes, salon-perfect tan and beautifully fitting designer slacks and silk shirt.

Bryce had also been watching the police. He turned

and took a couple of steps back toward us. Stephanie edged closer to him. He ignored her.

"What happened to Rusty?"

"Someone stuck a pitchfork through him," I answered.

I could hear Irma catch her breath.

"Oh! Ugh." Susannah went a little pale again.

A white van pulled up, the county Sheriff's logo on its doors. The uniformed officer let down the yellow tape, the van drove down the barn aisle. The officer must have been aware that we were all staring, transfixed, but without once looking in our direction, he pulled the tape up, then turned his back on us.

"How do you know it's Rusty?" Bryce finally said, breaking the spell.

Irma looked a little startled, Susannah hopeful. "Mom? You saw him. What did he look like?"

Like nothing I ever want to see again, I thought. Carrot-colored hair spilling over a still brow, freckles that frosted a sharp nose, the image of Rusty filled my mind.

"Did Rusty have red hair?"

Susannah nodded. "Freckles too."

"It was Rusty."

"But why would anyone kill him?" Bryce's voice sounded strangulated.

No one answered. We were all too busy watching Dan approach. He ducked under the yellow tape and stopped by Irma's chair.

"Good. Glad to see you're all still here." His eyes traveled over the whole group, but stopped at me.

I swallowed the remark I wanted to make.

"Are you the trainer, Bryce…?" Dan transferred his stare to Bryce and glanced at Susannah for help.

"Ellis," I supplied. Dan looked back at me impassively.

"Yes." Bryce straightened his shoulders and raised his chin a little as he faced Dan. "Who are you?"

"He's the top cop," I told him.

Dan's face told me he wasn't amused, although Susannah stifled a giggle. I wasn't sorry. Dan deserved it, and it perked Susannah up.

"Rusty. Is he really dead?" Bryce's voice began to crack.

"Someone is." If Dan felt any empathy for any of us right then, his face didn't show it. "I'm going to need you to identify the body in a few minutes, so stay here, all of you. I'll need statements, and I'll send someone over as soon as I can."

"Why do I have to identify him?" Bryce looked around, as if searching for support. "I don't want to see him."

"He worked for you, didn't he?"

"If it really is Rusty, yes."

"And you want one of the women to do it? Susannah, maybe?" Dan's voice wasn't any kinder than the look on his face.

"No, but…"

Dan neatly cut him off. "Good. I'll let you know when we're ready. In the meantime, don't move."

Stephanie had given up trying to hold on to Bryce's arm. Instead she took a step toward Dan. "That's mean. He shouldn't have to do it."

"Who are you?"

"Stephanie Knudsen." She said this with a toss of hair and a tone of voice that tried for arrogance. It didn't work.

Dan paused, obviously bit back a remark and finally said, "All right. Did you know this Rusty?"

"No. Yes. Sort of," Stephanie stammered, looking toward Bryce for support. She didn't get any.

"Well, Stephanie Knudsen, unless you want to do the honors, I suggest you go sit down someplace and let us get on with our job. The coroner is here. We're all going to wait until he's finished. Now, please stay put. All of you."

Dan gave us one last long stern look, said something to the uniformed officer standing by the yellow tape and headed back to where all the action was.

"He certainly is rude." Bryce's voice mirrored the petulant look on his face. "We can't stay here. The Championship's coming up."

"Oh my God, the Championship." Irma's hand flew to her mouth, her eyes stricken. "We have to do something. We can't miss it. We just can't."

"Last Challenge has to show." Stephanie's eyes were round with horror. "Bryce has worked so hard. That awful policeman can't make him miss that."

"Yes," murmured Susannah. "It would be terrible to disappoint Bryce. He works so hard."

The sarcasm in her voice didn't escape Stephanie. "He does. You don't know, he's…"

"Shut up, Steph." Bryce chewed the fingers of his glove, looking a little wild-eyed. "What can we do?"

"Nothing." I thought Irma was going to burst into tears. "We can't even get to the horse. We'll have to forfeit."

Before I could ask why this class was so vital, a voice shouting, "Irma" interrupted us. "Bryce. Tell this guy to let me in."

A tall, paunchy cowboy type was standing in the

main aisleway, trying to look past the stubborn shoulders of a uniformed policeman. His stomach overlapped the top of his jeans and rested on the shiny headlamp of a belt buckle. Probably the effect of a lifetime of too many beers. His bright red tractor cap was decorated with silver letters that said LONG'S HORSE HAULING over a black horse's head, but his sunglasses would have been right at home beside any Hollywood swimming pool.

"Who's he?" I whispered to Susannah as both Irma and Bryce rushed over to the policeman, urging him to let this new person into our little group.

"That's Wes Fowler. He and his wife, Linda, run Irma's horse transport company. He's here to take the horses home."

There was something guarded in Susannah's tone. I was beginning to wonder what was wrong with horse show people.

"What the hell's goin' on around here?" Wes's voice was loud with a faint Texas drawl. "Talkin' to that cop is like tryin' to get information from a clam."

"Someone murdered Rusty." Susannah's voice sounded distant in contrast.

"Murdered!" Wes exclaimed. He went on more thoughtfully, "You don't say. What happened?"

"He got himself skewered on a pitchfork."

I couldn't believe Susannah had said that. I also couldn't believe the way Wes looked at her, examining the way her jeans curved over her hips, the way her tee shirt clung to her breasts. He took time to give Pat and me the same treatment, but the exam was less thorough and a lot quicker. Stephanie he ignored.

"A pitchfork. Sounds like someone lost his temper big-time." Wes looked around our little group. "Can't say I'm surprised though," he drawled. "The kid was no good. Told you not to hire him." This was belligerently addressed to Bryce. "Why did you?"

"He was the only one I could get," Bryce answered sourly. "A little fact you already knew."

"I told you I'd groom for you, Bryce." Stephanie reached for his arm again. Bryce sidestepped.

Wes dismissed them both and bent down toward Irma, patting her shoulder a little awkwardly. "Don't you worry none. That kid's got nothin' to do with you. All this'll be over real soon." Straightening, he looked directly at Pat and me, a "who are you and what are you doing here" frown evident behind those magnificent glasses.

Susannah sighed. "This is Pat Bennington, Neil's mom. And this is my Mom, Ellen. She found him."

Wes said nothing for a moment, just stared at me from behind those glasses, his expression impossible to read. Finally he said, "That's too bad. It must have been real…gruesome."

"It wasn't very nice." Just saying it made me a little lightheaded again.

Wes wasn't listening. All the official vehicles, haphazardly parked up and down the aisle, had captured his attention. Or maybe by the woman in the short shirt taking pictures of the feed room door. He barely glanced at the back of the patrolman who had returned to stand guard behind his yellow ribbon, then turned back to Irma. "Did Challenge win?"

"Of course he did." Bryce's tone made that win a foregone conclusion "It's almost time for the Championship. Only, they won't let us leave." He chewed his glove again and started to pace. "We could have won this too, I know we could have. Why did this have to happen, especially now?'

Stephanie tried again to grab his arm, but he brushed her aside and continued to pace. "Do something, Susannah. You know that policeman." He was almost wailing.

"Right. I'll waltz right up to Chief Dunham and say, oh please…look."

"Oh, I don't think…" Irma began but Susannah interrupted her.

"Look," she said again. "There, at the end of the barn aisle. Be quiet, don't say anything."

We all turned to look at the main aisle that led to the show arena. There was Chovalo, determinedly holding on to a restless Last Challenge. The colt arched his neck and snorted at the strange vehicles and the flapping yellow ribbon, giving every indication he thought leaving was a great idea. Chovalo tried to soothe him while waving at us and pointing toward the arena.

"Go." I could hear Susannah's harsh whisper as she gestured toward Bryce. With one quick backward glance at the policeman guarding the yellow tape, his back still turned to us, Bryce grabbed his whip and fled.

"Go on, follow him." Susannah turned toward Irma. "You can't miss this."

"She's right." Wes's voice was soft, but his grip wasn't. He took Irma's hand, pulled her out of her chair and practically dragged her around the corner of the barn. "You too." He motioned at Susannah. "We'll need you on the rail."

Susannah nodded, picked up a pail she'd set down by her chair and followed.

Like commandos, they slipped around the corner and were lost to sight. Stephanie made a little whimpering noise and scampered after them.

"Rail?" I asked.

"Why is this Championship thing such a big deal?" Pat asked.

"I have no idea. We can go find out."

"And we can get in a lot of trouble."

"It's been quite a morning for trouble. You think there can be more?"

"Doesn't seem likely."

We grinned at each other, took a good look at the back of the policeman, then Pat said, with an expansive gesture, "After you." We too slipped around the corner.

THREE

IT WAS EARLY EVENING and the "biggest little fair on California's central coast" was in full swing. Susannah, Pat and I were back at the fairgrounds, only this time we were sitting at a picnic table on one of the green areas, surrounded by passersby on their way to 4H exhibits, the midway or the commercial display buildings. You could buy almost anything there; fake antique tables, the amazing Ginzu knife or wooden shoes straight from Holland. The smells of deep-fried zucchini, egg rolls and cotton candy were overlaid with the aroma of barbecue smoke. Music floated toward us from all directions, mixed with the chatter of voices, the cries of tired babies and the roar of golf carts bringing more supplies to the myriad of crowded food stands.

We had discussed the murder at length. Pat's husband, Carl, and her son, Neil, were horrified and wanted every detail. We didn't have many.

"Does Dan, I mean do the police, have any idea who did it?" Carl asked.

"Dan didn't say much." Pat was careful not to look at me. The one thing we hadn't mentioned to Neil and Carl was Dan's cold, distant behavior.

"I think the way you got Challenge into the Championship was brilliant." Neil moved the subject away from murder and Dan, back to horses, his biggest love next to Susannah. He gave her an admiring look. "I knew he'd win."

"I still don't understand," said Pat, pouring beer from a large pitcher into paper cups. She pushed a cup over to her husband, Carl, another my way and somewhat reluctantly, handed one to her son. "Why was that Championship class so important?"

Susannah took a sip of her Coke before she answered Pat's question.

"The winners of the breeding classes have to go back in for a final judging," she began. "That's when they choose a Show Champion Stallion and Mare. You need to win a local Championship to qualify to show at a Regional or National level."

"Besides," Neil wiped some foam off his face with the back of his hand, ignoring his mother's offered napkin, "winning is what gets a stallion mares."

"What?" Pat and I both stared at him, but this time I was the one who voiced the question.

"The way you make money with a stallion is to have people who own mares breed them to him. For a fee."

Neil, a scant twenty-one, was enjoying his role as adult as well as instructor. He kept giving Susannah little glances and was rewarded with a beatific smile. He took another gulp of his beer and went on.

"The more a horse wins in the show ring, the more mares he is likely to be bred to. If his foals—"

"Those are baby horses," Susannah put in kindly.

"Thank you, dear," I said.

Neil dismissed our interruption with a wave of his cup.

"If his foals also start to win, then his breeding fee can go up. But it starts with the stallion winning at small shows held at fairs in small towns, just like this one."

"Why didn't you tell me about all this horse breeding stuff?" Pat turned to her husband indignantly.

"I'm a small-animal vet," Carl reminded her complacently. "The day I graduated from vet school I vowed never to work on anything larger than a Great Dane. A vow I've kept. Good beer."

"Oh, you." Pat turned with exasperation back to her son just as I commented, "So the whole thing boils down to money."

"Most things do," said a voice in my ear. "Move over. Hello, Carl. Neil." Dan Dunham slipped onto the bench beside me, picked up the last paper cup and reached for the pitcher. "Did you save some for me? Where are we eating?"

"Aren't you even going to say hello to the rest of us?" Susannah asked him, falling into the trap.

"I haven't decided yet." He carefully tilted his cup while he filled it, looking sideways at Carl and Neil. "Did they tell you about this morning?"

"Some," Carl replied, with a straight face. "Probably not all."

"But they told you about finding that kid murdered."

"In detail. Not a pleasant experience for a couple of innocent citizens."

"No," Dan agreed. "Not pleasant for anybody. But when innocent citizens stumble across something like that they have an obligation to cooperate with the police. Don't you agree?"

"That seems reasonable." Carl nodded, avoiding Pat's gaze.

"Because the police have a procedure that needs to be followed. Evidence, crime scenes, questions that need answering. Anyone who has watched TV in the last twenty years knows that."

Carl wisely buried his smile in his cup.

"Did they tell you they escaped?"

"I don't think I heard that part."

"We didn't escape." The thought seemed to make Susannah indignant. "We absolutely had to get the colt into the Championship. We came right back."

"You couldn't expect them to miss that." Neil seemed to believe that leaving the scene of a murder to partici- pate in a horse show made complete sense.

Dan looked at him, opened his mouth to say some- thing, then changed his mind and buried his own face. He came up with foam on his mustache.

"My entire crime scene could have been jeopar- dized." He still addressed only Carl. "All my witnesses disappeared, my…"

"We really did come back." Susannah also addressed Carl and included Neil.

"You're foaming." I handed Dan a napkin. "How long are we going to do this?"

"I thought maybe through dinner, maybe even until the Oak Ridge Boys come on."

"Oh?" I raised an eyebrow. "Aunt Mary's been rav- ing about the flower show this year, and I understand the 4H beginning-cooking exhibit is a 'must see.' Then there's always the home canning."

"OK." He grinned at me as he conceded. He put his arm around me and gave me the kiss I'd been expect- ing all day. "But you're still not completely forgiven, any of you."

"You sure were mad." Susannah looked relieved as she turned to Neil. "You should've seen his face when we got back to the barn. It was sort of purple."

"Susannah," I said, warningly. I wasn't in the mood for another frosty episode. It had been a terrible day and I wanted a smooth, peaceful evening. But privately, I thought I had some forgiving of my own to do. Dan had been furious when we all returned, triumphant. That was understandable, but he hadn't had to treat me with cold hostility. By the time I was allowed to leave, I was livid. Some of my anger wore off as the afternoon passed. I started to think the excitement of Last Challenge winning the Championship and Dan's unexpected behavior had pushed the real tragedy, the murder of a young man, into a backseat. I had never met the boy, and it seemed no one else really knew him, but still.

Now, my old buddy Dan was back and everything was back to normal. Or was it? I thought Dan owed me an explanation and later, when we were alone, I was going to ask for it. Or would I? Twenty years of marriage to Dr. Brian McKenzie had taught me to avoid personal confrontations like the plague. If I'd asked Brian for an explanation, no matter how carefully, I would have had to listen to an hour dissertation on how unreasonable I was, how selfish, how demanding. But Dan was different. Or he had been until today.

"Bryce was the most interesting color." I shifted the conversation back to this afternoon. Awful as it had been, it was better than thinking about my ex. "He was the meanest shade of green I've ever seen."

"Who's Bryce?" Carl asked.

"Irma's horse trainer," Neil replied. He looked like he'd just eaten a sour pickle.

"Why did he turn green?" Carl pressed. "You people are leaving gaps in the story."

"Dan made him identify Rusty's body." Susannah had just a hint of a smile.

"He spent quite a bit of time in the bathroom after he came out of the feed room." Pat looked a little amused, but she hadn't seen Rusty. I had, and Bryce had my sympathy.

"Tell us, who did it and why?" I started to pour a little more beer into Dan's cup, but stopped in mid pour. "You are off duty?"

"Now, Ellie, you know 'top cops' are never off duty." He managed that sentence with only a trace of sarcasm. "I'm delegating. As for our little problem, we don't know who or why, and you know I wouldn't tell you if I did." He turned to Susannah. "Who hired Rusty? You or Bryce?"

"Bryce did. I don't think he was too happy about it, but he needed someone. Chovalo's nephew had been working for him; only he died in some kind of accident last month. I guess Rusty was all he could find."

"What's her name? Stephanie. Why didn't Bryce use her?" Dan pushed on.

"Irma wouldn't let him. She, well, Stephanie gets in the way." Susannah started to slowly twirl her Coke can.

"What do you mean?" Pat put down her half-full cup on the table. "She seemed to know about horses."

"It's not that." Susannah kept her eyes on her Coke can. "She thinks she's in love with Bryce and won't let him alone. It's hard to get work out of him any time, and when she's there, it's impossible."

"Did Bryce know Rusty had a reputation for drug use? Also for selling?" Dan's voice was gentle as he asked his question, almost offhand.

"I think so. Stephanie sure did." Susannah twisted her can faster, looking everywhere but at me.

"Drugs?" My voice wasn't gentle. Alarm bells sounded in it. "What kind of drugs?"

"How do you know?" Dan pressed gently.

"I was in the grooming stall, rolling leg wraps," Susannah started.

"Leg wraps?" Pat asked. No one bothered to explain.

"Bryce and Stephanie were outside, arguing. Stephanie kept saying the only reason Bryce had hired Rusty was to buy drugs and that he'd promised her."

"Promised her what?" Neil reached over and removed the now squashed can and held Susannah's hand in his. She didn't pull it away.

"I don't know," she went on. "They walked off about then, but it sounded like Bryce had been playing around with that stuff and had promised Stephanie he'd quit."

"Did they say anything more?" Dan's voice was grim. Good, I thought. Just the way I was feeling.

"Stephanie said if Bryce didn't get rid of Rusty, she would. She was pretty upset." Susannah sounded pretty upset herself.

"When was this?" Dan's voice wasn't so gentle now, either. It sounded downright grim.

"Early this morning. Before the first class."

"What did you think of this Rusty?" Dan persisted.

"I never saw him before this morning. Do you really think he was taking drugs? And selling them?" The only good thing about this conversation was the look of consternation on Susannah's face.

"He had the reputation" was Dan's cryptic reply.

Something Susannah said earlier suddenly clicked. "What happened to Chovalo's nephew?"

"Drug overdose," Dan said.

"You must have read about it, Ellen." Pat sounded miserable. She pushed her cup around in circles, watching the beer left in it slosh against the sides. "It was all over the paper and the local TV station had a field day."

I nodded slowly, remembering the picture of a nice-looking young boy with beautiful eyes, tragically and unexpectedly dead at seventeen. There'd been a hue and cry about the availability of drugs for a week or so, but it had died down.

"You know, I never quite believed all that." Carl's cup was still as he stared down into it but his voice held the same sorrow. "Miguel worked for me part-time, he was serious about school, got great grades. He was up for a scholarship. He didn't even smoke."

"But he was full of meth. Lab test proved it."

"I know, Dan." Carl sighed. "You told me before. But it just doesn't make sense."

"I hate all this talk of drugs—Rusty, Bryce, Chovalo's nephew. Is there anyone else?" I could hear my voice getting a little shrill, but I couldn't help it.

"Mom. Of course not." Susannah abruptly looked up at me. "How could you even think that?"

"Easily. Three people in your little horse world are taking drugs. Two of them are dead. That tends to make me nervous. Dan, what are you going to do about Bryce?"

"At the moment, nothing." Dan tilted his cup up, ready to drain it. "What I think is we need to eat. I didn't have any lunch. I was a little busy, and I'm darn near starved."

"I doubt it," I started to say, but Carl, with a look at his watch, sided with Dan.

"We'd better eat. Pat and I don't want to miss the sheepdog trials. Ribs or Tri-tip?"

"Ribs," said Neil. Pat nodded and Dan was already reaching for his wallet.

"Here." He handed Neil a roll of bills. "Can you and Susannah manage six plates?"

Neil nodded and, still holding Susannah's hand, trotted off toward the Barbecue stand.

"That all right with you, Ellie?" He'd asked some-what after the fact.

"Sure." I smiled brightly, then crossed my fingers, hoping the ribs wouldn't drip with too much grease. "Now, tell us about Rusty."

I shook my head at Dan's offer to top off the beer in my cup. Pat refused as well, so he poured most of what was left in the pitcher into Carl's, reserving a little for Neil. Pat frowned at him and started to say something, but Carl interrupted.

"Neil's a man now, Pat, whether you like it or not."

"I don't like it, and I don't believe it." Pat set her cup down on the table more forcefully than necessary. I would have laughed but I felt much the same way. Motherhood!

"Listen. Quit changing the subject. I want to know about Rusty before the kids come back." Drugs, mur-der and my daughter only too close to it. I wanted reas-surance that Dan knew all about that boy, that he had a good idea who'd killed him, and that whoever it was had nothing to do with Irma, her barn and especially Susannah.

"Rusty was a no-good kid." Dan started slow and with what appeared to be some reluctance. "He was well known in this area. We couldn't find one person who had anything nice to say. They'd either fired him or knew someone who had."

"Why?" asked Pat. "Because he used drugs?"

"That, but much more. Selling, methamphetamine mostly, started doing that in grade school. Petty thiev-ery started in grade school too, first from his mother and then from the other kids. He graduated to simple breaking and entering, a try or two at blackmail, even a car theft. Anything to keep his own habit going. He's been a frequent visitor at juvenile hall, where they had him pegged as a habitual. Rusty, if he'd lived, would have been a perfect candidate for our 'three strikes and you're out' law."

"So now what do you do?" The thought that Susannah had been anywhere near someone like that made me furious. I wondered what Irma would have said if she'd known ahead of time who Bryce was hiring.

"What we always do." Dan smiled a grim little smile at me. "Just put one foot in front of the other until we get to the end."

"That's not what I mean and you know it," I started, but Pat had a question of her own.

"I keep hearing about the methamphetamine stuff. What is it? Do you grow it, like marijuana?"

"You make it, and it's deadly," Dan answered. "We have a real problem with it in this county because there's still so much open country, and we're close to big cities. LA to the south, the Bay area to the north, both only a few hours away. They're huge, open markets for this stuff."

"What does open country have to do with drugs?"

"Lots. It only takes a week to ten days to brew up a batch of that poison, so the scum making it scout out old barns not being used, or they'll rent a mobile home on a ranch or find a vacant one. Any place where they can set up shop for a while and visitors aren't too likely. They can, and too often do, have the stuff distilled, the powder packaged and are on their way before we even find out they were there. We know when they blow themselves up or set themselves on fire, but otherwise all we find is the mess they leave behind."

"Then you think whoever killed the kid is somehow connected with making drugs and selling them?" I felt a shudder run through me. I'd assumed Rusty's murderer, like Rusty, was a stranger, but now I wondered. Could someone at Irma's barn be involved?

"I didn't say that, so don't go jumping to conclusions." Dan's frown changed to a large grin as a heavy paper plate loaded with ribs, beans and limp salad was placed in front of his six foot four inch frame.

"We're going to have to make two trips." Neil charged back toward the Barbecue stand. Susannah slid a plate in front of me and set another down in front of Pat.

"I got you two the small plate. Is that all right? You can have some of mine if that's not enough."

Enough! An entire dogsled team could have lived for a week on what was on my plate. Besides, I'd caught sight of the ice cream bars on a stick, the ones rolled in peanuts. Childhood memories stirred and I decided on a little dessert.

For a while, no one spoke. I expected Dan, Carl and Neil to finish off the huge pile of ribs on their plates, but, as usual, Susannah surprised me. Slender, feminine Susannah could out eat any lumberjack. I had one rib left, looked at the pile of bones on Susannah's plate and slipped it onto Dan's.

The conversation started again, centered on the evening's events.

"Are you sure you don't want to watch the sheepdogs?" Carl asked us all forlornly.

"Positive." Pat placed her last nude bone in the trashcan and wiped her face. "I'm going to look at the quilts, and I want to see who placed where in the wine making, and forget about murder, drugs or anything else."

Dan looked a little apprehensive. It must have been

the mention of quilts, because he brightened up when I suggested the livestock barn.

"Are you two going to the horse show?" I asked Susannah.

"Not tonight. No classes. Besides, I've had enough horror and horses for one day. We're going to the midway."

The only thing we all agreed on was that we would meet for the nine thirty Oak Ridge Boys show.

"Nine thirty in front of the fountain," Dan told everybody for the tenth time as we dumped our plates in the trash and headed our separate ways.

Dan and I wandered our way through the cows, sheep and goats, stopping often to chat with proud parents who pointed out their children's award-winning 4H animals, or acquaintances who urged us not to miss something or other. Ladies Lead was starting.

"Let's watch." I tugged at his hand.

"Why do you want to watch decorated sheep?" Dan tugged back, looking toward the beef cows.

"They aren't decorated, they're dressed up to match the girls leading them. It's a fashion show showing how to use wool."

Dan wasn't impressed. He led me over to the next barn. "Now, that's showmanship."

A half dozen small 4H boys and girls were showing swine. Or maybe it was the other way around. The pigs were huge, the children weren't, and the canes they were using to tap the pigs in a desired direction didn't always work. We watched long enough to see a father jump over the rail with what looked like half of an old door, shove it between two pigs who were clearly mortal enemies and jump out again.

"I'd call that a draw." Dan's grin was wide. We

moved on toward the exhibits and were standing before an enormous selection of portable spas, all churning away, when I saw him.

I clutched Dan's arm. "Dan, look."

"I am." He was watching the blond woman in too tight black spandex pants demonstrate the bubble maker.

"Not her." I made my answer as scathing as possible. "Look. My pirate."

"Your what?" Dan, with perhaps a little reluctance, turned back toward me.

"My pirate. I ran into him today. He has a very rude parrot."

The pirate was surrounded by a growing group of people, listening to his chatter, admiring his parrots. I pulled on Dan's arm and headed toward them. "Come on. I want to see this."

Dan smiled broadly but didn't move any too fast. I practically had to push him forward into the circle where the pirate was showing off his birds, letting them hang upside down from his arms. He put birdseed between his teeth for one of the birds, the rude one I thought, to gently remove. A little girl, about ten, jumped up and down with delight and the pirate put his hand out to her.

"Here, girlie." His gruff tone didn't faze the child, but her mother reached out as if to snatch her back. The pirate pulled the child a little further into the center of the circle and offered her a bird. Awestruck, she put out her arm and the bird obediently hopped on.

"Want to give him a treat?" the pirate asked. Before she could answer or her mother reach her, he had placed a seed between her lips. The bird gently reached for it, then squawked and flew back to its perch on the pirate hat. The crowd exploded with applause.

"How about the rest of you?" The pirate circled slowly, addressing the crowd, holding out his hand filled with birdseed. "Any brave souls here?"

He started around the circle, offering the bird. When he came to us, he stopped.

"How about you? Want to feed the bird?" He looked directly at Dan. Their eyes seemed to meet and I could have sworn he nodded. Then he laughed. "Or maybe your girlfriend's the brave one."

"We'll take a rain check." Dan smiled but his eyes didn't look too friendly. He took me by the hand and we were on the outside of the circle, drifting away from it.

"Quite an act. How did you say you met him?"

"I didn't. I ran into him this morning, right after I found Rusty."

"What do you mean, you ran into him?" Dan's smile lingered.

"Exactly that. I was watching the horses and didn't see him. I ran into him."

"Why doesn't that surprise me?" Dan laughed. "And his parrot was rude to you."

"He was," I replied with dignity.

"He was by the horse barns?" He glanced back at the pirate, his expression thoughtful.

"You know him, don't you." I knew that pirate nodded at him. "Who is he? Why shouldn't he have been by the barns?"

"What makes you think I know him?" He turned his back and started to walk off.

"Don't try to get evasive with me, Dan Dunham." I grabbed him by the arm and tried to make him face me.

"Where do you know that pirate from? Did you arrest him? You suspect him of something. What?"

"Ellie, I guarantee you, I have never arrested that pirate, and the only thing I suspect him of is being more rude than his parrot. Come on."

I glanced back at the group surrounding the pirate and stopped short.

"Dan, look."

Bryce and Stephanie were now part of the circle. Stephanie had substituted jeans for shorts and had tucked in her shirt. Her sunburn had faded, and her eyes sparkled. She was almost pretty.

Makeup. That was it; she'd tried a little makeup. It must have helped. She had a firm grip on Bryce's arm, and he wasn't brushing her off.

"What do you suppose that means?" We continued walking.

"That Bryce has interesting taste in women."

We were almost at the horse barns, but neither of us really noticed.

"Dan." I tried to stop, but Dan just kept walking. "Do you think his being near the barns this morning could mean something? Could he have known Rusty? And how about Stephanie? Could she—Dan, answer me. What's the matter?"

The faintly amused expression on Dan's face had changed. Abruptly, he stopped.

"Isn't that Chovalo?"

A tall thin figure in boots, jeans, Western shirt and black sombrero was striding purposefully toward the barns. He disappeared as a fat lady trying to eat cotton candy pushed a stroller in front of us.

"So, what if it is?"

"Go get some ice cream." Dan thrust a bill into my hand and almost tripped over the stroller.

"Where are you going?"

"I'll meet you at the fountain in, oh, forty-five minutes." He glared at the fat woman, stepped around the stroller and was gone.

"Well." She pulled off a long strand of gooey stuff and fed it slowly into her mouth. "Where's he going in such a hurry?"

Exactly what I was wondering. He must be following Chovalo. The only reason could be Rusty. That brought the murder closer to the barn, which meant closer to Susannah. Ice cream forgotten, I followed Dan.

FOUR

"DO YOU SEE HIM?" Dan had stopped in front of a closed stall door directly across from Irma's barn. I tried to peer around him.

"What the hell do you think you're doing?" he hissed. "Didn't I tell you to go get ice cream?"

He was irritated again. I chose to ignore it.

"Why are you following Chovalo? What do you care where he goes? There, he's stopped. Right in front of Irma's barn, where he belongs. Satisfied?"

"No. There aren't any classes tonight. So I, ah, was curious, that's all. What's he doing back here?"

"Maybe he came to feed. Or give the horses water. Or kiss them all good night. Horse people have some strange ideas. Why are we skulking?"

"Police chiefs don't skulk. We observe. And if you won't go away, will you please be quiet?"

It looked like skulking to me, but I kept my opinion to myself and followed close behind Dan. He stopped again and pulled me into the deep shadows of the quiet barn.

"If he's kissing horses good night, why isn't he putting on the lights?" Dan whispered into my ear as we crept down the line of closed stalls. Most of the barns were dark; the only sounds the occasional snort of horses, the rustle of straw. From a couple of aisles over came the blare of a radio, someone laughed, clippers buzzed. We could make out a faint glow of light, but it didn't reach Chovalo or us. The clop clop of hoofs froze us in place. A man rode by, whistling softly to himself, then disappeared around the corner of the barn.

"He didn't come to feed." Dan nudged me and pointed toward the far end of the barn.

Hay bales, hurriedly brought from Irma's ranch to replace the inaccessible ones sealed in the feed room by crime scene tape, were stacked at the far end of the aisle. Sacks of grain and a couple of pails sat beside them. A single light burned over the hay, making only a small pool before it faded away again to darkness. Chovalo walked slowly down the aisle, shined his flashlight on each door, paused at each tack trunk, but didn't go near the feed. A burst of laughter from the workers in the next barn over made him pause and turn, flashing his light toward the shadow where we crouched. Dan pulled me tightly against him as we flattened ourselves against a stall door. The beam returned to Irma's barn and became a warm glow. The yellow crime scene tape was still up, but now it cordoned off only the feed room and the grooming room where the pretty mare had stood. The tape moved a little, followed by the protesting squeak of a door. It evidently had not impressed our sombrero-hatted man with its importance.

"I thought so." Dan still whispered, but with what sounded like satisfaction. "He's gone into the feed room."

"But why?" I whispered back.

"Hush. He'll hear you. I don't know why."

"Yeah? Then why are you so pleased?"

"I'm not. Will you pipe down?"

"He won't hear me. You're talking louder than I am. Are you sure it's Chovalo?"

"Of course I'm sure and he's looking for something.

Stay here, Ellie. I'm going to try to get closer. I want a better look at him when he comes out."

"Why not just arrest him? Isn't it against the law to break into a crime scene, or whatever?"

"I want to see what he's doing, what he's after. Stay here."

"In your dreams." I muttered under my breath and waited until Dan crept down the barn aisle to a better vantage point, then I crept right along behind him. After all, he was hardly in a position to yell at me. Though he could—and did—glare.

We heard the squeak again and the soft glow shone briefly. Almost immediately a figure appeared, bent down and ducked under the yellow tape, stood straight, looked around carefully and hurried off toward the main part of the fair.

I didn't realize I'd been holding my breath until I let it out. "It was him." I said that too loudly. "That mustache. I'd recognize it anywhere."

"I told you it was Chovalo." Dan resumed his normal voice. "But I don't think he was carrying anything. I wonder… Come on."

We hurried after him, dodging groups heading for the main stage show. The crowd was thick and no one was in any hurry, so it didn't take long for us to lose sight of him.

"Is that him, over there?" A black sombrero bobbed for a moment above the crowd and we headed its way. Unfortunately, under it was a young man clutching his giggling girlfriend.

"Damn." Dan looked at the young man with unde-served disgust.

"Buy me an ice cream and let's go toward the fountain." I glanced at my watch. "It's almost time to meet the others."

Dan hesitated, looked around once more and shrugged. "Here, you go stand in line. I've got to make a phone call."

"Who are you going to call?"

Dan just looked at me. "Go buy the ice cream."

Poor Chovalo, I thought as I bought our ice cream. He's going to have a few visitors with some unwelcome questions tonight.

"All set." Dan took one of the sticks and began to bite off the chocolate. "Let's sit down."

We found a spot on a bench facing the fountain. Neither of us said anything for a moment, then Dan started to mumble.

"I can't understand one word. What did you say?"

"I said, I'm sorry about this morning." His face was a little red and he made quite a show of taking another mouthful of ice cream.

"Oh." I wasn't sure how to respond. I'd been building up courage to ask him about this morning, and here he was, offering. I hadn't expected that. "OK, but why were you so mad? It wasn't my idea to find a dead body."

"I know." He sighed. "Remember the day I met you after you came home?"

How could I forget! It was my first real estate appointment and there was a dead body in the house.

"Remember what happened later?"

I shuddered. "I almost got killed. So did Susannah."

"Yeah." He paused, looked down at his ice cream but didn't take a bite. Instead, he sighed. "I've lost one family already," he went on, not looking at me. "I heard you'd found another body and Susannah was also there and I, well, I got a little—upset. It wasn't very, ah, professional, and I'm sorry. Still friends?"

I hadn't forgotten Dan's wife and son had been killed in a head-on collision with a drunk driver, but hadn't thought he'd transfer that into protective feelings for me, or Susannah. And he apologized. I wasn't used to apologies. In all the years I'd been married to Brian, he never once offered one. He assumed he was right, I was wrong and that was that. For the first few years, I felt guilt every time something happened Brian didn't like. Later I learned to tune him out and eventually to stop caring. I had felt an unexpected surge of relief, mixed with a lot of other things, when his attorney notified me he wanted a divorce, that he wanted to marry someone else. I hadn't expected Brian to apologize, or even explain, and he hadn't. So, an apology was something new, and I didn't know how to handle it. Besides, I suspected there was another reason for Dan's flare of bad temper.

For about a month or more before Susannah arrived home for the summer, Dan's evening visits had turned into overnight stays. I amazed myself. I enjoyed them, just flat-out enjoyed every minute. I'd never cheated on Brian, way more than could be said for him, but I was no longer married and having Dan as a companion, day or night, no strings attached, was great fun. Only the nights were becoming more frequent, Dan's shaving kit seemed to have taken up permanent residence, and I found myself feeling—trapped.

I decided to take the summer off.

Dan was hurt, I knew, and certainly confused, but I mumbled something about Susannah, appearances and all that. Didn't mean we couldn't see each other, after all, we were still friends.

At first Dan protested, then he got thoughtful and finally said, "OK, I'm a patient man. For the rest of the summer, we'll be friends. Just friends." I'd heaved a quiet sigh of relief that I'd postponed a commitment I wasn't ready to make. But this! All this protection stuff! This didn't feel like plain old friendship. I had no idea how I felt about that and I wasn't ready to find out. So, not having any idea what to say, I reached over with the hand not holding ice cream and slipped it into his. He squeezed. I squeezed back. I said, "Friends," and changed the subject.

"Dan, what exactly is going on? I know you think Rusty was somehow mixed up with these drugs you were telling us about, and it seems Bryce has more than a nodding acquaintance with them. Do you think Chovalo is involved in all that also?"

Dan took a careful bite, studying how the chocolate cracked instead of looking at me.

"Come on, Dan. We're friends. I'm worried about Susannah. Should I be?"

"You know, Ellie," he finally said, "police work is largely a matter of elimination. We look at everybody who could have, who might have, and start narrowing the field. Chovalo was around the barn at about the time Rusty was killed. That's all."

"If that's all, why were we chasing him through the horse barns?"

"Why are you so curious about Chovalo?"

"Because my daughter works with him! And with that ego on two legs, Bryce. I don't like all this talk of drugs, and murder makes me nervous."

"It should. It makes me nervous too."

Dan looked very serious. Suddenly, I felt the need to

push this terrible murder and everything connected with it as far away from my daughter and me as possible.

"Of course," I bit the last bit of ice cream off the stick, "the most logical explanation is that whoever murdered Rusty had no connection with Irma's at all. From what you said, he sounds like he could have had a whole crop of enemies."

"That's certainly possible. Probably even likely." Dan looked around for a trashcan for his empty stick. I took it and dumped it and my own in the can close to our bench.

"But I'd still like to know what Chovalo wanted in that feed room tonight." He said that almost as an afterthought.

"Maybe he was just checking on the horses. Or looking for extra buckets or halters or whatever they use."

Dan looked at me pityingly. "Did you see any buckets? Did you see him open even one stall door? If you were checking horses, wouldn't you turn on lights?"

I wouldn't check on horses at all, if I could avoid it, but was saved from answering when Susannah and Neil arrived, proudly waving a plastic bag. Neil had won three goldfish and it only cost him ten dollars. Wonderful.

Carl arrived, full of the wonders performed by the sheepdogs, followed closely by Pat. She'd met my Aunt Mary while examining the home canning and had filled her in on the events of this morning, not that she needed to. Aunt Mary's grapevine was extensive and efficient. I was sure she knew more than I did, and probably as much as Dan. Anyway, Pat said I was to call Aunt Mary in the morning. Susannah laughed, I nodded, and we all went in to see the Oak Ridge Boys. Even the goldfish.

FIVE

SUSANNAH RODE HOME with me, to my mild surprise. She had to be at Bryce's barn early because she'd be the only one around to feed horses, answer the phone and prepare the stalls for the returning show participants. Several had evidently been scheduled to come home after the Saturday classes, but the events of this morning turned lots of plans upside down.

"Who's going to help Bryce at the show grounds? Stephanie?"

"Hardly. Although I'm sure she'll be there. No. Chovalo is. He volunteered. I didn't expect that. He can't stand Bryce. I guess he's doing it for Irma."

Really, I thought. Or another chance at whatever is in that feed room. I wondered if Dan's men had found him yet and if so, where. What kind of questions would they ask him? Dan and I hadn't seen him take anything. He did work there. So— My thoughts were interrupted by the clatter of dishes in my cupboard.

"What are you doing?" I addressed that to Susannah, or rather the back end of Susannah. She was on her knees, pulling out a pile of mixing bowls.

"This one will do, don't you think?" She held up my favorite large earthenware bowl.

"For what? You aren't going to start baking at this time of night, are you?" My tone was probably a little incredulous, but I couldn't figure out why she wanted the bowl.

"Of course not." She was at the sink, filling the bowl with water and, before I could stop her, the three gold-fish were plopped into it.

I was going to protest, strongly, but she put her arm around me and gave me a peck on the cheek. "I love you, Mom. And I love this town. I'm so glad we moved here."

Speechless for once, I tried to give her a kiss back, but she danced around the kitchen, paused to pick up her bowl of fish, putting them down in the middle of the chopping block.

"Just think. If you and Dad hadn't gotten divorced you would never have moved to Santa Louisa, you wouldn't have met Dan again after all those years, and I wouldn't have met Neil. Isn't it wonderful how things work out?" She danced out of the kitchen and toward the stairs before I could start the inquisition that immediately came to mind.

Had something happened between those two tonight, something, well, more? It was much too soon for them to start making any kind of plans except those that involved finishing school. Neil still had three more years of vet school, and Susannah at least two, maybe three, before she got her bachelor's degree.

I decided, as I slowly climbed the stairs, I didn't want to deal with this tonight, after everything else that had happened. Jake, my big yellow tom, sat in the hall star-ing at Susannah's already closed door. I joined him for a second, wondering if I should knock and say some-thing then shrugged, slipped into my nightgown and crawled into bed, Jake right behind me.

Sleep took a while. So many thoughts kept whirling in my head, so many emotions I didn't want to face. My six months in Santa Louisa hadn't yet buffered me from the trauma of my sudden divorce and the abrupt change from dependent housewife to independent full-time real estate agent. I'd run home, reaching backwards for the roots and stability that had been yanked from under me, to find myself living in the house where I'd grown up, renting it from my absent parents, starting a new life that was just beginning to feel right.

Dan had returned earlier, but for similar reasons. After the accident that killed his family, he gave up a promising career with the San Francisco Police Department to become Chief of our minuscule town force, where the most exciting event was the occasional painting of our park pioneer statue by the neighboring town's football team when we managed to beat them.

Dan. The boy next door. Literally. We'd grown up best friends, me tagging behind whenever he'd let me, him bossing, teasing and protecting me. Then he left for college. Two years later so had I, to find Brian, to have Susannah, and ultimately to be dumped by my now famous physician husband for his cute blond office nurse. I was grateful Dan was around while I licked my wounds and was pretty sure some of my feeling went beyond gratitude or friendship for the boy next door. We'd both outgrown that. But something else was happening to me, other feelings and realizations were emerging, and I liked them. I hadn't sorted them out yet, but it had a lot to do with independence and it felt good. Only, tonight I didn't want to sort. Tonight I wanted to sleep. Right after I quit worrying about Susannah, about her perhaps too close relationship with Neil, about the possibility that Rusty's death might touch her in any way, about… About here I fell asleep, Jake firmly wrapped around my feet.

SIX

THE PHONE WAS RINGING. I opened one eye and stared at the clock on my bed table. Seven thirty. On a Sunday morning. I fumbled for the receiver and pressed it to the ear not attached to my pillow.

"Humph," I muttered.

"Ellie. That you?" Dan's voice was disgustingly cheerful.

"Who else were you expecting?"

"Are you still asleep?"

"Not anymore."

"Are you all right?"

"I haven't been awake long enough to find out." I struggled to sit up, to wake up, but my normally sunny disposition wouldn't kick in until I had my first cup of coffee.

"I guess mornings aren't your thing." Some people don't know when to quit. "It's a beautiful day, Ellie. A beautiful day. And I hear it's going to be a nice night. Lots like last night. Just perfect for a barbecue."

I can take a hint, even half asleep.

"And you think my backyard would do fine." I sniffed the air. Coffee. Just a faint aroma, but definitely coffee. Thank God. "I guess we can do that. Susannah will probably be home and that means Neil. Pat and Carl?"

"Sure. If they want to. Let's have hamburgers. I'll bring beer. See you about, when. Six?"

"Fine." I hung up. I needed to follow my nose toward the coffee while I contemplated my now full day. Beer? That's all he was bringing? Beer?

Bless Susannah. The coffee pot was almost full and there was a note on the table. "See you at Irma's at one. Don't forget." As if I could, I thought as I sipped.

I'd been both looking forward to and dreading this afternoon's appointment. Irma Long owned an eighty-acre ranch not too far outside of town. Actually, it was two adjacent forty-acre pieces. Irma lived on the back parcel, where she maintained her horse breeding operation and the barn that she rented to Bryce. The front forty was used for the transport business Wes and Linda Fowler ran for her. The mobile home the Fowlers lived in was there, as well as the transport office and the barns that housed the trucks and trailers. It was this parcel, along with the horse vans, that Irma was thinking of selling. I was to give Irma some idea of what the land was worth.

Right. I had never, in my vast six months' experience as a real estate agent, sold or listed a piece of ranch property and was terrified I'd make a mistake. Irma had become Susannah's friend over the last few weeks. I didn't want to let her, or my daughter, down.

Not that I hadn't done my homework. My broker, Bo Chutsky, an old friend of my parents, had put me through a crash course on ranches, wells, cost of fencing and so on. I felt somewhat prepared, and was excited by the opportunity to do this new thing. Also relieved that I had someone to back me up when I ran out of knowledge.

My mood greatly improved with coffee. I called Pat. "We're barbecuing tonight. Dan's bringing the beer. We get to do the rest. You and Carl want to come?"

"Of course. The first one of the season. What fun. Let's see, I have avocados, some shrimp, how about if I improvise?"

"Sounds wonderful. I'm going to call Aunt Mary. She'll bring potato salad, she always does. At least she used to."

"Did Dan say anything more about that poor boy?"

"Rusty? No. Actually he didn't say much of anything except he would see us tonight." I didn't tell her I hadn't given him a chance.

"I hope they find out who killed him soon and what it's all about. Drugs and all that really worry me. You don't expect it in a small, quiet town like this."

"No, you don't," I agreed. "LA, it's everywhere, but not here." We hung up, but I kept thinking about Rusty. Could anyone connected with Irma's barn…? No, of course not.

"I wish that kid had gotten himself murdered in someone else's barn," I told Jake, who was sitting in the middle of the chopping block contemplating the goldfish, "then I wouldn't have to worry about Susannah."

Jake jumped down, sat in front of his empty bowl and looked at me. I took this to be disapproval of his lack of breakfast, not my callous statement. "If you were a mother, you'd feel the same way." I filled his bowl before reaching for the phone.

Aunt Mary was home from church and more than willing to barbecue.

"I'd love to come," she said immediately. "What shall I bring?"

"Potato salad. Everybody used to say yours was the best."

"Imagine you remembering that. About five thirty?

I hope Dan has some information for us. I don't like this talk of drugs one little bit."

I had long since given up wondering where Aunt Mary got her information, but she always knew everything and somehow she always had it right! Age of information nothing, Aunt Mary was light years ahead.

Humming, I put out a jar of sun tea and started the hunt for my summer dishes, tablecloths and outdoor candles. I still had boxes of stuff unpacked, stuff Brian hadn't had the guts to refuse to let me take. I knew I could lay my hands right on it. An hour later, and quite a bit grumpier, I found everything in a box labeled "Christmas decorations."

I had just enough time to hit the shower and head for Irma's. I'd stop at the store on my way home and pick up meat, buns, ice cream and fresh corn. Tonight we would feast.

SEVEN

IRMA'S PLACE WAS only about ten minutes out of town, but it was a different world. The two-lane road wandered through a gently rolling countryside filled with grapevines, barley fields and cows. The pale gold of the grass showed off the emerald leaves of the vines and the black-green of the massive oak trees. The sky was the clearest of blues and the few fat white clouds lay still, looking like mounds of whipped cream. Dan was right. It was a beautiful day.

I drove slowly through Irma's gates and down her wide driveway, examining the front part of the ranch as I went. The drive was on the extreme right side of the property. I could see the almost new doublewide mobile where Wes and Linda lived. A few plants grew reluctantly against its side, but no lawn, no flowerbeds, no pots of color. Oh well, I thought, gardening takes time and work, and it isn't their property.

All the action took place in the huge two-story metal barn behind the mobile. Horse vans were housed, washed and repaired there. The business office, with its maps, charts and two-way radio, was located along one side. Long's ran two cross-country transport vans as well as three pickup trucks that could be combined with two four-horse trailers and one two-horse trailer for more local needs. All in all, they represented a huge investment and, I imagined, a lot of income for Irma. I wondered again why she wanted to sell.

A woman appeared in the doorway of the office, watching my slow progress down the drive. She was dressed in a plaid shirt, jeans tight over skinny hips and the kind of running shoes that fasten with Velcro. Her hair was skinned back in a tight ponytail, and crow's feet shadowed her eyes as she squinted. I passed her close enough to tell she wore no makeup and, more than likely, moisturizer wasn't on her shopping list, either. She nodded at me, just once. I nodded back. Who was she? Why was she standing there, arms folded, watching me? I glanced at her again in my rearview mirror. Who on earth—Wes's wife, Linda. She couldn't be anyone else.

No wonder he eyed every pretty young thing that passed by.

She still watched me as I passed through the open gate that marked the horse ranch.

IRMA'S HOME WASN'T LARGE, but the setting was perfect, a low ranch-style house with huge windows, set on a knoll surrounded by oak trees. She could view her entire property as well as miles of country around. A short drive went up the hill toward her home, a longer one led to a complex of barns and outbuildings on the flat area below. That was where I now headed. Large pastures were filled with curious young horses that raced me along the fence line. The older ones contented themselves with lifting their heads and watching my progress as they guarded their shaded places under the oak trees. A dark red pickup truck with a long silver horse trailer attached was parked in front of what seemed to be the main barn. A silver L was painted on the truck door and red letters on the trailer said, "There is a LONG way to go." Cute.

The barn had two tall sliding doors that opened onto a wide aisleway, with what looked like horse stalls on each side. Another pickup truck, with some sort of open camper shell in the back, was pulled up halfway inside the doors.

That's a strange place to park, I thought, as I chose a shady spot, got out and walked toward the barn, looking around as I went. Pipe pens in neat rows flanked one side of the main barn, all with metal covers over them. Almost all were filled with horses. A few housed mares with babies by their sides. I was tempted to take a detour, but I was sure Irma would show me around later. Another barn, more like the ones at the show ground, stretched out behind them. The stalls were in a row, with the roof overhanging about six feet, creating a walkway. The top doors were open and all seemed to be empty. Maybe the horses in the pastures spent their nights here? Then again, maybe not. Off to the side, an enormous pile of baled hay rested under a tall roof held up by, of all things, telephone poles.

I heard voices as I neared the main barn, and I got a better look at the truck. That was no camper shell. The tilted-up sides showed exposed shelves of bottles, pulled out drawers filled with syringes. A metal pail sat in the dirt with a lethal-looking soft plastic tube inside it. I paused, then hurried into the barn. The truck had to belong to a vet. Even I knew that meant trouble.

The beautiful little mare that I had met at the fairgrounds was standing in the barn aisle, head down, anything but beautiful now. Dark sweat marks showed behind her ears and down her shoulders, her large inquisitive eyes dulled with pain.

The group surrounding her hardly noticed me as I walked up. A short, rather chubby man with a face that looked like it was used to laughing, was worriedly telling Irma, "We don't have much time. She has to go immediately."

Neil appeared with a cellular phone. The man grabbed it and walked back toward the truck, punching in a number. Susannah stood beside the horse, a lead rope draped over her arm. She looked up, saw me, started to say something when Neil called out. "Watch out. She's going down." The mare swayed, her knees buckling. Neil leaped forward, grabbed the lead, snatching up the mare's head.

"Don't let her lie down. We'll never get her up into that trailer if she does." His face was grim. "Walk her, Susannah. Slowly, easy does it."

Susannah glanced at me, her eyes wide and scared, but she obeyed, pulling the mare gently forward. Neil was behind the horse, tapping her on the rump, making clucking noises. The mare tried, stopped, then seemed to gain a little confidence and slowly, painfully, moved off beside Susannah.

"What's happening?" I stood beside an ashen-faced Irma and whispered as if I was in a hospital room. "What's wrong with her?"

"Colic." Irma seemed to feel the one word was enough.

Neil took pity on me. "Horses have miles of intestines and not much stomach. Sometimes the intestine gets blocked or gets twisted back on itself."

"Is that what happened to her?" I pointed at the mare staggering down the barn aisle, trying to follow Susannah. "How do you cure it?"

"You don't, not when it's this bad." The chubby man shoved the phone at Neil. "You operate and pray like hell that you get in there before her gut strangulates.

The clinic's expecting you, Irma, so let's get going. That's your rig out there, isn't it? Where are the keys?"

"In the ignition," called out Susannah.

"OK. Neil, go throw in some straw and make sure this mare has room to go down if she has to. Irma, who's going with you?"

Irma looked around somewhat blankly. She'd said only one word since I had arrived and seemed to be in only a little less pain than the mare.

"I can't." Susannah stopped by us, the horse more than willing to quit moving. "Bryce and Chovalo will be bringing the rest of the horses back from the show pretty soon. Neil?"

"No. I need him. We have another emergency as soon as we leave here. How about you?" The vet pointed at me.

"Who, me?"

"Of course. Mom will go." Helpful Susannah!

"But I don't know anything about horses."

"You know how to work a phone, don't you?" The vet swung away from me abruptly. "Let's get that horse in the trailer."

I could hear clanging and banging in front of the barn and reluctantly followed the rest out into the sunlight. The double doors at the back of the trailer were wide open, showing a large open space. Neil emerged covered with straw.

"Ready. Bring her in."

The vet took the lead from Susannah. Gently, but very firmly, he led the horse up to Neil, who disappeared with her into the trailer. Then the vet whirled around toward me.

"Here." He handed me a plastic sack filled with syringes. "Do you know how to give shots? I've filled her pretty full of painkillers, but you might need to give her some more if she goes down and starts to thrash."

He'd lost his mind. I had never given anything a shot in my life and wasn't about to learn on a thousand-pound horse thrashing around on the bottom of a trailer.

Irma was heading for the cab of the truck, so with a deep breath I hitched my purse under my arm, climbed into the passenger seat and deposited the bag of syringes on the dashboard.

"Hey, wait. Where're you going with that truck?"

A woman's face appeared at Irma's window. Her faint Midwest twang was strong with agitation.

"Get out of the way, Linda." Irma had the truck started and was trying to put it in gear. Her legs didn't quite reach the clutch and she was fumbling under her seat. "Ellen, see if there's a lever or something under your side. This damn thing won't budge."

"Where're you going?" Linda had a hand on Irma's door handle and looked like she was going to open it.

"Valley Oak Clinic," Irma barked out. The seat slid forward with a jolt, and the gearshift slid down into first. "That's got it. Let's go."

The vet took Linda by the arm and pulled her away from the truck. "They're taking Mariah for colic surgery and they haven't got time to waste. What's the matter with you, woman? They need to leave."

"Not in that rig. Wes needs it to go get horses from the show grounds." Her voice was brittle with irritation. She pushed at the vet, trying to get back toward the truck.

Irma had paused, her foot on the clutch, staring at the woman in apparent amazement. "Tell him to use the big van or wait until we get back, but we're leaving. Now!" She let the clutch out and we were finally slowly moving.

"The truck's still got show gear on it," Linda shouted after us. "I've got a two-horse that's empty. Why can't you use it?"

"The mare stays where she is until she gets to the clinic," the vet said. "The gear will still be there when they get back." He was determinedly holding on to the still squirming Linda, letting go only when we were halfway up the drive.

I looked back as we made a slow turn onto the paved road. She strode up the driveway toward the van yard and her office, pausing only to watch us.

"What was all that about?" I fought with my seat belt as we picked up speed, heading for the freeway I guessed.

"Linda probably figures Wes'll pitch a fit. I'm sure she thinks I should have checked with him before taking this truck."

"But it's your truck."

"You're right there."

"Where is Wes?"

"No idea. Did you ever use one of these cellular phones, Ellen?"

I had one, but not that kind, so we spent the next few minutes going over its simple mysteries.

"Where are we going?" I replaced the phone in its holder. Irma glanced sideways at me, obviously surprised. "Why, the Valley Oak Clinic!"

I must have looked unusually blank because she gave a little snort and said, "I keep forgetting you're not a horse person. It's the only clinic around that's equipped to do surgery on horses and, lucky for us, it's one of the best in the country. If she's savable, they'll do it."

"She's a beautiful horse." I'd momentarily forgotten the horse and its distress in the commotion of getting away. Now the horror of what might be happening in the trailer behind us returned.

"Surgery. It must be terribly, ah—" I didn't know how to finish. I was certain surgery to a horse, like surgery on a person, wouldn't come cheap. Irma's decision seemed already made. Was this horse worth it? I wasn't sure how to tactfully ask such a painfully practical question. Once, years ago, Susannah's dog had been hit by a car. I agreed to the surgery, putting the dog through unnecessary agony before it mercifully died. All this couldn't be less agonizing for the horse and probably twice as expensive.

"Expensive? And is she worth it?" Irma finished my question for me. "Yes, in several ways. I bred her, and she's always been a favorite of mine. Not my biggest winner, but a real sweetheart. Besides, she's carrying a foal, sixty days into it. And the sire is Last Challenge. His first foal and the only mare I bred to him this year. If I lose her, well, it won't be easy." Then, very softly, "Seems like it's been my year to lose things. Hasn't been a year yet since Bud, oh, dear God, that terrible accident. I still can't think about it."

Her hands tightened on the wheel, the knuckles white. She reached up under her dark glasses and wiped her eye, then downshifted a little too abruptly as we slowed for traffic.

Now what do I say? I wondered. I knew Irma was a widow, but nobody had said anything about an accident, especially one so recent. I twisted in my seat to look out the side-view mirror at the trailer, and my hand hit something. The folder I had brought with me, with the information that Irma wanted. I picked it up, uncertainly. Was now a good time? At least it would change the subject.

"Is that the stuff you brought for me?" Irma asked, glancing sideways at me.

"Yes." I started to open the folder. "Do you want me to go over these numbers? We've got quite a way to go yet, don't we?" Figures were the last thing I wanted to think about right then, but maybe it would take Irma's mind off the potential tragedy riding in the trailer behind us.

"Let's wait, Ellen. I'm not in the mood." She paused, then reached up and settled her sunglasses more firmly on her nose. "Ed Brady will just have to be patient. Anyway, they're all driving me crazy."

"Who's driving you crazy?"

"Ed Brady, Wes and Linda, all of them. Ed's our biggest competitor. He wants to buy me out. Wes and Linda don't think I should sell. They say we're doing just fine."

"Are you?"

"I guess so. But Ed keeps telling me I'd be better off. I'd get a nice monthly check and wouldn't have to worry. Don't know how selling would keep me from worrying. It'd just be about something different, that's all. Anyway, Linda writes me a good-sized check every month."

I was beginning to feel a little lost and said so. "I don't understand. You're getting a check, but you don't know what the business is doing?"

Irma's neck turned a pale pink. Her eyes never left the road. "Linda and Wes do a great job. When they're not fighting. Sometimes I think they do too good a job."

"How can someone do too good a job?"

"I guess I'm just grousing, Ellen. I feel, well, left out. I don't know what's going on, can't tell if we're making money or losing it. Hell, I don't even know the drivers anymore."

"But you have the books, it's your business."

The pink spread up to her cheeks. "It's all on computer, has been since right after Wes and Linda came to work for me. She gives me these long things with figures going every which way and says it comes from some fancy program named after a flower."

"Lotus?" I asked with deep sympathy. I had seen those printouts. They made no sense to me, either.

"That's it. She goes over those things with me. She's real nice about trying to explain everything, but all I ever get out of it is a headache."

Irma paused to change gears. We were leaving the downtown section of San Luis Obispo and traffic was, for our slow-moving part of the world, heavy. A little sports car darted out of the fast lane, cut close in front of us and zipped down the off ramp.

"Idiot," Irma said. The trailer lurched.

I strained against my seat belt to look out the back window. "Is she all right? Did she go down?"

"I don't know about all right." Irma picked up speed again. "She's still on her feet. That's a good sign." She paused and changed the subject. "You know, Ellen, I don't want you to think I don't appreciate Linda."

The abrupt backwards jump in the conversation took me a little by surprise. I took one more quick look in the mirror at a trailer that was not telling me a thing and concentrated on Irma, who was.

"Linda's a whiz at that stuff and she's better at scheduling than I was. She gets on the radio, finds out where every rig is, what horse got picked up, who got dropped off and makes sure the rigs are on time. Wes is great with the drivers, all that good ol' boy stuff, but they do what he tells them."

Before I could say anything, the cellular phone beeped. Irma picked it up, listened for a minute or two. Her expression changed. A darker color crept up the back of her neck and filled in the hollows of her cheeks. When she spoke her voice came out harsh and overloud.

"You listen to me, Wes Fowler. This is my rig, my business. It's my horse that's trying to die. How dare you call me up and—and—" She paused, but only for a second. "This horse is one hell of a lot more important than yours or Linda's schedule. No, I couldn't wait for you. I didn't need you. I'm perfectly capable of driving this rig." She paused again. "Then take the big van and go get the rest of the horses. I don't care. But, Wes, don't ever talk like that to me again. Don't forget, I'm your boss, not your wife." She snapped the phone off with a vicious click and threw it on the seat. "If it rings, don't answer. We're almost there. Right now I don't need to be any more upset than I already am."

We pulled off the freeway and slowly wound our way through the charming business center of some small town. Where, I had no idea, but I didn't care.

"What did he say to you?" I was too shocked by Irma's end of the conversation to worry about tact.

"Started to bawl me out like he does Linda. That's another reason I don't stay in the office much. All the fighting, I hate it. He said I shouldn't have taken the truck and trailer without consulting him, he should have driven, I would need him when we got to the clinic, drivel like that. Wes doesn't think there's a woman alive who can survive without a man's supervision, especially his." She sighed and the tight lips and staccato sentences started to soften a little. "He means well, he really thinks he's supposed to act like that, but it gets on my nerves."

"Sounds like it gets on Linda's too." Irma didn't answer.

We slowed down and Irma carefully turned into a driveway blocked by iron gates, with a sign that proclaimed "Valley Oak Equine Clinic." She pushed a button, the gates opened and we drove down a gravel driveway toward the low, white hospital buildings.

EIGHT

"HOP OUT, ELLEN, tell 'em we're here."

I didn't need to. Double doors on the side of the low, white building opened and a tiny Chinese woman, who looked more like a girl, emerged followed by a tall, lanky, Hispanic man.

"I'm Dr. Woo," she told Irma, pausing for a second by the truck window. "This is Dr. Hidalgo. Dr. Williams is inside, waiting. Let's get her out."

Irma opened the trailer doors, and Dr. Hidalgo went in. Almost immediately, the horse staggered out, the vet beside her, crooning sympathetically in Spanish. They headed toward the open doors. Dr. Woo hurried along behind, asking Irma all kinds of questions, making notes on a clip board as she went. I followed slowly, feeling about as useful as the fifth person on a double date.

I was torn between thinking Irma might need me and being certain I might get in the way, but the doors were still opened and no one said anything as I eased my way inside a large, open room. The concrete floor was covered with rubber mats, a hose hung from an overhead pulley. White cupboards, each closed door with a label identifying its contents, lined another wall. The horse was being scanned by what I guessed was an ultrasound machine. The screen flickered with indecipherable images as the probe moved gently over her belly.

A tall, skinny, completely bald man stared at the

screen. "Only two choices, Irma. Operate or put her down." He turned inquiringly back toward Irma, his eyes resting briefly, sympathetically, on the suffering horse.

"You know the answer, Charlie." Irma looked almost as bad as the mare and my heart went out to her. I started to take a step forward until I saw her shoulders straighten. I stayed where I was. "Do I need to sign something?"

"Just the permission slip. After all these years, I guess we know where to find you." The vet gave a bark of a laugh and waved toward the horse. "Let's get her ready."

The tiny Dr. Woo and the tall Dr. Hidalgo immediately ran off in different directions while we followed the bald vet into a dark office.

"I guess I can find what we need. Don't know why we don't have office staff on Sundays, seems they're always the worst day of the week. Permission forms, where does Nancy keep—here, here's one." He pushed a paper in front of Irma and shoved a pen in her hand.

"You doing all right, Irma? Haven't seen you since Bud's funeral. Terrible thing. If there's anything I can do…" He broke off, looking a little uncomfortable.

"I'm getting along, Charlie. It's taken a while, but I'm managing. What you can do is save that mare. The foal she's carrying is by Last Challenge. His first. I'd really hate to lose it. Kinda like to keep the mare too."

"We'll do our best, you know that. Where do you want me to call you? Just write the number down there." He shoved a prescription pad at Irma, squinting to read the number, then nodded. "Good. Be a while, you know." He gave Irma a pat on the shoulder and disappeared.

I felt a little disoriented by the speed of all this, but Irma seemed to take it as a matter of course.

"Let's move. Nothing more we can do around here." She blinked a time or two and headed for the truck. I was glad to be going, but nonetheless suffered vague guilt about leaving. It didn't somehow seem right. I hesitated a little and Irma gave a small, grim smile.

"If the mare lives she won't know or care if we're here. If she doesn't make it, I'd rather be home when I get the news."

NINE

THE RIDE BACK seemed miles longer. Irma was quiet for the first thirty minutes or so. I wasn't sure how, or if, I should break the silence. When she finally spoke I was surprised where her thoughts had been.

"You never met Bud, did you, Ellen?"

I shook my head.

"You've been back, how long, about six months?" I nodded. "It was in all the papers, the accident, but you wouldn't have seen them. The TV made a big thing about it. See that gully there? That's where he went over."

We had just started the long uphill climb that separated the north and south sections of our county. She pointed to the bank at the end of the treacherous downhill side. This roller coaster descent had been the scene of more than one accident over the years. The Homecoming football game of my senior year in high school flashed through my mind. Three football players and two cheerleaders had gone over the side, right about here, after celebrating our victory with forbidden beer. It had been my first brush with tragedy. I shuddered and listened as Irma went on.

"I never really understood what happened." Her eyes were on the road, but I wondered if she wasn't seeing something else. "Bud was a careful man. He'd spent a lifetime pulling a rig. He'd never jackknifed one before in his life. Highway Patrol thinks the storm that day, it was the first one of the season and the pavement was slick. That and the fact he was pulling empty. I don't know. Guess we never will."

There was a pause, then Irma gave a deep sigh and went on.

"He died in my arms. He waited till I got there and then he died."

I had no idea what to say, so mumbled the obvious. "I'm so sorry."

"Yeah. Well, it's been hard. Bud and I never had children, maybe that's why we were so—close." Her eyes blinked rapidly for a moment. "Bud ran the transport business, and I ran the breeding business. Then we'd sit at dinner and tell each other all about everything. It's taken a while, but I'm gettin' there." She gave a rueful little laugh. "That was one time I could have used Wes's bossiness. Chovalo, bless him, wasn't in much better shape. He did the best he could, but grief is a hard taskmaster. Anyway, after a couple of months Chovalo said we had to get someone, there was too much work for the two of us. So I hired Wes and Linda."

"How did you find them?"

"They found me. Wes appeared one day and said he heard I was looking for someone experienced to run the hauling business. He had good references from people I know back East. Bud had been talking about getting some help before he died. So we could have more free time, he said. We'd earned it. He'd even bought the mobile home Wes and Linda live in. So, I hired them. I think they've retired me. I don't even do the little I did for Bud. One good thing, it gives me more time with the horses."

I really didn't know what to say, but picked up on the key word. Horses.

"Tell me about Last Challenge."

A smile broke through on her tired face.

"What do you want to know?"

"Anything. Everything. My knowledge of horses starts at zero."

"Well…" Irma's smile faded to a thoughtful look. We were at the top of the grade and she shifted gears before she went on. "Bud and I bred him. We knew from the beginning he was the best thing we'd ever had. His mamma is a great mare, had some darn good babies for us, but Bud always felt she could do a little better. We really scratched to pay the stud fee, but the minute he was on the ground we knew he was good."

"Everyone keeps talking about choosing a stallion, stud fees, breeding. Doesn't sound like anyone ever consults the mares."

Irma gave a surprised laugh. "Guess women's lib hasn't gotten that far, but they don't get much choice in the wild, either. Mares run in herds. They breed with whatever stallion can fight off all the others. Not too much different now except the stallions battle it out in the show ring."

"Neil started talking about that last night, but I still don't really understand."

"Not too hard. If a horse wins a lot, people notice. People who own mares. If the horse wins big, like Regional shows and especially at the National level, people will send him mares from all over the country. Or, we can transport the semen. It's big business and you can make good money, but the cost of getting to that level is pretty heavy. You need to advertise, go to lots of shows and have the best handler you can find. Or afford."

Which brought us to Bryce, but before I could ask her about him, Irma switched subjects.

"Neil Bennington. He's a nice boy, comes from a good family. He'll be just right for a smart girl like Susannah. They'd have good-looking kids too."

What? What was she talking about? "They're friends," I protested, "just friends." All this talk of breeding was getting out of hand.

"Can't stop nature, Ellen. And they're at the age."

That's what she thought. Susannah and I were going to have a talk, tonight I vowed, as we bumped through Irma's gate.

"Looks like Wes figured it out."

A large silver transport van was parked in front of Irma's barn, facing us. Red letters spelled out "There's a LONG Way to Go" brilliantly against the silver metal. The side door was open and a ramp stretched to the ground. The van appeared empty, but the barn wasn't. Loud voices came from it, or rather one loud one. Another, softer, belonged to Susannah and that sent me hurrying through the barn door, Irma on my heels.

All the noise came from a room directly inside the barn on the right, where saddles sat on racks, halters, bridles and other strange equipment hung from pegs. Shelves held neatly folded blankets, bins and pails were full of brushes, combs, jars and cans of stuff. I had just time to notice how orderly and clean it all was before my attention was consumed by an ongoing soap opera. Bryce stood in the middle of the room, facing Chovalo over an open red and white trunk, the same kind that had propped up Rusty. An angry flush stained Bryce's normally tanned face. He was still yelling as we came in.

"Never again. Do you hear me? Never again."

"Never again what?" Irma's voice was soft, but it plainly said she would tolerate no nonsense.

Bryce whirled around at the sound of her voice, his face turning an even deeper red. Chovalo looked steadily at Irma, his expression unreadable, hidden under hat and mustache. Maybe Irma saw something I couldn't, because she stared back at him. It was a long minute before she went on. "What's going on here?"

Stephanie stood beside Bryce, Susannah behind Chovalo. She looked relieved to see us. "Bryce is accusing Chovalo of going through his things."

"He is. Was. I caught him."

"That's right," Stephanie contributed. "We both saw him. He quit when we came in."

Ignoring her, Bryce angrily pointed down at the open trunk. The top tray was on the floor, filled with brushes and bottles. The trunk seemed to be filled with a variety of things, the most obvious several beautiful fine leather halters decorated with silver. Clean white towels were neatly stacked on the floor. One lone empty beer can lay on its side beside the tray. I wondered how it had gotten there.

Susannah didn't bother to hide the exasperation in her voice. "It's a tack trunk, Bryce." She ran her fingers through her hair in a gesture I knew only too well. "The farm's tack trunk. Irma's tack trunk. Irma's tack. Chovalo was unpacking it, which I for one appreciate. It's your job, but I usually get stuck doing it."

"He was snooping. Looking for stuff." Bryce insisted stubbornly on making his point, ignoring Susannah's little jab.

"Looking for what. This?" Susannah kicked the beer can. It clattered across the concrete floor and came to rest in a corner under a saddle rack.

"I rent this part of the barn," Bryce kept on. "He's

got no right to be in here. He hates me. He'd do anything to make me look bad."

"Why, Bryce?" Susannah asked, her tone dripping with sarcasm. "Is there something in there we're not supposed to see?"

"Of course not." Bryce tried hard to project injured dignity. "Go ahead and look if you want. But he was going to do something." He glared at Chovalo, hanging on to his grievance like a Jack Russell terrier hangs on to the end of a sock.

"He's always picking on Bryce." Stephanie's voice was filled with hostility. "You all pick on him. You don't give him credit."

Susannah snorted.

"I do not need your opinion, Stephanie. Chovalo is the farm manager here, not Bryce." Irma's lips were tight. "He goes anywhere and does anything he wants on this ranch, with my blessing." She turned to Bryce, fury in her eyes. "With everything Chovalo's got to do, you should thank him for helping."

Bryce opened his mouth and Irma threw up her hand. "I'm in no mood for one of your tantrums."

She sagged a little and lifted one wrinkled hand to a face suspiciously gray. Susannah produced a stool from somewhere. Chovalo took Irma gently by the arm and eased her down on it. Straightening, he turned slowly to face Bryce.

"The son of my cousin will begin work for you tomorrow, as agreed. His English is good, so you will not need me here. However, I will take care of the colt. You will not touch him unless I am there." The expression on his face didn't change but his tone said plenty.

Bryce started to protest, but Chovalo went on in that same low dangerous voice.

"You push hard, Bryce. Be careful. Someday you will push someone too far."

"There you are." The voice coming out of the shadows of the barn aisle made us all jump. "What are you all doing here? Irma, the clinic called."

Wes walked in the room holding a cellular phone like a trophy, followed closely by Linda. He stopped abruptly, looking first at Bryce, then at Chovalo before he turned back toward Irma. Linda, who had almost run into him, glanced quickly around the room, then curiously at the open trunk before she too turned toward Irma.

"Oh" was all Irma said as she reached out for the phone, but quickly drew her hand back.

It was Chovalo who asked, "The news. Good or bad?"

"So far, so good." Wes chuckled. "She made it through the surgery just fine and is in recovery. Doc says if she does OK the next twenty-four hours, she'll probably make it and so will the foal."

You'd never know this was the same man whose only concern a few hours earlier had been for his trailer.

"Dear God, thank you." Irma looked a little less gray. "I'd been trying to resign myself to losing her, but it wasn't working any too well. Now…well, we'll wait and see."

Chovalo hadn't moved from beside Irma. He lightly patted her arm.

"Good. She is *muy especial*, that one. Now Señora Irma, go home. There is nothing more you can do here. There is nothing more any of us can do here. I will finish outside and will see you tomorrow."

He took one more hard look at Bryce, who studied

the far wall, glanced briefly at Stephanie, who looked mulish, then turned back to Irma.

"Yes. Home sounds about right. A snifter of brandy, a hot tub and maybe I'll start to feel human again."

Chovalo smiled at her. A full-on smile, the first I'd ever seen him give anybody. He smiled only a shade less broadly at Susannah. He nodded gravely to me, not quite so amicably to Wes and Linda, ignored Bryce and Stephanie and left.

That seemed to bring Bryce back to life. He moved in on Irma, neatly cutting off Wes, who had taken a step forward.

"Let us drive you up. We're leaving anyway. I'm sure Susannah won't mind putting the rest of this stuff away."

Susannah started to open her mouth, but I got there first.

"Susannah's not doing one more thing. She's as tired as anyone else and I think I heard her say that all this," I waved at the tack trunk and tray, "is your responsibility, Bryce."

"Mom," Susannah started, dividing her angry look between Bryce and me. This time Irma stopped her.

"If Bryce wants to stay, that's fine." She struggled to her feet. "Ellen's right. Susannah is going home. As far as I'm concerned that stuff can just stay where it is until tomorrow." She paused. "The horses. They've all been taken care of?"

Bryce looked blank, but Susannah answered promptly.

"Of course. Fed, bedded and blanketed."

"I knew I could count on you. Bryce, go on. Take Stephanie with you. I'm going to ride up the hill with Wes and Linda. We've got some talking to do."

Wes looked a little taken aback, but not nearly as much as Bryce.

"I didn't mean…ah, Susannah, I'm sorry." It wasn't hard to see how Bryce charmed his way through life. Not only was he beautiful when he turned on that smile, but he looked amazingly sincere. "You always do so much and do it so well, I didn't mean for you to do my job, or Rusty's, either. If he hadn't gone and gotten himself killed, making us all suffer like this…"

"Rusty did a little suffering of his own." Susannah looked at him with disgust. "Furthermore…"

"Go home, Bryce," Irma interrupted tiredly.

Bryce looked at each of us in turn, even me, then with an injured air said, "All right. I have to meet clients for dinner anyway. Important ones. People who might have mares to breed to Challenge."

He paused for a moment, waiting for praise I supposed. He got some.

"Good," said Irma. "I know you'll make sure they're quality mares. Let me know tomorrow how it goes."

Apparently mollified, Bryce left, with a scowling Stephanie on his heels. No one said anything until we heard the roar of his sports-car engine. Then Wes broke the silence.

"Arrogant little son of a bitch. And that pet amazon of his is just as bad. Come on, Irma. I'll trade you an apology for a glass of that brandy." A little awkwardly, he reached out to help her off the stool.

"I'll take you up on that apology, and the ride up the hill," Irma said. "I'll even throw in the brandy. But the bath I'm taking by myself. Ellen, take your child home."

Irma started for the door followed by Wes, who chuckled at Irma's tired joke. Linda hung back for a second.

"Irma, you sure you don't want me to stay and put this stuff away? I'd be happy to, only take me a minute."

"Well, that's real nice of you, Linda." Irma paused, looking at her with obvious surprise. "But no, don't bother. The stuff's not going anywhere." A small smile appeared for the first time in a while. "Besides, since Bryce is so hung up on no one touching 'his' equipment, we'll let it wait for him."

She walked out the door, Wes trailing her. Linda paused again, gave the trunk an uncertain look, gave Susannah and me a backward glance, shrugged and followed.

I watched them out the door. I turned back to see Susannah looking thoughtfully at the unpacked trunk.

"You wouldn't," I said. "Tell me you're not…"

"I'm not. I'm not as compulsive as Linda. I'm going home and I'm going to shower, long and hard, then sit in the backyard and let Neil serve me hamburgers and potato salad."

"Hamburgers. Potato salad. Oh my God, I forgot. What time is it?" My watch announced it was after five. "I still have to go to the store. Everyone's coming to our house for… How did you know? You were gone this morning."

"Guess."

"It was either Aunt Mary or Neil. Neil?"

She grinned. "You got it. If anyone's there, I'll tell them you'll be along just as soon as you get the buns. Do we have cheese?"

I assured her we did and with one last quick look around, we both left.

TEN

THE PARTY HAD STARTED without me. Dan stood in front of my open refrigerator door, a beer in each hand. I let the screen door slam as I staggered into the kitchen loaded down with sacks.

"You're late. It's after six."

"The grocery store was packed."

"Did you remember to get charcoal?" He watched me heave the sacks onto the counter.

Silently I pointed toward the back porch.

"Great." He planted a quick kiss on my cheek. "Should I start the barbecue now?"

"No. Give me a few." I stifled a sigh. My feet hurt, so did my shoulders. I was thinking I didn't want to shuck corn or make hamburger patties.

"Gotcha. I'll just go give this to Carl."

"Do that."

Dan stopped, one foot holding the screen door open. "Aren't you coming?"

"Soon. Soon." I listened to the screen slam again.

"Why are you standing there staring at those sacks?"

I hadn't heard Susannah come downstairs, but there she was, long, tanned legs showing under white shorts, dark hair damply curling, violet eyes quizzing me.

"I was thinking."

"About what?"

"How happy I'd be if I never found another dead body."

"You're safe. There aren't any in the backyard, but there's a bunch of live ones. Everyone's here and probably starved. At least I am." She started pulling things out of the sacks and putting them in cupboards or stacking them on the counter. "OK. Ben and Jerry's Cherry Garcia ice cream. Way to go, Mom."

The screen door slammed again and Pat and Aunt Mary appeared. Pat looked trim and fit in light blue slacks and a white tee shirt. Aunt Mary looked like an early tribute to a Fourth of July parade. I gasped. Susannah swallowed a giggle, and we immediately started to talk about hamburger patties.

"I get the feeling you're impressed." Aunt Mary ran her hands down the legs of her satin-finish, bright red pants. The American flag fluttered across her front, rising and falling in time with her breathing. I expected drums to roll and fifes to sound any moment.

"Impressed is a good word. Where did you get it?"

"At the United Methodist rummage sale last week."

"Of course. Let me guess. You were chairwoman of the sale committee, right?"

She nodded.

"And that outfit wasn't going to sell and you felt guilty."

"The lady who brought it looked so disappointed when it was still there. It's my size so I bought it. After all, we were raising money for the women's shelter."

"Are you doing any more soon?" I eyed her outfit. Her wardrobe consisted entirely of things purchased in the name of charity and then, of course, worn because you couldn't waste perfectly good money. Could you?

"Not soon." Aunt Mary smiled a little. "Susannah,

give me the corn. I'll shuck it outside. I could use a re-
fill when one of you brings out the wine bottle."

"Do you think we just got told to get a move on?"
laughed Pat. "Here. These patties are ready for the refrigerator."

"Sounds like it. I like the wine part. Grab a couple
of glasses and let's go outside."

"Go on," Pat said. "I've got a few little snacks I'll
bring."

I glanced at the plate she pulled out and quickly
snatched a shrimp before following Susannah and the
drinks into the backyard.

Dan, Carl and Neil were all standing around the barbecue, talking in low tones.

"What are you talking about?" Susannah asked.

"Nothing." Dan tried to look innocent. He didn't
succeed.

"Charcoal," Carl said hurriedly. "How much we're
going to need."

Neil broke away to take the tray from Susannah and
put it on the table. He poured a glass of wine and offered
it to me, letting Susannah pop the top off her Classic
Coke by herself.

"Here, Mrs. McKenzie. Sit down here."

"Her name's Ellen and she's not crippled," my com-
passionate daughter told him. She transferred her gaze
from the two older men to him.

Neil looked a little uncomfortable. I quickly said,
"By all means, call me Ellen," and sank gratefully on
the offered chair.

"Ellen," Neil tried. "Well, you've had quite a day.
Isn't the Valley Oak Clinic the greatest? I could spend
hours there."

If I hadn't been so tired, I'd have been suspicious also. This sounded a lot like subject changing.

"Hum. Wonderful."

"What were you doing at Valley Oak?" Carl asked.

"Neil made Mom go with Irma when she took a mare in for colic surgery." Susannah didn't look as if she was buying the change of subject attempt any more than I was.

Pat set a tray loaded with shrimp, avocado, crackers and some kind of wonderful dip in the middle of the table. I immediately helped myself.

"Why you?" Pat stopped passing out napkins to stare at me. "You don't know a thing about horses."

At the same time Neil was telling Susannah, "I did not make her go."

"Did too."

"Who did what?" Aunt Mary, who had taken the shucked corn into the kitchen, was now back with a tray of fruit, cheese and French bread. I wondered where she had gotten all the food. Certainly not out of my refrigerator.

"Neil made Mom go with Irma to the vet clinic. One of her mares coliced and they had to do surgery. None of the rest of us could leave."

"I'm glad you did." Aunt Mary nodded at me approvingly. "Irma's had a terrible year and what she doesn't need is more stress. Having someone sympathetic to talk to always helps."

"What you two see in horses, I don't know." I addressed that to Susannah and Neil, a little more crossly than I had intended. "As far as I can see they're nothing but hard work, tension and turmoil."

"You haven't seen the fun parts," Neil told me earnestly.

"Which are?" Aunt Mary asked.

"Showing is fun. And the foals. They're fun."

"Tons." Carl didn't bother removing the irony from his voice. "First you have the agony of trying to get the mare in foal, then you wait eleven months for the great event. When it's time, you spend night after night in the barn waiting for the old girl to do her thing, only to find that she spit it out while you were in the house having a cup of coffee. Horses are perverse animals."

"If it's such an agony, why does Irma keep doing it?" Dan popped two more beer cans and handed one to Carl.

"It's an addiction." Carl's voice was serious as he accepted his beer. "She loves her dogs and cats, but she's addicted to horses."

"Addiction seems to be a key word around here." Pat refilled our wine glasses. She tipped the bottle up, examined the few drops left and poured them into Aunt Mary's glass.

"What do you mean?" Carl poked the coals with the hand not holding the beer. He didn't sound as if he was paying a lot of attention.

"I was thinking about Bryce, about what Susannah said yesterday. And about that poor boy, Rusty."

"I'm not sure Rusty was worth wasting sympathy on."

Dan surprised me. I'd heard police work can harden you, but so far, I hadn't seen any signs of it in him.

"Everyone is worth sympathy." Aunt Mary sounded a little surprised as well. "I never met the boy, or this Bryce, either, but they both sound like sad, lost souls to me."

"Maybe so," Dan grudgingly admitted, "but dangerous ones. The Rustys of this world can do a lot of damage. That kid peddled dope to his friends when he was in grade school." His eyes took on a steely look as he talked. "I wonder how many got hooked because they were curious, or thought it would be fun to try." He paused, as if to make sure his thought came out right. "It doesn't excuse murder. We're going to catch whoever did it, but I'm not going to grieve that Rusty's gone."

"The Bryces aren't too safe, either." Pat nodded at Dan as if in agreement and settled herself in a chair next to Carl. "He impressed me as a selfish, arrogant young man, a user. Maybe he won't hurt people the same way Rusty did, by selling them drugs or robbing them, but he'll leave a lot of misery behind."

Neil looked down at the beer in his hand before contributing to the conversation. "Yeah, he's sure not doing Stephanie any favors. Every time I go over to Irma's, there she is, hanging on him. I can't figure what he wants her for, but whatever it is, when he's done, he'll dump her."

"Stephanie." Aunt Mary's eyes opened wide and her mouth pursed a little. "Would that be Stephanie Knudsen?"

"How did you know?" Susannah seemed genuinely surprised.

Pat and I glanced at each other, but we shouldn't have. It was hard to keep a straight face. Of course she knew.

"Money's what he sees in her." Aunt Mary frowned, almost scowled. "The Knudsens have a lot and Fiona spends it. Especially on Stephanie. I think she's compensating." She took a piece of French bread, put a little cheese on top and bit down hard.

"Compensating for what?"

"Her guilt feelings. Stephanie's not exactly the prettiest child and she's always been a little, well, hefty."

"Robust," murmured Pat.

"Yes." Aunt Mary almost smiled. "Very tactfully put. Anyway, Heidi, Stephanie's younger sister, is all the things Fiona expected in a daughter. Tiny, pretty, sweet. And smart. So Fiona never disciplined Stephanie, never made her control her wicked temper, never said no to anything. Don't feel sorry for this Bryce. He may be a user, but he sounds weak. Stephanie's single-minded, selfish and strong. If Bryce doesn't do what Stephanie wants, well, he'll be the one to feel sorry for."

"Say good-bye to Bryce's drug habit," Pat laughed. "If he has one. It sounds like Susannah heard right, Stephanie's set to take away his toys."

"This is all very interesting." I finished the last of the wine in my glass and reached for the last shrimp as well. "Dan, you still haven't told us who you think killed Rusty. You must have some idea by now." I wasn't happy with this conversation and wanted reassurance that Rusty's death had nothing to do with anyone connected to Irma's barn.

Dan twirled his can around, tilted it to check how much was left, took a deep swallow and sighed with exaggerated satisfaction. We all waited, saying nothing. Finally, he couldn't stand it. "You know I can't talk about an ongoing investigation."

"For God's sake, Dan, we're involved. Sort of."

He raised one eyebrow at me.

"We aren't asking for state secrets, but you can at least tell us if you have a suspect outside of, ah…"

"Irma's people?" Dan's smile was a lot too knowing.

"Of course it's not any of us." Susannah was empathic. Clearly, there was no doubt in her mind. I wished there wasn't in mine.

"The only one who could possibly be a suspect is Bryce, the little creep, and he was in the show ring."

"Or sweet Stephanie," murmured Pat.

"Where was Stephanie?" I wheeled around to look at her. "I don't remember seeing her until we got back to the barn."

"No one seems to know." Dan injected that mildly.

"How do you know that?" I turned back to stare at him. "Do you know where everyone was?"

"Well, I know you and Pat were in the stands."

Pat gasped a little. After a quick intake of breath I had to laugh. "Nice to know we aren't suspects. Who else?"

"Susannah and Irma were with you and Bryce was in the ring. That leaves only one other person unaccounted for."

"You've got to be kidding," Susannah exclaimed at the same time Neil protested, "No way."

"Hey." Dan threw up his hands. "You asked if I knew where everyone was and I'm telling you. I don't. That's all. But it would be nice to know. It's always so much tidier when you can eliminate people."

"Who are they talking about?" Aunt Mary looked from one of us to the next. Clearly, she didn't like not knowing.

"Chovalo." Susannah's voice and face were grim. "How the thought could even cross your mind is beyond me." This last was crisply addressed to Dan.

"Besides," Neil thoughtfully contributed, "it's Bryce Chovalo hates. He didn't even know this Rusty. Did he?"

"No one knew him."

"Someone did," Carl put in quietly.

"Exactly." Susannah issued her statement with satisfaction. "Only, none of us did."

"Finding out where Chovalo was shouldn't be hard." I had a hard time taking Chovalo seriously as a murderer. "I'm a little more interested in Stephanie. The first time I saw her was back at the barn."

"You couldn't miss her." Pat's mouth pursed in distaste. "She hung on Bryce like her life depended on it."

"You're right." Susannah was almost gleeful. "We never saw her in the stands. I didn't spot her on the rail, either."

"You heard Aunt Mary. She has a wicked temper. You might want to ask her a few questions." I turned back toward Dan. He wasn't pleased.

"We already have. We've talked to Wes, to the grooms in the barn across the aisle, to the guy selling hot dogs and to the man who runs around in the golf cart with a chart in his hands."

"I'll bet you haven't talked to the pirate." My glass of wine was making me reckless.

"You're wrong. We did."

Now that was interesting, but before I had a chance to pursue it Susannah got in a question.

"Why Wes? He got there after everything was over."

"So it seems. But you never know who saw what, when" was Dan's vague answer.

"Wes was there?" Neil's normally amused tone turned sharp. "Did he…?"

"No."

"If he says one word to you or puts one hand on you, I'll kill him."

I was struck dumb by Neil's thundercloud face. I looked over at Pat. She seemed equally taken aback. Not so Susannah.

"Wes is harmless. He's the type who thinks he's doing you a favor by looking. He's never even offered to touch." She paused for a second, flicked a lock of hair over her shoulder with a toss of her head before going on. "Besides, I can take of myself."

"I think we've had enough of this for one evening. Let's talk about something more interesting. Like sheepdogs." Carl picked up his empty beer can, collected Dan's and Neil's and headed for the trash. "Or starting the barbecue."

We got up and started to clear away the debris left on the platters. Susannah disappeared into the kitchen and came back with plates and my basket of silverware, Pat brought out a tray loaded with the hamburger toppings. Barbecue smoke started to lazily fill the backyard.

But we weren't quite finished with murder.

Aunt Mary put down her bowl of potato salad and picked up the subject again.

"Dan, are you sure Irma's all right? Except for Susannah, it seems to me not very nice people surround her. I'm deeply disappointed in Chovalo. Stephanie Knudsen I know and she is, well, I've already said all I'm going to. This Bryce sounds as bad and I've heard rumors about Wes Fowler."

She unfolded my picnic cloth with a sharp crack before laying it on the table. "I feel sorry for his poor wife. Susannah needs to stay way away from him."

"Don't worry about Wes." Neil's voice once more was grim. "I've already strongly suggested he keep away from Susannah."

"You did?"

There was an odd expression on Susannah's face, as if she wasn't too sure she liked, or needed, a white knight.

"What's all this about pirates?" Aunt Mary went on. "How do pirates fit?"

Pat laughed. "Ellen ran into one. Literally. She said his parrots were rude."

"Parrots?" Carl's professional interest perked up. "What parrots?"

"He was by the horse barns yesterday morning and he had no business there."

"I didn't see a pirate," mused Susannah. "He sounds like he'd be hard to miss."

"He was there. Dan knows him, only he won't admit it."

Dan laughed. "That pirate is a professional entertainer who's paid by the fair to wander around and, well, entertain. He's likely to show up anywhere. I can assure you neither he nor his parrots ran the pitchfork through your friend Rusty."

"He was no friend of mine." I shuddered.

"Rusty wasn't anyone's friend. Whoever murdered him was someone none of us ever heard of." Susannah shook her head emphatically, making her curls bounce. "I'm sick of the subject. Let's eat."

By mutual consent the conversation changed direction as we finished getting dinner on the table. Murder, drugs and pirates were not mentioned again, but the pirate sat in the back of my mind, refusing to go away.

It was close to ten o'clock when Aunt Mary yawned and stated she was heading for home. She started to gather her empty bowls and platters, packing them in a carton box.

"Where's your car, Mary?" Dan asked. "I don't remember seeing it."

"That's because it's home in my garage where it belongs. You don't think I'd get that thing out for only four blocks, do you?"

"You carried all this stuff over here?" Neil looked at her, shocked.

He was rewarded with a pitying look.

"Well, you aren't carrying it back," Dan stated. "Come on. I'll drive you."

Pat and Carl gathered their things up as well and even Neil, who had driven over with his parents, got up to leave. He didn't look too anxious to go, but Susannah looked as tired as I felt and tactfully shooed him toward the door.

"See you tomorrow, Ellie." It wasn't a question Dan asked as he balanced Aunt Mary's box, and the kiss he leaned down to deliver was more than a peck. Susannah raised one eyebrow on her way upstairs, leaving me to turn off porch lights and lock doors before following her. Jake hadn't waited for me, either. He was already a yellow ball of fur curled up tight on my pillow. I shoved him over when I was ready to crawl in, reached for my book, decided I was too tired and switched off the light. Only sleep didn't come. I realized I hadn't quizzed Susannah about Neil and wondered if I should do it now. Probably not a good idea. Tomorrow, I would make time, just the two of us. I envisioned a nice mother/daughter talk; one where I did the talking and she did the listening. It might even happen.

My thoughts turned to Dan and our relationship. I knew, deep down, that Dan's protective feelings, in my opinion his overprotective feelings, weren't misplaced male superiority. He truly cared, about me and about Susannah. Only, I wasn't sure that was what I wanted. No, that wasn't right. I wasn't sure I was ready for the commitment that kind of caring brought with it. For the first time I felt my life was my own. I called the shots, a feeling I was beginning to like. A lot. How I fit Dan, commitment and independence together, or even if I wanted to try, I wasn't sure.

Now, of course, I was wide-awake. Irma, Susannah, murder, pirates, Dan. They refused to go away. The pirate. There was something about him—more, lots more, than Dan was admitting. He was connected to all this, but how? And, how did I find out? It was obvious Dan wasn't going to tell me, so who would?

Thoroughly irritated, I sat up in bed, snapped on the light and grabbed my book. It was equally obvious I wasn't going to make any headway solving these problems tonight, so I might as well see if I could figure out how the heroine in my latest thriller solved hers. Maybe she'd give me some ideas about what to do next.

ELEVEN

THE RED LIGHT on my desk phone flashed. I looked at it in alarm. I'd made an appointment with an about-to-be-transferred young couple to list their house. Surely this wasn't them calling back, changing their mind.

It was Dan.

"You sound surprised to hear from me. Are you?"

"Of course not." I was, not to hear from him but because a hectic Monday morning had raced by so fast.

"It's lunch time. We are meeting for lunch? The Yum Yum?"

"Sure." I pushed papers back into a file. "Ten minutes, all right?"

"No more than. I'm starved." The line went dead.

I smiled a little ruefully and started to shuffle more papers into priority piles. Of course we were having lunch. We had been to lunch almost every day in the week since the murder. The police station was only three blocks from my office and the Yum Yum was right in the middle, making it easy for both of us. Dinner was harder, but Dan had shown up at my house three evenings and had taken me out Saturday night. Sunday, we had packed a picnic and gone to the beach.

I loved being with Dan. I missed sleeping with him, waking up with him beside me, sharing coffee and the morning news. I was pretty sure where our relationship had been headed until I'd stalled it at "friendship." I had an uneasy feeling that it wasn't going to stay stalled forever and pretty soon I was going to have to make up my mind what I wanted and how I wanted it. Not, however, this afternoon.

A few months earlier I would have had all the time in the world for lunch, but as I learned my new business, I found my days filling up. I'd closed a few sales and had more than a few listings. My knowledge level rose with every transaction I closed and every listing I won, as did my confidence. I was actually having fun.

Brian and I had married the summer before my senior year of college. Susannah and graduation had arrived together. As wife of an up-and-coming obstetrician, my "job" was hostess, charity bazaar volunteer, country club member and, of course, mother. Never anything that paid a salary. Brian made more than enough money, a fact he told me often. As long as I spent it in ways that reflected his idea of our social position, he was generous. Gradually the idea of "wife" as "partner" faded. "Wife" as "job" took its place. It became more and more clear that the job didn't carry a lifetime guarantee. One day Brian's lawyer informed me my husband wanted a divorce so that he could marry again. I had known about his affairs but had tried to ignore them, telling myself all kinds of lies. Down deep, I knew I was putting off the inevitable. The only part that came as a shock was my strong feeling of relief, mixed, of course, with fury that this last time he had been cheating with a blond piece of fluff not too much older than Susannah.

My lawyer, a true barracuda, told me to be grateful. It opened up a whole range of settlement possibilities. I left it all to her, enrolled in real estate school, got my license and headed north. Coming "home" to Santa

Louisa had probably been my Linus blanket. If so, it was working.

I had been afraid that moving into my parents' home would make me feel like a child again, but my parents were happy in Scottsdale, my things had settled into the old house as though they had been made for it. I felt, for the first time, I had a home truly mine. My life was taking shape, and for once I was doing the shaping.

My lawyer made sure Susannah had a huge trust fund. I'd ended up with a block of stocks that provided me a very nice monthly check, but nothing compared to the feeling each real estate commission check gave me. Money I'd earned. Each check said I was a competent, intelligent woman, capable of directing my life as I saw fit, capable of sharing my life as I saw fit. I cherished that feeling more each day.

I told Rosie, our secretary, to put all messages on my voice mail and headed across the street and through the park toward the Yum Yum, humming under my breath. The trees were full, the sky was blue, the air felt gentle on my cheeks. Life was good.

Dan was already seated and in deep conversation with Ruthie, the Yum Yum's head waitress and part owner. I waved to several people I knew and slid into the chair opposite him.

"We were talkin' about the kid that got killed at the fair," Ruthie told me. "Pretty gruesome way to die, but it's one punk less we have to pay to keep in jail. Want the special, Ellen?"

Ruthie's hand, which never seemed free of a coffee pot, hovered over the empty cup in front of me.

"Iced tea please, Ruthie. What's the special?"

She pointed proudly at a blackboard that sat on an

easel just inside the front door. I'd missed it entirely as I came in.

"New?"

"My idea. Pretty good, huh?"

"Great." I squinted at the cramped writing. "What's the chicken oriental salad?"

"It's new too. You'll love it. Dan's having the Swiss steak. Be right back with your tea." She topped off his cup and trotted off.

"I'll bet it comes with mashed potatoes, gravy, rolls which you plan to lather with butter and more blue cheese dressing than salad."

"As a matter of fact, yes." Dan grinned at me as he poured cream in his coffee. "You look pretty today. That's a good color on you."

I refused to be distracted. "Dan Dunham, don't you ever think about your arteries?"

"Sure. Every night when I have a beer. Scientific research has discovered beer helps keep everything flowing right along."

"I thought that was red wine."

"That too."

I gave up on the subject of food, with or without drink. I wasn't going to win anyway. I tried murder.

"Have you come up with anything new?"

"New?"

"Yes, new. About Rusty. Remember? Murder? Fairgrounds?"

"I remember all right. I was hoping you wouldn't. At least until lunch was over."

"Too bad. Well?"

"Did anyone ever tell you about curiosity and the cat?"

"Yes. This isn't curiosity. I found him. My daughter

works with people who might be connected to Rusty somehow. I want to know if I should be worried. Go on."

"Murder is always something to worry about."

"You sound like a pompous police chief. Well?"

"All right." He smiled at me. A nice smile. "Evidently this Rusty had quite a reputation among the local horse people." Dan's voice became thoughtful and the smile in his eyes faded. "Everyone either knew him or knew of him, and none of them would hire him."

"Why? He must have known something about horses."

"Evidently. Everyone agrees he was good with them but completely unreliable. It seems he'd be fine for a few days and then he'd just disappear. They'd find the horses, no feed or water, stalls filthy, that kind of thing. I think some of these people would have forgiven him his drug habit, even his part-time dealing and pilfering, if he'd never neglected the horses."

"Why did Bryce hire him?"

"Excellent question. One I asked our friend Bryce."

"And?"

"He says he didn't know a thing about Rusty's reputation. He had to have someone for this show, Rusty seemed to know what he was doing, so he hired him."

"Only you don't believe him."

"Every other horse person we talked to knew Rusty, or knew about him. Besides, Chovalo's nephew's been dead over a month. Seems enough time to have found someone. But having met Bryce, maybe not."

Gooseflesh started up my arms, and I didn't think it had anything to do with the air-conditioning. "You think there's some connection between Bryce and Rusty. Some drug kind of connection. Don't you?"

This was one time I wanted Dan to scoff and tell me

I had too much imagination. Instead he paused, took a sip of coffee and kept looking serious.

"I don't know what to believe quite yet. You know, Ellie, we, ah, my department, we sort of knew about Rusty."

The gooseflesh spread. "You already told us. About his record and everything." I watched Dan's face carefully. He was leading up to something, something he wasn't too happy about. I had a feeling it wasn't going to make me happy, either.

"Right. His record. Actually, it's because of his record we knew about him. A while back the Sheriff's Department asked us for a little help. We're all stretched pretty thin in this county, you know, and…"

"I know, I know. You tell me all the time. Exactly what kind of help and what does it have to do with Rusty?" I wanted to add, or Bryce? but couldn't get the words out.

"The Sheriff's drug task force is pretty sure Rusty was mixed up with the noble citizens responsible for manufacturing and moving methamphetamine. We've been helping them keep an eye on him, hoping we could get a line on how and when the shipments are being made. Rusty wasn't too bright. We were sure he'd slip up some way and we could spot his contact. Unfortunately, we weren't watching him quite closely enough."

Before I could say anything, Ruthie appeared. She slipped a beautiful plate full of salad in front of me and a brimming platter of cholesterol in front of Dan.

I stared at his mountain of food and shook my head. "It's going to take more power than one poor little beer can muster to push all that through your veins."

"I may have to have a second one. Just to make sure."

The teasing look was back in his eyes, and a satisfied smile on his face.

"Dan works hard. He needs to eat." This from toothpick thin Ruthie, who was on her feet over twelve hours a day, who trotted God alone knew how many miles, lugging loaded trays, not to mention the coffee pot. Ruthie, who was a vegetarian. She patted him lightly on the back, gave me a conspiratorial grin and trotted off.

I watched Dan's plate empty while I picked at my salad, thought for a moment and said, "You didn't answer me about Bryce. Do you think he has some connection with this drug thing? Is that why he hired Rusty?"

The thought of flamboyant, flighty Bryce in league with real criminals didn't seem possible.

"It does seem a stretch." Dan mopped up the last of the gravy with a roll. "No, I think it's more likely Rusty was his source."

"Source! Then you do think Bryce uses drugs."

"I don't think there's much doubt" was the not terribly reassuring reply.

"But you don't think Bryce killed him."

"No. I don't."

"Then it had to be Rusty's suppliers or whatever they're called." An anonymous person who had no reason to come near anyone I knew, that was what I wanted.

"Maybe. Maybe not. I'm afraid it's a little closer to home."

"I don't think Stephanie would kill Rusty just because he was selling Bryce drugs. Would she?" I thought about it. I could actually picture the scene. Rusty jeering at her, Stephanie losing her temper, picking up the pitchfork, threatening, Rusty daring her, Stephanie thrusting, then…wham. I almost gagged.

Dan watched me. "We can't rule it out. We can't rule anything out, but that's not what I think happened."

"You're not thinking what I think you're thinking?" There was only one scenario left and it was not a welcome one.

Dan looked blank, so I tried again.

"You can't be talking about Chovalo?"

"You know I am."

"I don't believe it."

"You're letting Susannah's opinion color your judgment."

"I am not. There's not one thing that points to Chovalo. Why, he's been with Irma for years, practically runs the ranch. She says she can't get along without him, and he's obviously devoted to her. Hardly the picture of a murderer."

"There are a few other things."

"Like?"

Dan speared the last piece of meat into his mouth before answering, evidently giving himself time to decide just how much he wanted to tell me.

"Rusty talked to one of the grooms across the barn aisle about the time everyone left to go watch Irma's horse. Everyone but Chovalo. Rusty was killed between the time the groom left and all of you returned. No one else we can find saw anyone near Irma's stalls."

"Not even the pirate?"

"Not even the pirate."

"I can't imagine Chovalo not watching that class." I put down my fork and thought about it. "It meant so much to all of them for Last Challenge to win."

"He was there, on the rail. But he arrived just as the

class was ending. The person who told us was surprised, couldn't believe Chovalo would miss most of the class. Says all he talked about was how wonderful that colt was. So—makes us think."

It made me think too, but I wasn't convinced. Not yet. "You'll have to do a lot better than that, Dan Dunham. People don't go around sticking pitchforks into other people without some reason. Chovalo didn't even know Rusty."

"Don't be so sure. Listen, there are a couple of reasons we're looking at Chovalo Gutierrez." He held up his hand and pushed down the first finger. "First. He was in the right place at the right time. Second, and more important, Mr. Gutierrez has recently won a place on our select list of people to watch."

"What are you talking about?" I pushed my salad plate away and found myself sitting a little straighter in my chair.

"Chovalo has been keeping company with the bunch we suspect are manufacturing the methamphetamine, the same ones Rusty was working for, the group we've been trying to get enough evidence on to make an arrest."

"You've been spying on him! That's not fair."

"It's not spying. It's watching. Besides, it's the guys making the stuff we've been watching, but we can't find out where, and we don't know how they're moving it. All of a sudden, Chovalo turned up. We don't know what his connection is with them, but we're pretty sure they're not getting together to watch Monday night football. You know," Dan's tone got a little softer, "I'm sure Bud had a long-term financial arrangement with Chovalo and while he was alive, they were doing real well. Now Chovalo may be wondering, actually he's been talking, about his own future. If Irma sells the hauling business, there may be no place for him on the ranch. She's already leased out one barn to Bryce. Her breeding business is small. Then what does he do?"

"Irma would never let anything happen to Chovalo. There has to be some other explanation." I tried to think of one.

"Maybe. But all this started about the same time his nephew died. The kid died from an overdose. He got the stuff somewhere but as far as we could tell, he wasn't a user."

"You can't possibly think Chovalo had anything to do with his nephew's death?"

"Not directly, I don't. But it's possible Rusty might have. Don't forget, Miguel worked for Bryce. We're pretty sure Bryce has a habit and has to supply it from somewhere, which brings us back to Rusty. And Chovalo. Chovalo has to know about Bryce's habit. We think he knew Rusty, knew he was a two-bit peddler and knew Bryce was buying from him. So why didn't he say something?"

"I don't understand. Why would Chovalo…?"

"Revenge. If he thought Rusty got Miguel started and gave him an overdose…"

"Oh, I don't think so." I shook my head emphatically. "If Chovalo thought that, he'd have gone straight to the police."

"Would you go to the police if you were involved in drug peddling?"

"You don't know he's involved," I said stubbornly.

"Oh, he's involved somehow." Dan paused to take a sip of coffee but he never took his eyes off me. "Remember the fair? He was up to something. People don't creep around places with a flashlight unless they don't want to be seen creeping."

I didn't have an answer to that one, but suddenly something clicked. "It was the pirate."

"What?" Dan looked totally confused. "The pirate what?"

"The pirate was around the barn when Rusty was killed. Or just after. Remember? I ran into him. And, Dan, think what a good disguise that costume would be for someone doing something illegal."

Dan's mouth opened and closed a couple of times before he finally spoke. "Ellie, I've told you. The pirate's a fair entertainer. We've checked. Forget him, will you? He's not our problem."

He sounded exasperated. Why, I wondered. Another question occurred. Why was Dan, the closed mouth cop, telling me all this?

"OK. What's all this about? Usually dragging information out is harder than dragging a Scottie out of a rabbit hole, so why all this volunteering?"

I watched several emotions pass over his face. He had a reason all right, and he didn't think I was going to like it. He paused before answering, looked down at his empty plate, took a deep breath, looked directly at me and spoke in a stern tone. "I want you to keep away from these people. Something is happening out there at Irma's ranch, something already has. I don't want you involved."

I carefully set down my iced tea. "Involved? It's a little late, isn't it? Did you forget Irma's a client of mine? I like her. She's involved. Evidently a lot more than she realizes. Then there's another tiny detail. I have a daughter working for 'those people.' She's involved, and if she's involved, so am I. What are you suggesting? That I walk away and ignore this?"

I was heating up pretty good and didn't mind at all that Dan was getting red in the face.

"Of course not. Keep your voice down. Everyone in this place is going to have a crick in their neck trying to hear what you're saying."

"Let them. I can't believe you think I would turn my back on friends. Or is it some kind of police order?" My voice was lower, but dripping with sarcasm. I hoped.

"Ellie, for God's sake. Look, I talked to Carl and he can use Susannah for the rest of the summer at his clinic. She can start tomorrow. I want her to quit working for Bryce and take Carl's job, and I want you both to stay the hell away from Irma's place."

"So, you and Carl have it all worked out. Is that what you were talking about last week in my backyard? Figuring out how to protect the little women, who we all know can't possibly manage on their own?" I was furious. I was actually beyond fury. How could Dan, my friend, be such a jerk? What happened to discussion, to respect for my judgment, to faith in my ability to take care of my child or myself? Or hadn't that ever been there?

"Did either of you talk this over with Pat?" I managed to get out.

"No, but Neil..." Dan's face got quite red, and there was a hint of embarrassment in his voice. But no apology.

"Neil!" I exploded. "Well, of course, you'd want his opinion."

"Ellie, will you please get off your liberated high horse and listen? I'm speaking as a policeman as well as a friend."

That was the one that blew the cork out of the bottle. "Liberated? From what? Evidently not from men who think I'm incapable of thought. Policeman, right. What are you going to do next, read me my rights?"

"You seem to have a good grasp on them." It sounded as if he said that through clenched teeth. "Ellie, will you please listen?"

"Of course." I pushed back my chair and reached for my purse. "Just as soon as you're willing to sit down with Susannah and me and discuss this. Not tell us what to do, but discuss. As though we were capable adults, able to reach conclusions and arrive at decisions. When that time comes, call me."

"Ellie." Dan tried again, pushed his chair back too fast, got his foot caught in it, tripped, caught himself by grabbing the table edge, then tipped over his coffee cup. "God damn it." He watched the light brown liquid soak into the check.

"Thanks for lunch," I told him, then stalked out the door.

Unfortunately, righteous indignation only lasted until I got to the office. Then the implications of Dan's suspicions started to sink in. I wasn't in the least concerned for myself. After all, I was on the outermost fringes of whatever it was that was happening, but Susannah. That was different. I had to think of how I was going to protect her. The only solution I could come up with was Dan's.

TWELVE

"I THOUGHT THIS Dan of yours was supposed to be smart."

Susannah scowled at me over the top of a glass of orange juice. Strands of damp hair had escaped the discipline of her headband, drying in tendrils around her face, giving her a Medusa look.

"He is, and he's not mine."

I'd come home from work early, fortified myself with a glass of white wine and tried to get us seated in the two wicker rockers on the front porch where we could explore the subject of Susannah's job change together. And, of course, arrive at the mutual decision that she'd quit and go to work for Carl. Instead, we were standing in the kitchen, facing each other like a couple of cats about to do battle.

"He's yours if you want him." Susannah gestured with the glass. The orange juice swayed dangerously. "No one with any smarts at all would suspect Chovalo of doing anything illegal, certainly nothing that would hurt Irma or the ranch. And definitely nothing that would have hurt his nephew. He loved his nephew. Irma says Miguel was like the son Chovalo and his wife never had. To think Chovalo could…that's…it's stupid!"

Her eyes blazed at me and more hair escaped as she slammed down her juice glass. "Another thing. Where do these men get off running our lives? Who elected them God? Who elected them anything?" She picked up her glass, scowled at the remaining orange juice and slammed it back down. She gave me a withering look when I winced, but the glass didn't break.

"We've done OK making our own decisions." She mercifully left the glass on the table. "I sure as shit don't plan on stopping now. If you want Dan to tell you what to do, fine, but he's not telling me and neither is Neil. I am not going to quit my job."

I got the message. I also understood her fury, but my worry overrode my natural sympathy. So I counterattacked.

"We don't use words like that in this house. Is that the kind of language you learn hanging around barns?"

She suddenly grinned, catching me off guard. "Well, there's plenty of it around there, as well as a few other places I could name. And I am not quitting."

"Give me one good reason why not," I said in my sternest mother voice and knew instantly I had made a tactical mistake.

"I'll give you three. Irma needs me to keep Bryce organized through the rest of the summer shows and I won't let her down. Second, Bryce is spoiled and weak and much too busy destroying himself to be a threat to anyone else. Third, Chovalo didn't kill that awful Rusty and he's not selling drugs. So why should I quit?"

"God damn it, Susannah."

"We don't use language like that in this house," she said sweetly.

Only a knock on the screen door kept me from going after her with the meat mallet.

"Hi." Neil strolled into the kitchen. He smiled slowly as he took in Susannah standing there, the blue of her shirt showing off the blue of her eyes, the curve of her body evident under the cling of her white jeans, the rich darkness of her hair as it fell over her shoulders. That smile wasn't destined to last long. Good, I thought with sour pleasure.

"Will you look who's here." She pulled off her head-band, setting the curls free.

"You knew I was coming." Neil looked mystified. "We arranged it. We're going back to the fair, to watch the rodeo." This last was addressed to me.

"Of course I knew you were coming. But I didn't know we'd have so much to talk about." Sugar dripped from Susannah's voice. Dangerous stuff, sugar.

"Uh, talk about?" Neil's expression changed, taking on a wary look. "What do we have to talk about?"

"Oh, jobs and things."

"I told those two guys. So did my Mom." Neil sighed.

"What did you tell them?" Susannah asked guard-edly.

"That you'd never leave Irma if you thought she needed you and that you'd especially never leave if you got ordered. But, honey, they do have a point."

Honey?

Susannah's expression, which had started to soften, immediately hardened again. I felt a twinge of sympathy for Neil. He was in for one wild night, but I didn't care. He'd asked for what he was about to get. After all, he was one of the enemy, wasn't he? Only I found myself hoping he'd win. I wanted her to quit too. So whose side did that put me on? And why were we even having sides?

"Shall we go?" Susannah picked up her straw bag, settled her sunglasses firmly on her nose and headed for the back door.

"Might as well." Neil followed her out forlornly. The

sound of their voices was drowned out by the clatter of his pickup's tired engine.

He had more sense than his father or the wonderful Dan Dunham. I'd give him that. I refilled my glass and headed for the front porch by myself. Of course, he had a sensible mother. Maybe they'd talk it through. Maybe he wouldn't lose his temper when Susannah dug in her heels, and maybe he'd convince her to go to work for his father. Yeah and maybe the moon was made of cream cheese.

Before I could set the rocker going, Jake jumped up and planted himself on my lap. Absently I stroked his ears while I sipped, rocked and thought. The cat purred.

At least he expects her to have opinions. He seems to think she is capable of making a rational decision. Unlike some people I know.

"Your friend," I told the cat, accusingly. "He thinks he's the only person in the whole world with ideas that count."

The cat slept on.

"You wouldn't believe how he treated me this afternoon. Ordering me around, telling me how to take care of my daughter, trying to run my life."

I rocked a little harder, then stopped as another thought appeared, one I wasn't willing to give voice to.

Isn't that the way I approached Susannah? Telling her what to do, not giving her credit for being able to assess the situation? Not respecting her ideas, her priorities?

"Of course not," I said out loud. Evidently, quite loud. Jake opened one eye. I took a quick sip as I thought this over. "I'm her mother, she's my daughter. I love her and part of my job is to protect her."

Sure, came the unwelcome voice again, but love doesn't mean dictatorship. She's old enough and certainly bright enough to discuss something this serious in a sane way. You didn't give her a chance, and she has a right to be mad. You did to her what Dan did to you.

"That is ridiculous." I got up, unceremoniously dumping Jake on the porch. He gave me a reproachful look and jumped into the other rocker, turned around on the cushion and lay down with his back to me.

"So be that way. I'm going for a walk."

Jake, to no one's surprise, ignored me. Also to no one's surprise, my walk ended at Aunt Mary's back door.

THIRTEEN

SHE WAS MAKING strawberry jam. There was a large pot simmering slowly on the stove, giving off subtle aromas that were heavy with memories. Lines of clear, clean jars waited on the old oak table and the sink was filled with bright red berries complete with little green stems.

"Well." Aunt Mary looked up as I let the screen slam. "You're a sight for sore eyes. And feet. If ever I needed a little help, it's now."

She took in my white polo shirt and gestured at the apron hanging on the peg under the O'Dell's Funeral Home calendar. I sighed inwardly and pulled it on over my head.

I'd spent many summer hours of my childhood helping my mother or one of my aunts pit apricots, peel tomatoes, snap green beans or stem strawberries. "Why don't the boys have to?" my cousins, my sister and I would wail.

"They hoe the garden and mow the lawn. They rake the leaves and help chop firewood. You'll be glad this winter when you don't have to" was always the answer. Secretly, I thought chopping wood sounded like fun, but I didn't get to find out. After I married Brian, I never canned another jar or made another pint of jam. But here I was, back removing little green stems from strawberries.

"Why do you do this?" I watched as she poured another batch of berries into the sink. "Who's going to eat all this?"

"Fair question. Sometimes I think the only reason I do it is because I always have. But it'll all get eaten. Those pretty jars," she pointed to a row of pint jars with fruit embossed on the side, "I'll top with little rounds of gingham and tie it off with ribbon. They'll sell at the Christmas Bazaar we hold just before Thanksgiving. Young women buy them to give away. Probably let everybody think they made it too. Well, it's their conscience."

I gave a start and quickly looked over my shoulder. I was one of those women and wondered if she suspected.

"Hear you and Dan had a little spat today." She carefully filled the front line.

"It wasn't exactly a spat. More a disagreement in principle."

"What principle?"

"The principle that says I have the right to run my own life."

"Oh. That principle." She finished filling the jars and brought the pot over to the sink and started rinsing it out. She handed it to me along with a knife and a measuring cup.

"Don't lose count of how many cups you put in there or I'll never get the sugar right."

She took a pitcher of sun tea out of the refrigerator, got two glasses from the cupboard, filled them both, handed me one, then lowered herself into a chair beside the old table.

"My, that feels good. I'm getting too old to do this. Now, just how is Dan trying to run your life?"

Years rolled back. I was ten again, standing in this same spot, telling Aunt Mary how my life had come to an end because Catherine, my older sister, got to go to Girl Scout Camp and I wasn't allowed; at thirteen how I was never going back to school because I was the only girl who had nothing to put in a bra; at seventeen how my mean mother wouldn't let me wear a strapless dress to my senior prom. So many crises in my life had been explored and gotten through in this kitchen, and here I was again. Not that this was a crisis. I was grown, and this was just a discussion.

"Ten cups." I held my hands under the tap and dried them on the flour sack towel before joining Aunt Mary at the table. "Dan wants me to have nothing more to do with Irma, and wants Susannah to quit and go to work for Carl. He practically ordered me! He and Carl had it all arranged."

"What did you tell him?"

"I told him I was perfectly capable of making my own decisions, both for myself and my child."

She looked at me over the top of her glass and took a sip. "Then what did you do?"

The woman was uncanny. How did she know?

"I went home and told Susannah she had to quit."

"To go to work for Carl?"

"Yes."

"What did she say?"

I started to giggle. I couldn't stop and caught Aunt Mary grinning right along with me.

"You know perfectly well what she said."

"Guess I do at that. How many cups did you say?"

She pushed her chair heavily away from the table and started pouring sugar over the berries, squeezed lemon over the whole thing and set the pot over a slow flame before she returned to me and the subject of Dan.

"What's going on at Irma's that's got Dan so nervous? Oh, I know the boy getting killed was enough to scare anyone silly, but from what I hear he didn't have any real connection with Irma or Susannah or anyone else there. He was just temporary, wasn't he?"

I wondered how much I should tell her, how much of what Dan told me was in confidence, but a lifetime of habit was too strong.

"Dan thinks Chovalo's somehow involved with the people who're making methamphetamine. Not only that, he suspects him of having killed that awful Rusty."

For the first time I could remember, Aunt Mary looked shocked. I'd seen her surprised, sorrowful, angry, but never shocked.

"It's not possible." There was no doubt in her voice. "I've known Irma for years, not too well, but I've known her. Your Uncle Sam and her husband, Bud, belonged to Rotary. They were wonderful to me when Sam died, and I was on the church committee that did the food when Bud had his accident."

No surprise there, but what did it have to do with Chovalo?

"Do you know Chovalo?"

"No. He and his wife go to St. Boniface, the Catholic Church. But Irma and Bud have been singing not only his praises but his whole family's for years. Gutierrez, that's their name. Chovalo and Maria Rosa, I think that's right, never had children so they helped raise their nieces and nephews. They've spent a small fortune helping all those kids through school."

Sort of like another Aunt I knew, I thought, but said nothing as she continued.

"Bud used to tell Sam he'd never have been able to get his hauling business going if it wasn't for Chovalo. He could do anything, fix an engine, load a horse no one else could touch. Bud said he was one of the finest men he'd ever met and one of the most honest. He and Irma built a house on the back of their property for Chovalo and Maria Rosa. Seems to me I heard Bud and Chovalo had some kind of long-term financial arrangement too. Bud sure didn't want to lose him. Said so all the time."

She got thoughtful, eyed her glass, then mine. "More tea?"

"I'll get it."

"Good. While you're up, give that pot a stir, make sure it's not cooking too fast and skim the top."

You should never volunteer for anything.

"I wonder," Aunt Mary continued.

"You wonder what?" I carefully skimmed the jam and checked the syrup to see if it was clear yet, surprised I remembered what to do after all these years.

"Well, I wonder how Chovalo liked having Wes and Linda move in."

"What do you mean, move in?" I gingerly put my finger on the hot juice on the spoon. I blew on it before putting my finger in my mouth. Perfect. "I think this is ready."

"Let me see." I held out a spoonful of jam. "No, not quite."

I shrugged and put the spoon back down. It looked ready to me. "Go on. Why would Chovalo not want Wes and Linda around?"

"Irma and I were talking after church a couple of months after Bud died. She'd just hired this Wes and Linda Fowler. Said that it had been hard to do, but she thought they were going to work out just fine. Linda's a whiz on the computer and Irma doesn't know one thing about them. Wes knew a lot about those huge van things, and they both spoke Spanish. Which I guess is a real plus, lots of the, what do you call the people who take care of the horses…?"

"Grooms."

"Yes. Well, I guess lots of them speak Spanish. Some of the drivers do also. Anyway, Irma said the business had changed so much she didn't understand it anymore. She thought it was time to let younger people take over."

"Which would let Chovalo out?"

"She didn't say that, but it seems like it might have."

"Did you know Irma's thinking of selling the transport business?"

"Why would she want to do that?" She put her glass down abruptly and stared at me.

How about that? I finally had a fact Aunt Mary didn't have first.

"I don't know. I think it's making money and I doubt the horse breeding is. From what Irma says it's going to cost a fortune to show Last Challenge, the stallion she's so hot on. I'd think she'd want to keep the one part that's paying the bills."

Aunt Mary had been listening intently to what I was saying, but suddenly she started to sniff the air. "Oh, oh. Better check that jam." She heaved herself to her feet and headed for the stove where she ladled out a spoonful of jam and examined it. Turning off the flame, she moved the pot over to a cool burner before turning back to me. "Go on. Surely Irma wouldn't sell the hauling business and then put all the money into a horse. Would she? Who is it wants to buy?"

"Somebody she's known for a long time."

"Is this person going to buy the land also? If she sells, what happens to Wes and Linda?"

"I guess they'd go to work for the new owner. I don't know about the land. It's one of the things I'm supposed to talk to her about, but every time we get started, something happens. I don't know a thing about businesses."

I didn't know much about land, either, but it was easier to figure out.

"So what's Irma going to do?"

"I don't know. I think she should talk to Bo."

Bo Chutsky, my broker, had been in town for close to a million years. He knew every business, every ranch and every house around and had probably sold each of them at least once.

"That's a good idea. Not that you're not capable, Ellen. It's just that Bo has, well, been doing this kind of thing longer."

I laughed. We both knew I wasn't capable, at least not yet, but bless her for not saying so.

"Why don't you help me fill these jars?"

I got to my feet, took both empty tea glasses over to the sink and picked up the big ladle.

"There must be other suspects besides Chovalo." Aunt Mary abandoned Irma's business transactions and returned to the thing worrying both of us. Susannah's safety. She put empty jars in front of me as fast as I filled them.

"I suggested Dan take a better look at Stephanie Knudsen. She could easily have been at the barn during the crucial half hour and she's strong enough."

"Oh dear." Aunt Mary's hand shook a little, spilling some of the jam over the side of the jar she held. She absently wiped it off with her finger. "What a horrible thought. Poor Fiona. But you're right. Stephanie has the temperament to do something awful. Why do either Chovalo or Stephanie have to be mixed up in this? Maybe it was somebody we never heard of, somebody

Rusty was involved with who has nothing to do with Irma, Chovalo, Bryce or anybody."

"Like the pirate?"

"Why yes. Your pirate." She laughed ruefully. "Wouldn't that be convenient. But, Ellen, you can't pick on him because he's available. Why do you keep coming back to him?"

I stopped ladling for a minute. I had to think this out. "Maybe because he was so…there. And because he was supposed to be entertaining at the fair, not the horse show. Only, both times I saw him, it was around the horse barns, and the first time no one else was around. Doesn't that seem strange?"

"I don't know." She sighed. "I'm afraid we're looking for something, anything, that doesn't lead to Chovalo, Irma or Susannah."

"Maybe." I picked up the ladle, filled a couple more jars and put it back down. "You know, the more I think about that pirate, the more I think he's involved. I'll bet Dan thinks so too. He gets real nervous when I try and bring him up. I wonder how I can find out more about him."

She watched me ladle the last of the jam into a jar, lick the ladle like I used to when I was ten and start to wash out the pot.

"Becky Monahan."

"Who?" I turned away from the sink to stare at her. "Who's Becky Monahan?"

"Rebecca Silverman. Remember her? She was in your graduating class."

Of course I remembered her. She'd been class president, a cheerleader, homecoming queen and a straight-A student. Every mother's dream and every teenage wallflower's nightmare. "What about her?"

"Becky married Paul Monahan." She seemed to think that explained everything.

"I'd heard that." I leaned against the sink. "Amazing. Paul was always so shy and quiet, Becky so energetic. But why bring them up now?"

"Paul outgrew his shyness. He's our state senator." She paused to let me take in that unexpected piece of news and continued, "and Becky's on the fair board."

She looked at me triumphantly but I still didn't get it.

"Good for her, but…"

"For heaven's sake, Ellen. You want to know about the pirate, don't you? What better place to start than at the top? Call Becky and ask her to find out about him."

I felt my mouth gap open. She'd done it again. "Becky Silverman. Monahan. Well, well. I'll call her in the morning." I almost laughed. If Susannah wouldn't quit and Dan wouldn't supply me with information to help me protect her, I'd do it myself. With Aunt Mary's help, of course.

"So, what're you going to do about Dan?" She broke into my burgeoning plan of investigation and neatly brought the conversation full circle.

"Guess I'll let him apologize and then we'll see."

"Are you going to apologize to Susannah?"

"Ah." I hid my face while I mopped up the jam I'd spilled on the sink. "Why would I want to do that?"

"You probably don't." She paused, evidently waiting for me to say something.

I have never been very fond of logic when it ends up making me look at something I would just as soon avoid. This was no exception. I could feel the corners of my mouth tighten down.

"People do not always act smart when they get scared, and being scared for someone else is the worst."

Aunt Mary knew I wasn't looking at her but that I was listening. The same as I did when I was fifteen. Her voice was soft, firm and irritatingly logical. "Dan's already lost one family. Things like that you never get over. Tends to make you overreact. I know what you went through with Brian, and I understand how you feel now. Independence is a wonderful thing, but so is loving someone and having him love you. Remember, we pay a price for everything. Trick is to make sure you're getting what you paid for."

"Are you saying I shouldn't be mad at Dan?" I was all set to defend my position.

"I've said all I'm going to say. You're a grown woman. It's up to you."

Neither Dan nor Susannah were mentioned again. I walked home richer by two jars of strawberry jam and with some thoughts that weren't nearly as sweet.

FOURTEEN

DAMN. I WENT INTO the kitchen, letting the screen door slam behind me. The man was impossible. He walks back into my life, acting all easy and funny, making me like him, making me feel… Damn and double damn. Things had been just great for a while. We went to lunch—a lot. He came to dinner a couple of nights a week and stayed. No pressure, no commitment and no trying to boss me around. But could he be happy with that? Oh no. He had to leave his shaving kit in my bathroom, he had to start talking about "plans," he had to get all protective. He had to scare the shit out of me. Oops. Where did that come from? Did the thought of having Dan around on a permanent basis, having anyone around on a permanent basis, really scare me? Oh, course not. Yes, it did. To hell with it. I was going to think about something else.

The house seemed quiet, way too quiet. I found myself wandering around the kitchen, putting away the jam, looking into a cupboard, drumming my fingers on the drain board. I needed something to distract me. It was too dark to garden. There was nothing on TV but re-runs of things I hadn't wanted to watch the first time. I hadn't had dinner but I had no interest in any more kitchen projects. Finally, I made a peanut butter and strawberry jam sandwich, poured a glass of milk and headed for the front porch.

I had no more plopped down in my rocking chair

than Jake jumped into my lap. He rubbed against me, purring loudly, then took a mouthful of my sandwich.

"Thief." He rolled the peanut butter around in his mouth, then dug it out with his paw and dropped it on the porch. He sniffed once more at the sandwich, shook himself and, after turning around several times with his claws out, settled down in my lap.

"Thanks for nothing." I ate the half Jake had rejected and sipped my milk. Now what? I wasn't about to let Police Chief Dunham into my thoughts. That just made me mad. I'd think about Susannah instead. Susannah, who might be somehow mixed up in a murder. That thought made me shudder. She obviously wasn't going to quit going to the barn. I had no idea if she was in any kind of real danger, what it might be and what I should do about it. I couldn't, I wouldn't, ask the great Police Chief for help. He'd already offered, no, told me, his solution. I was going to have to figure this out on my own. Which, of course, I was quite capable of doing.

I put my glass down on the porch, sat up straighter and started rocking. Rather fast. Jake woke up, growled something under his breath, set his claws into my legs to balance himself and jumped down. "Yikes." He ignored me, jumped into the other rocker and resumed his nap.

Sure would be nice being a cat, I thought. Nothing to worry about, just eat and sleep. But I wasn't a cat and I had plenty to worry about. For openers, how did I protect my daughter? The only way I could think of was to find out who had stuck the pitchfork through Rusty. Now, how was I going to do that?

I'd start by finding out about the pirate. I rocked some more. If he was involved somehow in transporting drugs, then he could have killed Rusty. He was there at the right time. But why would he? I didn't know, but Becky, bless her little heart, was going to help me find out.

Next, Chovalo. He had been with Irma and her husband, Bud, for some twenty years. Then Wes and Linda Fowler had come to take over what sounded like Bud's job and a large part of Chovalo's. One he must have loved and taken pride in doing. He ran the horse breeding half of Irma's businesses, but was that what he'd expected? It was the horse hauling part that made the money, and if the prospective buyer had not included a job for Chovalo, could the breeding farm still pay his salary?

The only thing I knew about horses was the little I had gleaned from Susannah, but one stallion and a handful of mares didn't seem like a big money-making enterprise. Irma must be about sixty, Chovalo looked about the same. Not an age when you are eager to start over. It sounded like lots of his and Maria Rosa's savings had been spent on helping put those nephews and nieces through school. Was it possible that co-operating with these drug people seemed like a hedge against possible later bankruptcy? How did I go about finding out? I could hardly ask Irma. There had to be a way. Only, I couldn't think of one right now.

That brought me to Bryce. The beautiful Bryce Ellis, poor spoiled, vain Bryce, talented, lazy, with one very dangerous habit. If he really took drugs, how long could Irma afford to put up with him? Bryce made me think of Stephanie. She was not an attractive girl, in looks or in personality, so maybe Aunt Mary was right. Her only hold on Bryce was money. Evidently, she owned a couple of the horses Bryce trained and showed. According to Susannah, she was trying to talk her parents into buying another, a very expensive one. If that didn't

happen, how long would Bryce be willing to tolerate
Stephanie's possessiveness? She must feel she had a lot
of control over him or she wouldn't have read him the
riot act about hiring Rusty. Would she? Or, maybe she
felt her control slipping. Maybe she thought, if it was her
or Rusty—would she do that? I pictured Stephanie and
her obvious obsession with Bryce and with getting her
own way and decided yes. Stephanie was a true suspect.
What did I do about it? I could find out where Stephanie was while Bryce was in the ring. I wasn't sure how
I'd go about that, but I'd figure it out.

My thoughts turned to Irma. She'd certainly surrounded herself with an interesting cast. I hoped Wes
and Linda were more stable than her barn staff seemed
to be. Now there was a pair. Wes, lightly balding,
paunchy, with his good ol' boy attitude and his pen-
chant for pretty women. I was sure he was popular with
his beer-drinking buddies, but his "pat the little dears
on the head but don't take them seriously" attitude was
grating to a woman. Linda's reputed efficiency was evidently not enough for her husband. Her plain Iowa farm
woman look, no-nonsense expression, flat Midwestern
twang, were not the stuff to keep his eyes fixed firmly at
home. I wondered why they stayed together. Maybe she
had hidden talents. Anyway, they seemed to be moving horses around the country with ease, which wasn't
a job I'd want to tackle.

The living room clock struck ten. I yawned. I wasn't
going to come up with any answers tonight so I might
as well go to bed. I stretched, covered another yawn
with my hand and got up when I had another thought.
Susannah. Neil. Just how serious were those two? Did
I need to worry? Susannah was a woman now, or close.
She was much better prepared to manage her life than

I'd been at her age. I had jumped, starry eyed, into marriage with her father, then had closed my eyes to all the brewing problems long after the stars had died out. I didn't want the same thing to happen to Susannah. I wanted her to take her time; there was plenty of it. Neil had ahead of him the dedication vet school demanded and she was a long way from her own scholastic goal. Only, how did I tell her that? Did I need to?

This was getting me nowhere. I picked up my empty glass, brushed the crumbs off the front of my shirt and decided what I really needed was ice cream and my newest library book. I'd let Carolyn Hart transport me to a different state and present me with a whole new set of problems I didn't have to solve.

The answering machine light was blinking when I entered my bedroom. Good. Dan had called. Had he apologized? I felt a little complacent as I punched the button. It was the voice of my latest client, excitedly telling me someone had already shown their house. Wasn't it wonderful?

"Wonderful." The machine clicked off. "Absolutely wonderful."

FIFTEEN

DAN DIDN'T CALL for three days, but Becky Monahan did. So did Irma.

Becky was delighted to get my message. Or, so she said. "I can't believe you came back to this sleepy little town, Ellen," she gushed. "If I'd lived in southern California, Newport Beach no less, you wouldn't have gotten me out with dynamite. Don't you miss all that? Parties, theater, good restaurants?"

Traffic, parties where your husband's drunken friends try to paw you, women with nothing to do but have lunch, shop and talk about each other, boredom, traffic. "Not really," I said, truthfully. "I've found a lot to keep me busy."

"Right. I heard about you and Dan."

Aren't small towns wonderful! "Actually, Becky," I turned completely away from that subject, "I wanted to ask you something."

I described the pirate and asked if she could help me find him. "You know, his name, address, that kind of thing."

"Why?" she asked.

"I'm sort of planning this party," I lied, "and I thought, you know, if he's not too expensive…"

"I'll see what I can find out, but, Ellen, I don't see how you could have run into him way out by the horse barns. All our roving entertainers are told to stay by the main exhibits or by the midway. They're never supposed to be by the livestock at all. If this guy was there, I'll have to put that in his record, in case we think about hiring him again. I'll call you."

So! The pirate wasn't supposed to be by the barns. He just happened to be there when Rusty was killed. Coincidence? I didn't think so. But, I was going to need a lot more before I confronted Dan. Whom I hadn't heard from. Damn.

The phone rang. It was Irma.

"How's the mare?" was the first thing I asked her.

"So far, so good. If she can get through the next couple of days without doing something silly, well, we'll see."

I wanted to ask her what silly thing a horse could do confined in a horse hospital, but Irma was tuned into something else.

"I need to talk to you about selling my horse hauling business. Ed Brady keeps at me and I don't know what to do. He wants to buy the business and the land, but I'm not sure I want to sell the land. Bud always said, never sell your land. We've had this place a long time, it's all paid for. I just don't know."

"You want to sell him the business? The vans and everything?"

"I'm thinkin' about it. Wes keeps tellin' me not to be a fool, that I'm makin' good money with them runnin' it, and I guess that's true. Ed wants me to carry some kind of a note, says that will be better income. Suppose somethin' happens and he can't pay? Then what do I do? Or suppose he moves all the trucks somewhere else? Could he do that?"

I didn't see why not, but my knowledge was a whole lot too vague to give Irma an answer. So I settled for a suggestion.

"Irma, you know Bo Chutsky, don't you?"

"A little. Bud used to be in Rotary with him."

That was no surprise. Half the men in town were in Rotary.

"I think you need to talk to him. Bo knows all about this kind of stuff and I'm just learning. Want me to talk to him for you?"

I hated to turn down Irma's business, but I was positive I wouldn't know what to do with it if I got it.

The relief in Irma's voice matched my own. "Oh, will you? But you'll still help me too, won't you?"

I was flattered, I had to admit, and only too glad to reassure Irma I wouldn't desert her. Besides, I knew Bo liked nothing better than to "teach." Which meant he'd direct and I'd do all the boring paperwork, but I didn't mind. I'd never sold a business and it could be interesting. Besides, it would keep me up to date on any new developments in the Rusty situation.

We set up the meeting for Thursday morning and I almost missed it. I had a call to show my relocation listing to a young family moving into town and they only had that morning open. Not the kind of thing you turn down. They were interested, very interested. I took them over to one of our local lenders and left them there, going over figures and the horrendous list of documents needed to get a loan. I returned to our office about eleven thirty to find Irma and Bo finishing up the details.

"How'd it go?"

Bo grunted.

"Great," Irma said. "Bo helped me a lot. Ellen, you were an angel to suggest this."

"Thank you." I wanted to know what Bo had told

her, if she had made a decision, if I needed to go back out to the ranch. I didn't get the chance.

"I've got to go." She grabbed up a file folder full of papers. "I'll talk to you in a few days, Bo. See you, Ellen."

I watched her out the door and then turned to see if I could get any information out of my broker. Not a chance. Bo was getting ready to go to lunch, his most important appointment for the day.

I'd known Bo Chutsky all my life. My father had also attended Rotary. Bo had watched me grow up and I had watched him grow wide. There wasn't a belt made that would fit around his waistline and the stretch on his suspenders kept you from standing directly in front of him. But he was one of the smartest and best-informed real estate brokers I'd ever known. Bo had several codes he lived by. One was that real estate was a serious business; you were dealing with the most expensive purchase most people would ever make and you better get it right. Another was "least said, soonest mended."

"How did it go?"

"Fine." He barely looked up from examining blue prints of some kind.

"What does that mean?"

"Means fine."

"What did you tell Irma to do?"

"Nothing." The tone in his voice said "you're bothering me."

"You told her to do nothing?" My tone was incredulous, but I couldn't help it.

"Yep. Not yet anyway."

"Why?" I was starting to feel exasperated.

"Because I need more information." He looked up at me. "Pricing the land is easy, but Irma's not sure she wants to sell it. Frankly, I'm inclined to agree with her. Which leaves us the business to look at, and Irma doesn't have the books. I need an inventory list, a current P&L, the last couple of years' IRS returns, monthly income statements. I need expenses. I need information. So I sent her home to get it."

He pushed at the blue prints lying on his desk with a fat finger. "Seems all Irma knows anymore is what she pays those two and how much she pulls out of the business every month. She's not too sure about that. I don't know. Seems to me…" He looked up at me again and I could see his mouth close down on his words. "…that I need more information. Irma's coming back next week, after the Santa Barbara horse show they're all going to. How'd your showing go?"

What Santa Barbara horse show? Who was going? Certainly not Susannah.

Bo checked his watch and pushed his chair back, waited only long enough for me to tell him I thought I was going to write an offer that afternoon. He nodded approvingly and reminded me to make sure my people got a professional home inspector. Don't forget to ask the seller to pay for a Home Protection policy, he cautioned, then asked a couple of questions designed to make sure I had correctly explained the first time home buyer loan my young clients wanted. Satisfied I wouldn't let them get in over their heads, or make a fool of myself, he lumbered slowly toward the door. I watched him, wondering again why Irma seemed to know so little about her own business and why no one had mentioned anything about another horse show. Vowing to have a talk with Susannah that night and do a little law lying down, tactfully but firmly, I went back to my desk.

I had just sat down when the phone rang. It was Dan. The surge of pleasure I felt surprised me. I didn't want to analyze why.

"Hi." He was perhaps a hint hesitant.

"Hi," I said, trying to sound offhand.

"Want to try lunch again?" There was no doubt about the hesitation.

"I think I can manage that. The Yum Yum?"

"Of course. Ten minutes, OK? Don't be late, I'm starving." There was no mistaking the relief, mixed with what sounded like happiness.

"Me late? I'll beat you there." I didn't mind that I sounded happy too.

"Not a chance." The phone went dead.

I smiled as I hung up. Dan was going to win this one. The day was much too nice to rush a walk through our lovely park. Besides, I was suddenly feeling a tiny bit euphoric. I paused to watch a couple of little boys weigh the pleasures of wading in the fountain against the possible consequences, then took a second to feel the sun as it made its way through the leaves of the trees. A pang of nostalgia pricked as I stood for a moment at the steps leading up to our century-old brick library. Our small, dark and now empty library. Our soon-to-be-a-local-history-museum library. The new large, light, airy library was directly across the street. I made a mental note to pick up a new book before going home that evening and pushed open the door to the Yum Yum.

It was packed. There was Dan, holding down our regular table.

"You're late." He smiled.

"Mm" was my only comment, but I smiled at him too before looking around. Bo was easily spotted, blue prints by his chair, talking to the mayor, two of the city councilmen and a man I had never seen before. I wondered what he had up his sleeve now, but was distracted by Ruthie. A harassed Ruthie, frizzy hair in more disarray than usual.

"Can't believe how busy we are." She set an iced tea in front of me. "The special, Ellen?"

I glanced toward the blackboard, but it was effectively blocked by a large woman in plaid shorts.

"What is it?"

"Chicken potpie."

"No thanks. Do you have…?"

"Salad? Sure. Chef OK? Thousand island?" She was gone.

I laughed. "I guess it's fine. Bet you're having the potpie."

"I ordered the low-fat version but they're out."

"Right. Thanks for ordering me the iced tea."

"I wish I could take credit, but that was Ruthie's idea."

I nodded, looked up at Dan, at blue eyes that smiled, and I smiled back.

"Truce?" His voice was gentle.

"Truce."

"Good. I've missed you." He looked like he had a hard time getting that one out, but I was glad he did.

"Well, now that I think about it, I missed you too," I told him and meant every word.

"In that case, how about dinner tonight?"

"Can't you think of anything to do but eat?"

"Actually, I can think of one other thing." He studied the now visible chalkboard.

To my horror, I grinned. Or, I started to. The trouble was, the thought of the "other thing" appealed. A lot. What was the matter with me? We'd agreed to be friends only; at least until Susannah went back to school in the fall and then we'd see. Fall suddenly seemed a long way away.

He watched me. I thought I detected a suspicion of a smile behind that mustache. "I could take you out for a pizza if you want."

"No, no." I grabbed my napkin out of the way as Ruthie slid plates in front of us. "We'll do something on the barbecue. No problem."

I carefully poured a small amount of salad dressing over my salad, trying to keep my eyes on my plate. Dan said, "Ellie, I want to ask you something."

My hand jerked and the whole cup of dressing poured out, most of it on the salad. I mopped up the rest of it with my napkin, avoiding Dan's eyes. "Oh? What."

"I want you to go to a horse show with me."

"What?" My head jerked up as I stared at him, dripping napkin still in my hand.

"It's in Santa Barbara. This weekend."

"A horse show? You?" I was dumbfounded.

"Why not me? I seem to be stumbling over horses and horsey people every place I go lately. Might as well see what it's all about. Besides, a change of scene will do us both good."

Thoughts tripped over each other. That Dan had suddenly been smitten with a love of horses was one I instantly rejected. There was another reason, but what and where did I fit in?

"I thought we might go down Saturday afternoon," Dan said, looking everywhere but at me, "get a room by the beach, have a nice dinner and come back on Sunday evening."

"What?" Surely I could think of another word, but the surprises were coming a little too fast. Images of sandy beaches, the setting sun, white wine chilling in glasses flashed by, coupled with a glimpse of a shut motel room door. I gulped. I could feel my resolve to slow down our relationship dissolve. Nights with Dan were fun, Santa Barbara would be wonderful, and why did I think we should go slow anyway? I was forty, for God's sake. And, one night in Santa Barbara didn't mean anything more than—one night. But this horse show thing. Where would Susannah be? I needed to know. We had to talk about that.

"I can't just…I need to know…"

"Oh well, maybe another time."

Dan was irritatingly complacent about my hesitation. I wanted to throw the rest of the salad dressing at him.

"How about if we leave early, really early, Sunday morning. It's only two hours down there so we'll make a day of it. It'll give you a chance to keep an eye on Susannah."

"Susannah! How do you know if…"

"She's going? Bryce told me."

Everyone seemed to be finishing my sentences but me, but then, everyone seemed to know what was happening but me.

"Why were you talking to Bryce?" I decided to leave the subject of Susannah until tonight. When she and I were alone.

"I'm a policeman, remember? I'm still investigating a murder. The victim worked for Bryce and Irma. They seemed like good choices for interviews."

"What did Bryce have to say?" I pushed dripping lettuce around the plate.

"Not a lot." Dan paused to mop up the last of the potpie gravy with a roll and then ate the rest of the crust. I vowed to give him green beans and salad for dinner.

"Just kept saying he needed someone. Rusty turned up and said he had a lot of experience, so Bryce hired him. Irma says she knew nothing about him until she arrived at the show grounds."

"So, we're going to Santa Barbara because you like sea air and have taken a sudden interest in Arabian show horses?" I watched his all-too-innocent expression. "Is that right?"

"Something like that, yes. Want to go?"

"I wouldn't miss it for the world."

"Somehow I knew you'd say that. OK. It's a date. Now, how about if I come over around six tonight and the same time Sunday morning. Six a.m. You will be up, won't you?"

All the fiends in hell wouldn't be able to keep me in bed after five on Sunday morning, but I only smiled and said, "Oh, I think I can make it."

I silently vowed to do one other thing. Use our two-hour drive to make Dan tell me what he really expected to find in Santa Barbara.

SIXTEEN

THE PHONE WAS RINGING as I came in the front door. It was Irma.

"Wanted to thank you again for setting up that meeting with Bo. I told Wes what I needed and he said he'd have Linda get everything together for me. Said he thought she already had, but no one told me. Not that that's a surprise. Anyway, I'll pick up what she has ready and take it to Bo before we leave."

"Leave. Right. I need to talk…"

"Another thing. I got Susannah her own room in Santa Barbara. At the Willow Tree, right next to mine. I didn't want you to think, well, that I wasn't taking care of her or anything."

Another sentence interrupted, but this time I was glad. "I never thought that for a minute. But no one told me about this show."

"Why, this is Region II! Remember last week when Challenge won? We said then he'd go. We already had other horses entered but now, now it's really special."

"Irma, exactly what is a Region II?"

"My goodness, Ellen, it's the qualifying show for Nationals. It's going to be huge. And tough. Remember the chestnut colt that Lone Oak Farms has been showing this year? He's good. Challenge has a better hindquarter but…"

Of course I didn't remember any chestnut colt. I'd only been to one horse show. I knew chestnut was a color, but after that I was lost. Hindquarters, however, I was familiar with. Just that morning I'd taken a good look at my own and vowed to shed a couple of pounds.

"Irma, I have to go. I think I heard Susannah. I'll see you Sunday."

"You're coming? Wonderful. That's wonderful. Get an early start so you don't miss his class."

She was gone before I could ask her how early was early, but it hardly mattered. Susannah would know.

My daughter came through the back door, sweaty, smelly and smiling.

"Hi, Mom. Boy, am I beat. Is the washing machine empty? What's for dinner?"

"Susannah, we have to talk."

"Sure. Right after I have a shower. I smell like a horse."

She did. Even Jake wouldn't go near her. She stepped out of the shower and into a whirlwind of activity. First she stuffed the washing machine with dirty jeans and muddy tennis shoes. Next she started rummaging in the garage.

"What are you doing?"

"Looking for the duffel bag I brought back from school. I know I put it here somewhere."

"You left it in the downstairs closet behind your tennis stuff."

"Thanks, Mom," and she was off.

"Susannah, wait. We have to talk."

"As soon as I'm off the phone." She punched buttons as she pulled jeans from the dryer.

"Did they all get there?" She had the phone tucked under her chin. "How about the two-year-old. OK. Now if you send the four-horse down early tomorrow, it can take Challenge and the geldings. That frees the van for the Ohio trip. No? Oh."

She must be talking to Linda. The logistics of moving show horses around made moving the 5th Army look like a breeze.

The screen door slammed and Dan walked in.

"Looks like someone is going somewhere." He eyed the growing pile of clean jeans, shirts, socks and sweatshirts on the dining room table. "Guess we're going to eat outside."

"Unless you want laundry with your pasta."

"Pasta?"

"And salad. It's non-fat."

Susannah carved out enough time to join us for dinner. "This is wonderful, Mom." She quickly worked her way through an overflowing plate.

"Take your time. There's no prize for finishing first."

"Have to hurry." She swallowed the last bite. "Neil will be here any minute. We're going to the movies."

"I thought you told me Irma was picking you up at five thirty tomorrow morning."

"She is. But she's driving, so I can sleep on the way down."

"Nice to think you might work that into your schedule." My sarcasm fell, as usual, on deaf ears.

"Mom says you want me to quit my job." Susannah turned toward Dan.

"I do."

"Why haven't you asked me?" She had her head slightly cocked to one side, waiting for an answer.

"Because I can't make you and you're not going to. Are you."

"No. I'm not."

"OK. But I'll make you a deal." Dan leaned forward,

elbows resting on the table, giving Susannah serious consideration.

"What kind of deal?" Susannah looked at him suspiciously. I looked at him in amazement. Why hadn't he done this earlier?

"I'm going to give you a card with a couple of phone numbers on it. If anything happens during the horse show, anything makes you nervous, doesn't feel right, even if you don't know why, get to a phone and call one of these numbers."

"And someone will come running, sirens screaming?"

"No sirens." Dan leaned forward a little, watching her. "Someone will come, but quietly. If you'll promise, I won't say another word." Then he smiled at her. "It'll make your mother feel better. Agreed?"

Susannah said nothing for a moment, then a slow grin grew. "Agreed. You know, you might be all right after all. Whoops. There's Neil. See you."

There was no mistaking Neil's truck engine. Susannah took the card Dan handed her, examined the numbers, nodded to him, blew me a kiss and was gone.

"You're still worried, aren't you?" I wondered if I'd badly misread the situation and when I should start to panic.

"Ellie," Dan paused before he went on, "people who deal in drugs, on any level, do it for only one reason. Money. One man has already died, right here in our little backwater town. I'm not sure who is responsible, or how, but I take that seriously. It's obvious you and Susannah aren't going to shirk what you consider your responsibilities no matter what I say, and you're right. You're an adult. You can make your own decisions. However, I'm still a policeman, sworn to protect innocent citizens, and that's what I'm trying to do." He smiled at me. "Come on. I'll help you with the dishes. I brought a movie. You'll love it."

"I'll bet it's a cops and robbers type." I stacked dishes on a tray, hoping my face was hidden. Dan acted exactly like I thought he should, so why was I feeling— what was I feeling?

"It's not 'The Princess Diaries,'" he informed me cheerfully. "I don't suppose you have any ice cream."

Dan picked up the tray and started for the door. I held it open for him. "It's frozen yogurt for you, Dan Dunham. Someone has to look after your arteries."

"I'll bet they'd benefit by another beer. Yogurt sounds like an after-the-movie thing. Want another glass of wine?"

Why not, I thought as I stacked the last plate in the dishwasher. Dan's conversation with Susannah had rattled me and yogurt didn't sound very comforting. I joined Dan on the sofa, the movie already in the VCR, Jake on his lap. It was indeed a cops and robbers type. Dan regaled me throughout with all of the procedural mistakes in it, but he kept quiet during the love scenes. By the time it was over I was somehow curled up beside him, my head on his shoulder, his arm around me. It seemed so natural I wasn't sure when or how it happened. Dan flicked off the TV, stretched, put Jake on the floor and pulled me to my feet.

"I'll take a rain check on your yogurt. How about Saturday? Tell you what, I'll treat you to pizza and a movie. Just like in the old days. We may even venture over the hill to San Luis. OK?"

"Sure. But I get to pick the movie. After all that excitement, I think I need something tamer."

"I think you've turned back into a small-town girl."

Then he kissed me. A long kiss, filled with intensity, his hands doing things that made my body come alive in places I'd never known existed the whole time I was married to Brian. I felt myself press against him, felt my lips open slightly against his, felt my hands slide around his shoulders, then up toward the back of his neck where they could do nothing to stop what his were doing. Just as suddenly he let me go.

"You know, Ellen Page McKenzie," his voice a little hoarse and raspy, "patience only extends so far." That was all he said, but the way he looked at me wasn't calculated to reduce my now wildly surging nerve endings, or restore my breathing to anything like normal.

"Dan" was all I got out. I felt as if the roller coaster I'd been riding had just hit bottom.

"See you Saturday," and the door closed behind him.

I stood there, as wrung out as an old dishrag. Why hadn't Dan stayed? God knew, in my melting Jell-O mood, we'd have been upstairs in another ten minutes. Hadn't he wanted to? If he hadn't, he'd given an Oscar-winning performance. What stopped him? My rules, that's what. I'd drawn the line. Dan had agreed not to step over it. I knew it was up to me to erase that line. Until I did— Damn. Double damn.

I fastened the dead bolt and switched off the porch light. Susannah would come in the back, so I left the kitchen light on and the screen unfastened and stood in the dark hallway, fretting, fuming and still tingling.

Jake jumped up on the bookcase, drawing my attention to the VCR. Dan had forgotten his movie. Just like a man, leaving me to return it. I punched the rewind button on the remote a little harder than necessary and stood staring at the tape whirring backwards, trying not to realize one of the reasons I was irritated with him was because he made me feel things I was—admit it, Ellen McKenzie—things I was afraid to feel. Things that had nothing to do with the bedroom.

I put the tape by my purse so I wouldn't forget it in the morning, paused, looked around the room for I didn't know what, sighed and went upstairs to my always reliable escape. Books. I didn't want to deal with my own world any more tonight. I'd read myself to sleep. I could count on being sound asleep by eleven. Only I couldn't get Dan off my mind. Or murder. Dan must have felt there was some kind of real danger, or he wouldn't have given Susannah those phone numbers. Maybe that was why we were going to Santa Barbara, maybe he was worried something more was going to happen. My hesitation about spending the night hadn't bothered him much, I thought sourly, and he hadn't pushed the issue tonight. Which, I told myself sternly, was exactly the way I wanted it. "Yeah, right," I told Jake, as, around one, I finally turned off the light.

SEVENTEEN

IRMA ARRIVED AT exactly five thirty. Susannah was up and ready. I was up. Doors had banged, the shower had steamed, the blow drier had blown, and I could no longer pretend that I slept. Especially as my door opened softly and a whispering voice asked, "Mom, can I borrow your green sweatshirt?"

She was going for three days, it was the middle of summer, and she had already packed six tee shirts and four sweatshirts. What on earth did she want with mine?

"Sure. Take it." I started to turn over when the smell of coffee got me. "What's that?"

I pushed the covers down a little. Susannah stood there with my favorite mug in her hand, steam lightly rising and drifting my way.

"I thought you might like to come down and say good-bye."

She hadn't wanted me to say good-bye when she left for college, but that hadn't been preceded by a murder. I yawned, pushed back the covers and reached for my robe. Might as well get into practice. Sunday would be here before I knew it.

Irma came before I had more than two sips swallowed or two sentences spoken. There was a burst of activity as Susannah lugged her stuff out to the car, then briefly panicked when she couldn't find her list of horses to be shown that day. It was under her coffee mug. Irma handed me phone numbers where they could be reached, finally the car door slammed and they were gone.

There was no point in going back to bed, so I contented myself with reading the morning paper. My shower was leisurely and I even had time to start a load of laundry. Mine.

I arrived at the office a half hour early.

I had just hung up the phone and was making notes on my conversation, when Pat walked in and plopped herself down in the chair beside my desk. "You busy?"

My desk was littered with papers and files and I had a stack of messages still waiting to be answered. "Not a bit. What's up?"

"Carl had an emergency surgery and I'm useless at that kind of thing, so I put the phones on answering service, closed the office for thirty minutes and came to kidnap you."

"OK. I'm more than ready for a break. Yum Yum?"

"Where else?"

The restaurant was quiet for once. The only customers were Saturday shoppers taking a coffee break between breakfast and lunch. Ruthie wasn't to be seen, which was amazing. A plump young girl with long blond hair in a braid down her back poured our coffee.

"Donuts?" she asked. "Or maybe a Danish? We've got really good Danish."

"Just coffee." The girl looked disappointed.

"Bet you Ruthie runs twenty pounds off her in a month," Pat commented.

"If she lasts that long. What's up?"

"What do you mean?" Pat was all innocence as she sipped her coffee. Only, I knew better.

"You don't shut your office for nothing. So, out with it."

She laughed a little. "Well, it's a couple of things. One interesting, but really just mild gossip. I'm not sure about the other."

"Gossip first?"

"Why not? But only if you promise not to squeal on me to Mary. You know how she feels about gossip."

"She's the only person I ever heard of who knows everything that goes on in town, but never gossips. Go on."

"OK. I was getting my hair cut," she patted her short, soft waves, "and Debbie, my hair dresser, also does a woman who's a cousin to Bryce Ellis's mother and doesn't mind parting with a little family history. It seems Bryce was a late-in-life child, an unexpected one. He has four older sisters and a father who died when he was little, leaving the family very well fixed. The mother always wanted a son and, with the father gone, doted on Bryce. He went to private schools and got kicked out of every one, the last couple for drinking and doing drugs. According to Debbie, there's something more but the cousin stopped short of telling her what it is."

She stopped and looked at me expectantly.

"You think Bryce might be selling drugs?" This opened up possibilities I hadn't thought of.

"Makes sense, especially with what's been going on. Doesn't it?"

"I guess it might. If he has a really bad habit, selling seems to be a next step. That could tie him more tightly to Rusty. But, where do the horses come in?"

"Evidently, they're an ego thing." She raised her coffee mug, stared at the empty bottom and set it back down. "The cousin said Bryce had failed at everything else he'd tried, but he really is good at showing horses."

"He's good at being charming." That sounded a little rueful. "Do you think Bryce has the guts to kill someone?"

"I doubt it." Pat was looking around, holding her empty cup in her hand. "Where is that girl? Oh, there she is." She smiled at the girl, who filled our cups before she wandered off again.

"But Stephanie might have. Aunt Mary's right. She is strong."

"I'll say."

I had to laugh at the expression on Pat's face. "I meant strong-minded. But, that too. She could easily have hefted that pitchfork. The only place she doesn't seem to be strong is where Bryce is concerned." I took a sip of coffee and thought about that. "We know she made him promise not to take any more drugs," I said slowly, feeling my way. "If she thought Rusty tempted him to break that promise, or worse, set Bryce up to help sell drugs, I don't suppose a little thing like murder would stop her."

"You may be right." Pat paused before starting off on another track. "There's something else, Ellen." Her expression changed and I didn't like it. She hadn't been comfortable telling me about Bryce, but now she looked worried.

"About Bryce?"

"No. About Chovalo." She paused before she went on, as though choosing her words carefully. "One of Carl's beloved sheepdogs came in this morning for a routine visit. Shots and stuff. I got to talking to the owner. He lives out by Irma and was at the fair. You know the horse show ended Sunday. Monday a lot of people went back to tear down before the rodeo people came in. Well, Chovalo was out there."

"So?"

"Irma's barn was already torn down. It was one of the few, according to this man. Chovalo went from barn to barn, not talking to owners but to the help, the grooms, whatever you call them. All the Spanish-speaking ones."

"I'm lost. What are you suggesting? That he was doing something wrong?"

"I don't know, but it's strange." Pat didn't look happy telling all this, but she plowed on. "His job at the fair-grounds was finished. Dan keeps talking about people being recruited to make this awful meth stuff and how the horse shows are somehow connected. What Chovalo was doing sounded a lot like recruitment to me. What do you think?"

I thought I didn't like what I was hearing. Another idea began to form, and I was getting scared again.

"How does that connect with Bryce? Chovalo and Bryce hate each other, so they can hardly be working together."

"They work together in Irma's barn," Pat pointed out.

"True." I thought about that. "You think they really might be in this together somehow?"

"Ellen, I don't know." Now Pat, my dear friend Pat, looked at me with miserable eyes. "Something isn't right. And whatever it is, it's dangerous. I'm scared, Ellen, for Susannah."

She wasn't the only one.

I found myself staring at her, coffee cup halfway to my slightly open mouth, thinking awful thoughts. Pat, the eternal optimist, who saw good in everything and evil nowhere, was worried. Once more, she was scared and that, somehow, was the most terrifying of all.

"Look, Ellen, I don't want to butt in, especially after

the high-handed way Dan and Carl tried to manage things, but we all care about you and Susannah." She took a deep breath and let the rest of her words out with a rush. "Can you get her to quit working with Bryce? That job with Carl is still open."

Loyalty be damned. Susannah might not know it, but her days as Bryce's girl Friday were ending on Sunday. I wasn't sure how I was going to pull it off, but somehow I had to.

Pat glanced at her watch. "I've got to go. Carl should be finished setting that cat's leg about now and I'd better open the office again." She pushed back her chair, then paused. "What are you going to do?"

"No idea. I'll think of something, though. And, Pat, thanks."

"Yeah. Right. Good luck." She dropped a dollar on the table and left.

I went more slowly. The day suddenly seemed a little too hot, the trees a little too dusty, the flowers a little wilted, even the breeze felt tired. Damn. Life was filled with decisions, problems, perils I wasn't sure how equipped I felt to deal with. Independence, pride that I was learning to do my new job well, was one thing. Coping with murder was another.

Had Chovalo known Rusty before the horse show? Was Rusty some kind of contact gone bad? There had to be one. A contact. The vague idea I'd had while talking to Pat returned, only now it had bright and shiny edges. The pirate. What better cover could there be? He was hired as an entertainer, his job was to wander the fair. He talked to hundreds of people every day. Both times I had seen him, he was either in the horse barns or close to them. The pirate had something to do with this, I was sure. Why, oh why, hadn't Becky called?

She had. I called her back immediately.

"Ellen, it's the strangest thing. That pirate, he wasn't hired by the fair."

"What? How can that be? He was there, I saw him."

"You and a bunch of other people. However, we have nothing on him, no paperwork of any kind. We never cut him a paycheck. If you hadn't asked about him, we'd never have known."

"How could you not have known? Doesn't someone check these people in? Give them passes or something?"

"Of course." She sounded a bit defensive. "We can't figure out how he got in, either, or why he was there. Anyway, we're continuing to check. If I find out any more, I'll let you know."

I hung up the phone and stared at my cluttered desk. But the papers waiting for my attention, the messages needing a return phone call, didn't register. Only Becky's news did. What did it mean? Only one thing I could think of. That pirate was closely connected to whatever was going on. This didn't prove he killed Rusty, but it sure put him first place in the suspect category and dropped Chovalo to the bottom. Or, did it? Next question, what should I do about this? Nothing was my answer. At least, not right now. Dan was so sure the pirate wasn't involved and Becky's bizarre tale probably wasn't enough to change Dan's mind. I'd wait for more information from her. In the meantime, I'd try to find out more about Chovalo. And, I reminded myself, this little tidbit didn't absolve sweet Stephanie. I sighed, sat down and started to answer my messages.

EIGHTEEN

SATURDAY NIGHT WAS balmy and beautiful. I had on my most flattering long skirt, a new silk sweater straight from the pages of the Nordstrom catalog and some killer perfume. I was slightly irritated at myself for taking so much trouble. After all, Dan and I were just friends. Sure, said my inner voice. He'd half moved in until you panicked. Of course that wasn't true. I just needed to slow things down so I could think. You panicked, my inner voice said again. Shut up, I told it savagely. I didn't, either. I had to admit, I'd missed him. Jake didn't cuddle nearly as well and he wasn't nearly as much fun to talk to. I sighed. Trying to figure out what I wanted out of this relationship was getting harder all the time. I'm not thinking about it anymore, I vowed, I'm only going to think about that blasted horse show and this afternoon's phone call from Susannah. The show was wonderful, she'd said. They had won several of their classes, Bryce wasn't being completely awful, Chovalo was a saint, Irma was a nervous wreck waiting for Sunday, the horse had never looked better, and she was having a great time. It was what she didn't say that made me happy. She didn't once mention murder.

Dan arrived a little early. He didn't say anything when he looked at me, but I thought his eyes lit up. "There's a new place in San Luis Obispo I'd thought we'd try. They have all kinds of weird stuff."

"That sounds nice." I made sure my skirt didn't get shut in the car door. "What kind of weird stuff?"

"Fish tacos and chicken Caesar salad. Sounds like something you might like."

"It does indeed." I smothered a smile.

I did like it. Judging by the empty plate, so did Dan. Afterward, we went to see "Calendar Girls." We were both still laughing when we headed up the grade toward home.

"Why did you turn off here?" The dark country road was somehow familiar, only I couldn't remember why. I knew it wasn't a shortcut back to town.

"There's a place I always wanted to go. With you. I thought we might go there tonight. Even if we are kind of old."

That place was Lookout Point.

"Dan," I said, when he pulled onto the small parking space. "This was where we all came to neck when we were in high school."

"I know." He turned to me and grinned. "I've been here before."

Then it hit me. "You always wanted to come here with me?"

"Well, not always. Actually, not until that year I went away to college. Before that, you were pretty scrawny. And you wore braces. But that year, you looked kind of promising."

"Kind of promising. I never knew you felt that way."

"I didn't want to say anything." He looked a little sheepish. "You know how boys are at that age, a little shy sometimes. Besides, we'd been playmates all our lives, looking at you as a girl didn't feel right. Then I left for college."

"How do I look now?"

"Kind of promising." He slid his arm around me and pulled me close.

At first I pushed away. Independence, my inner voice yelled. You're starting to establish your own life, don't let this happen. But things were happening and I didn't want them to stop. Thoughts of independence evaporated like fog on a sunny day.

NINETEEN

SUNDAY MORNING the doorbell rang promptly at six. I opened it, my most wide-awake smile determinedly in place.

"You look surprised," I told Dan smugly.

"I wasn't sure you'd be ready. I did leave here a little late."

He looked at me uncertainly, as though he wasn't sure what to expect. Thinking about Lookout Point, where we'd done a little more than identify stars, sent a faint flush up my cheeks for several reasons. I couldn't believe it, two middle-aged adults, one a police chief. How embarrassing it would have been if one of his patrol cars that routinely checked had found us. But they hadn't, and no one had disturbed us when we returned to my house, either.

Dan had walked me to the front door, opened it and gently pushed me inside. Then he locked the door. On the inside. He reached for me and I found myself going willingly into his arms. His lips brushed the hair at my temple and moved down toward my ear. His tongue explored that for a second, long enough for my legs to turn to putty, then soft kisses moved down toward my neck.

"Oh, Ellie," he murmured.

I wondered, briefly, if this meant Dan was tired of being patient, but I didn't care. Patience seemed, right then, a most unnecessary virtue. My hands, unbidden by me, reached for his shirt buttons, his somehow slipped under my sweater, my shoes were no longer on my feet, and we were working our way up the stairs. I remember thinking, who needs motels. There's no place like home.

It was after three when Dan finally went home.

There had been a whole lot more to our love making than surging hormones and tingling nerve endings and it had effectively put paid to my "we're just good friends" routine. From some of the things Dan had murmured in my ear, I knew he was planning something much different than an occasional repeat of that night's performance. How did I feel about that? I had no idea. I was certain of one thing; I wasn't ready to discuss it. I had some serious thinking to do.

Dan stood in the doorway, waiting for me to say something. "Uh, Ellie, about last night…" he finally started. "I know you wanted…"

"A nice adult friendship, as befits two middle-aged people." I couldn't keep a straight face and finally laughed. "Last night gave friendship a whole new meaning and it seems we're not so old after all."

"I never said you were old," he said, indignant. He looked me up and down. "I certainly would never have said that."

I silently gave thanks I still fit into my jeans and tucked my tee shirt in a little more firmly. "We'll talk about last night later. Right now, we better get going."

"Good idea. That wouldn't be coffee I smell, would it?" He looked hopeful and smiled for the first time. Evidently he too was happy to put off the inevitable discussion, the one entitled, now what?

"It is. Let's take it with us." I made a point of looking at my watch. "It's getting late."

"The army lost a good sergeant in you, Ellie." He

headed for the kitchen. I followed him and just in time. He lifted one of my best china cups off the open shelves.

"Oh no. Those don't leave this house. Here. Have this one." I handed him a large chipped white mug with a picture of a purple hippopotamus on the side. The words "a moment on the lips are forever on the hips" stood out sharply in black. He looked at it for a moment before filling it with coffee.

"Cream and sugar?"

"Very funny." He headed for the door.

THE TWO-HOUR DRIVE to Santa Barbara was spectacular. The low summer fog lingered just off the shore, making more than a promise of the blue sky showing above it. The waves were lazy, throwing only token spray over the rocks, but there were still a few diehard surfers determined to catch whatever mild thrills the ocean might surrender.

We had left the coast and started the climb over the mountains and through the San Marcos Pass that would drop us into Santa Barbara before I asked Dan the question that had never left my mind.

"You expect to find out something. What?"

His eyes stayed on the narrow winding road. "Didn't you want to come?"

"That's an evasion, not an answer. You're up to something and I want to know what."

"Now, Ellie."

"And don't 'now, Ellie' me either. Years ago I learned to tell when you were plotting something, and you haven't changed that much, Dan Dunham. So, tell me."

"Seems to me most of the scrapes we got into had your fine hand directing. I just did as I was told."

"Odd thing, memory. And, I am not going to be side-tracked. So, tell me again why we're doing this."

Dan glanced at me. His attention returned to the road. I waited.

"I thought it would make you feel better to see Su-sannah. I know how interested you've gotten in Irma's horse, and I haven't been to Santa Barbara in…"

His voice trailed off as I stared at him. He glanced over at me again and gave in.

"OK. You're my cover."

"Your what?"

"My cover. Well, not exactly a cover. More like an excuse."

"An excuse. For what?"

"For hanging around the horse show grounds. I told you we think, actually we know, methamphetamine is being manufactured in San Luis Obispo County. We also know that it's being shipped to dealers not only in LA and San Francisco, but to the Midwest, the East Coast and down South. Only, we don't know how. We think these horse shows are a link."

"I'm not sure I like being an excuse."

"Why not? You make a great excuse, for me to take a day off, to act the part of ardent admirer, only I don't need an excuse for that one, and for me to wander around and talk to people. Strange what sometimes turns up."

"No one's going to talk to you. Everyone knows you're a cop."

"True," he answered complacently. "They also know we're dating. What could be more natural than to drive you down here, to see the show, to bring Susannah home."

"Who knows we're dating?" I thought about last

night. I certainly didn't want information about that circulating freely around town.

"Everyone. We are, aren't we?" Dan took his eyes off the road long enough to glance at me. I didn't want to answer, so quickly changed the subject back to something safer. Chasing murderers.

"What about Chovalo? He's obviously still on your suspect list. Do you think he's part of that link?"

"He's done nothing to take himself off. He had another meeting Wednesday night with one of the people we think are manufacturing the meth, only we can't seem to nail the bastards. If we can find out how the supply line works we can not only stop the flow, but hopefully get some proof on this scum we can take into court."

He held up his hand, stopping me before I could comment.

"I know what you're going to say. No, I have no proof Chovalo's involved in anything more sinister than playing Monopoly, but if you can think of any legitimate reason for him to be setting up clandestine meetings with known drug dealers, I'd love to hear it."

I digested all this for a few minutes, not knowing what to say, but thinking about Pat's story of Chovalo's return to the fairgrounds. There was no doubt he was up to something. Did it include killing Rusty? I couldn't rule it out. I couldn't rule out the pirate, either. I wanted to tell Dan what I knew, how he hadn't been hired by the fair and that no one knew what he was doing there, but I hadn't heard from Becky. The guy could be some kook who thought delighting kids and scaring almost-middle-aged ladies was some kind of fun. I decided to keep quiet about the pirate until I had something real to tell.

"All right. What kind of questions do you want me to ask?"

"None at all." There was a tone of finality in his voice. "Your job is to make this whole day look normal. We're here to see the show, to cheer on Irma's horse. Nothing more."

"Why not?" Indignation started to build. "Don't you think I can do a good job?"

"Too good a one. You're smart and you're observant, qualities that could get you in a lot of trouble. Besides, I don't think you'd look nearly as pretty wearing a pitchfork through your middle. Neither would Susannah. So please, today play it my way. OK?"

I gulped. A mental picture of the dead Rusty appeared and my imagination substituted Susannah's face for his. I shuddered. Dan watched me out of the corner of his eye. Why, he had done that deliberately, to scare me, to keep me from doing—something. I started to say so when he pointed ahead.

"We're starting down. Will you look at that ocean?"

The promised blue had appeared, a few fat white clouds floated contentedly just off shore. Below us Santa Barbara spread itself out, waiting. I decided to wait also. Wait and watch, because who knew what interesting things the day might bring.

TWENTY

"I THINK I GOT OFF the freeway too soon."

We were stopped at another light on State Street where, at ten to eight on a Sunday morning, traffic crawled.

"Who are all these people?"

"Tourists," Dan said sourly.

"We're not?"

No answer. Instead we made a quick right turn down a less crowded street.

"I think it's down here." Dan slowed to read a street sign. "Yep. Here's the golf course. And there's the gate."

We swung into a parking lot crammed with campers and RVs. Deck chairs, portable barbecues and playpens for dogs, most of them yappingly full, were everywhere.

"Who are…" I started to say, but stopped as Dan slowly navigated through a sea of horse trailers and vans. Small two-horse trailers looked timid tucked between larger four-horse ones. All of them proudly announced farm names. Dwarfing them all were what appeared to be dozens of vans in several sizes ending in huge.

"Look." I rubbernecked like a fan on Oscar night. "There's Irma's. See the slogan?"

"Ellie, sit back. I can't see anything. I think the ordinary cars park right around this corner. Yes. Good God, will you look at that? Do you see a parking spot?"

"There. Right there."

"I can't get into that. Well, maybe. Hang on."

We seemed to have found the only parking spot left and we more or less invented it.

"I had no idea this many people came to horse shows. Especially in the morning."

Dan just grunted, grabbed me by the arm and hurried me along. We walked past an empty ticket booth into an also empty courtyard between two large buildings.

"Where are all the people? And the horses?"

"Down here I think."

I had to hurry to keep up with Dan's long-legged stride and almost tripped on the asphalt walk that ran along the side of the buildings. We could hear voices now, laughing, calling. A loudspeaker blared indistinguishable sounds. A horse whinnied. We rounded the corner to find ourselves in another world, a spectacular world brimming with medieval pageantry.

A narrow tunnel led into the building we were standing beside, its entrance jammed with people squeezing in and out. Next to the tunnel was a huge closed gate. In front of it milled more people and horses, very young, very excited horses. The people were more varied, equally excited, and they outnumbered the horses three to one. A man stood in a high booth beside the gate shouting something into a microphone and everyone milled around some more.

Beyond the waiting horses were two white-fenced arenas also filled with people. Some rode horses, some stood in the middle yelling at the riders. Others, carrying the ubiquitous pails, scurried back and forth like frightened mice. On each side and at the back of the arenas were barns, gaily decorated with canvas drapes stapled to their sides. Some were beautiful, some garish, all were more elaborate by far than at the show in Santa

Louisa. Ribbons hung on the drapes, trophies were displayed on tables or tack trunks set between deck chairs that seemed awash in a sea of potted plants. Farm names were spelled out everywhere, and brochures were available for the taking, all claiming the superiority of the horses housed behind the curtains. Or was it the superiority of the trainers who handled those horses?

"Heads up." A young horse thundered past me accompanied by a skinny, pimply-faced boy. They skidded to a stop before a short, bald man who snarled something at the boy and grabbed the lead from his hand. He whirled the horse around, tapped it lightly with his long whip, which he then quickly raised. The horse immediately struck the pose I had seen before. The man lowered his whip, patted the horse and snarled once more at the boy.

"Gate's open," shouted the loudspeaker. "Tom. You're first. Mike, you're next. Get number thirty-six out of the way. Where is seven oh two?"

"Let's go," said a voice behind us. Susannah had us each by the arm and dragged us toward the tunnel. I took a look at Dan as I followed her and almost laughed.

"You look like a kid watching his first circus."

"They're magnificent." He seemed a little embarrassed. "I had no idea."

We were in the stadium, looking down on the open arena. The stands were filling up fast and Susannah had disappeared.

"There she is." Dan pointed toward some seats close by the rail. We pushed our way through the crowd and slid into the front row beside her.

"I hope you didn't buy a program." She flipped pages in what looked like Santa Louisa's phone book. "I already got one. Look." She looked up from the program and pointed down into the ring. "Bryce is next. Nice colt, don't you think? It belongs to some friends of Irma."

The colt was beautiful, but then I thought they all were.

"Aren't those guys kind of little?" Dan watched the colt in front of the judge two-step in place, try an experimental rear or two, then refuse to move when it was time to trot off.

"They're yearlings and pretty unpredictable. That one just blew his chance. Not that he had one."

I shook my head. My daughter the expert. Bryce approached, one hand on the neck of his nervous charge, who looked all the more beautiful for his arched neck and light step.

"Watch this," Susannah said.

Suddenly Bryce whirled the colt and snapped his whip high in the air. The colt, startled, raised his neck, tightened his body and pricked his ears forward. It held the pose long enough for the judge to get a good look and, just as quickly, Bryce had the colt trotting away.

"You've got to give him credit. Most of this is timing and Bryce sure has that. Too bad he doesn't have a few other things."

"Like what?"

"Manners. Consideration. Self-control."

"What's he been doing?" asked Dan.

"You name it. He's been a royal pain since we got here. Temper tantrums, playing all night, only showing up in time to go into the ring, of course doing none of the work. I've just about had it."

Now there was a statement to make a mother's heart sing.

"Don't say that, Susannah." Irma stood by the row

of seats, looking forlorn. "You're the only thing keep-ing me sane."

"What's the matter now?" Susannah's exasperation was obvious. "Mom, why don't you guys move down one so Irma can sit by you. I'll take the aisle. I have to go back to the barn soon."

We all obediently moved over a seat, and Irma slid into the one beside me before she answered Susannah.

"There's a regular war going on back there. Poor Chovalo's nephew—what's his name?"

"Palo," supplied Susannah.

"Right. Anyway, he's trying, but he's new. Chovalo's giving him instructions, Bryce is yelling at him to do something else, and now Wes shows up and wants to start loading horses on the van."

"Loading horses?" Susannah wheeled away from watching the show to stare at Irma. "Well," she spoke slowly, "all the mares are finished. So is that colt." She pointed toward the ring. "He's not going to win this. Which means we get treated to another tantrum from our super star, but the colt can go home."

"Wes wants equipment loaded too. He's got a cross-country run leaving tonight, using this van, and he wants to get home. We can't tear down now, though."

"So they're all fighting." Susannah sighed. "How very pleasant."

"Bryce and Wes are fighting. Chovalo's ignoring them."

"But giving them that look only he can. I'll bet he's furious."

"Furious doesn't cover it. He wants Bryce gone. I've never seen him so down on anyone. I don't know what to do." Irma's voice trembled a little.

"Gone? Like fired gone?" I asked Irma.

She nodded.

"Wow." Susannah stared at her, open mouthed, the class in the ring forgotten. "That's—wow."

"Isn't that a little drastic?" I could tell Dan tried to keep the interest out of his voice. "Doesn't Bryce do a good job?"

"Only when he's doing that." Irma pointed toward the arena where horses and handlers were waiting impatiently for the results of their class. "He has the potential to be one of the best handlers in the country, but showing is only one part of this. Bryce is either useless, or simply not there when it's time to work horses, groom, clean stalls or feed."

"Is he supposed to do all those things?" Dan asked.

"All the horses on the ranch are fed by my staff, and my guys do all the cleaning. That way I know it's done right. Bryce is responsible for working, grooming and showing my horses. That's what I pay him for. I let him rent stalls for outside horses. He's supposed to either take care of them or hire someone to do it." Disgust was clear in Irma's voice. "Lately, he either lets Stephanie do it or Susannah."

"Work horses? You?" I squirmed around so I could look over Irma at my daughter. "You don't know how! Besides, what does that mean?"

"Does Bryce pay your salary?" Dan asked Susannah, much more calmly than I had.

She glanced at me, but chose to answer Dan. "Irma does. I'm supposed to keep Irma's records, make out the show entries and do Bryce's billing so he can pay Irma for the stalls he rents from her for the outside horses. Only, I seem to be doing a lot more."

"What is an outside horse," I demanded pretty emphatically, "and what do you do when you work one?"

"It's any horse that doesn't belong to me." Irma answered with more patience than I deserved. "If Chovalo has his way, they'll soon be gone along with Bryce."

"What will Chovalo do if you don't get rid of Bryce?" Dan pressed on.

"He didn't say." Irma shook her head. "Maybe things will sort themselves out if we can just get through the rest of today."

"That could prove interesting." Susannah reluctantly pushed herself out of her seat. "I'd better go see what horses can go home and what we can pack on the van. We've got five horses that are finished. Wes has to come back for the others this afternoon. Surely the rest of the stuff can go then."

"Sounds like refereeing a minor league hockey game would be easier than trying to keep this bunch apart. Good luck." Dan smiled up at her.

"Thanks. There's no doubt I'll need it."

Ribbons had been presented and the class left the ring. A scowling Bryce thrust the colt's lead and a fourth-place ribbon into the hands of a dark-haired boy as he stalked through the gate.

"He takes losing seriously."

"He takes it personally." Irma corrected me with a sigh. "That's part of what makes him good. It's also what makes him so damn difficult. One of the things. Watch. He'll come storming up here, telling me how unfair everything is, the judging, Wes, Chovalo, probably the owner of the next horse he's showing."

"I can hardly wait." Dan eyed Irma a little dubiously.

"You were right. There he is." I'd been watching the mouth of the tunnel. Bryce emerged, letting his scowl fade only when accepting tribute from his admirers. "He's certainly popular."

Bryce made his way toward us, switching his charm on and off.

"Until you get to know him. Then he wears real thin." Irma sighed again. "Chovalo has a point. I'm getting pretty tired of putting up with Bryce's antics."

"Are there new ones?" asked Dan, but I interrupted him.

"Who is that?"

Bryce stopped to talk with a tall, well-built man with softly curling, longish blond hair. He was clean-shaven, dressed in chinos and an expensive polo shirt that showed off evenly muscled and deeply tanned arms. He seemed vaguely familiar, but I couldn't place him.

Both Irma and Dan turned to look.

"Never saw him before." Irma turned away, not interested. "Probably some neophyte horse owner. If he's got any money, Bryce will smell it and have his horse in our barn before the man puts his check book away."

The conversation ended, the stranger headed out of the stands, Bryce spotted us and was on his way.

"Anyone for coffee?" Dan was also on his way. Out. The next class was entering, but his newfound interest in horses didn't seem to come close to his desire to avoid a Bryce Ellis scene.

"Coward," I told him.

He grinned. "Cream and sugar?"

Irma nodded, her attention on the rapidly approaching Bryce.

"Black, but you know that."

Dan grinned again, nodded at Bryce, who scowled deeper at the sight of him, and disappeared at a gallop down the stairs.

Bryce plopped himself into the aisle seat, barely acknowledged me and started on Irma. "Did you see that class? I made that jackass colt look like a million. I should have won. I know I should have. Old Roger is getting senile. Don't you think I should have won?"

"I would have placed it the same way Roger did." Irma's voice was mild, her eyes solidly fastened on the activity in the ring.

Bryce looked a little taken aback, but didn't say anything right away.

"Wes's back at the barn making a mess of everything." There was a pout on his face and in his voice. "He wants to start tearing down, keeps yelling about Linda and his schedule. I have four horses before Challenge goes in and I need everything left just as it is. Besides, if Challenge wins—and he's going to—I thought we could have a party."

"No party." Irma turned to face Bryce. "I mean it, so don't argue." She sighed. "But you're right about not tearing down. Susannah's back at the barn now, seeing what we can send home with the first load of horses. I guess we'd better get back there too. Chovalo and his nephew can't do everything."

Bryce looked a little surprised at the implied suggestion that he might help, but immediately turned smug, as though he had won some important battle.

"I'll wait here for Dan." No one had suggested I do anything else.

Irma nodded. Bryce didn't bother to go that far, only picked up his gloves and whip, tapping them impatiently against his leg before turning to leave.

Dan appeared as Irma stood up. "Here's your coffee."

"Oh. Yes. Thanks." She took the offered white cup and hurried after Bryce.

"What lovely manners that young man has." Dan handed me a cup and settled himself in Irma's vacant chair. "Good. They left the program. Maybe we can figure out what's going on."

"His poor mother." I shook my head. "Did you figure out what's going on here or back there?" I waved in the general direction of the barns.

"We're going to need more than a program to figure that out. I stopped by to see if Susannah needed help. She already had three horses on the van with two more ready. The nephew, Palo? Is worshipping at her feet. Chovalo is nowhere to be seen. Evidently Wes is leaving and will be back sometime after lunch for the rest of the horses and equipment. He threatened general mayhem if everything isn't ready to load when he gets back. Look at these names. Is this Arabic?"

Dan's nose was stuck in the program. He looked from it to the horses in the ring. I felt relieved Susannah seemed to be all right, but felt a little off balance Dan had been the one to think of checking on her.

"So, we're not going back there?"

"Not right yet. We're going to sit here like regular fans and watch the show." His complacency was irritating.

"OK. Then give me that thing." I took the program and started studying the list of horses' names, some clearly Arabic, some English, some a mystifying combination, untranslatable in any language.

"I'm voting for the one called 'Popeye.' At least I can say that."

The next couple of hours were fun, both of us rooting for the horses led in by women, but for different reasons.

"You're a dirty old man."

"Merely human. Besides, I saw you check out that blond kid in the tight green pants."

"I was admiring his horse." I told him that with

dignity. "I noticed you didn't cheer for the fat woman who kept bobbing up and down like a cork."

"Even her horse laughed at her." Before I could respond Irma and Susannah were back, Susannah clutching the required pail.

"We're next," Irma told us unnecessarily. She looked white, her face pinched.

"Here goes nothing." Susannah's face glowed with excitement. "Bryce is so nervous he's almost chewed the fingers out of his gloves."

"How about the horse? Is he nervous too?" Dan chuckled at his little joke.

"Hard to tell." Susannah smiled at him, but it was a nervous kind of smile. "He's feeling something. It's all Chovalo can do to keep all four feet on the ground."

"Chovalo!" I exclaimed. "Shouldn't Bryce have the horse by now?"

"Chovalo will hand him over right outside the gate." Irma's voice was tight. "This damned feud is getting out of hand."

I turned to Susannah, eyebrows raised. Then another thought struck me.

"Where's Stephanie?" I asked that as quietly as I could. "I can't believe she hasn't appeared."

"She's here all right." Irma had overheard me and her tone was grim. "I told her to sit someplace else."

I raised both eyebrows at Susannah.

"Tell you later," she mouthed. "Look. They're getting ready."

A man with a red coat, white trousers and a long horn blowing something you couldn't hear appeared in the center ring. The announcer screamed, "Ladies and Gentlemen, your Region eleven stallion contenders."

The huge gate that barred the way into the arena

opened and the first horse burst out of shadow into sunlight, led by or maybe leading, a somewhat chubby older man running for all he was worth. Horse after horse made its entrance when finally Irma clutched my arm. "There—there they are."

Horse and handler entered the ring, paused for only a fraction of a second, but it was long enough. All eyes were on them, on the elegant deep brown colt with burnished black legs and the equally handsome man by his side. They both seemed aware of the picture they created as they trotted into the ring, the colt with his coal-colored tail over his back, neck arched, nostrils flaring. The man's hair, dark and lustrous, was cut long and blew back like a mane. His long legs kept pace with the horse, the lead line loose, as most others had not been, letting the colt show himself. There was no doubt that this was partnership, the horse taking cues only from the man. They held all eyes as they made their way around the ring, including those of the three judges.

"Leave it to Bryce," I heard Susannah say gleefully, while beside me Irma gave a deep sigh and finally exhaled.

"I've never seen so many beautiful animals. How could anyone possibly choose?" I let out the breath I'd forgotten I was holding as I watched the first horse get ready to make his presentation to the first judge.

Irma's eyes never left the ring. "If you think this is tough, you should see the National Championship. It's in Kentucky this year. Long way to go, but if we qualify, we'll get there. Somehow."

"Explain that again, please." Susannah had spent hours regaling me with horse and horse show information. Sometimes I listened, sometimes I didn't.

"It's a point system, Mom. There are Arabian horses

and shows all over the country and the shows vary in size. To show at the National level you have to win so many points, which you only win by being Champion at a class A show. How many points depends on the number of horses entered. If you win a Regional Championship, or go top five in the class, you're qualified. Trick is, you also have to qualify to show at a Regional show by being a Show Champion."

"That's why all those horses are so wonderful? They're all Champions?"

Susannah nodded.

Dan hadn't taken his eyes off Bryce and the horse, but he'd obviously been listening because now he said, "That's why you were all having such a fit about getting Irma's horse in the Championship class last week? It was so important a little thing like murder didn't stop you?"

"That's why. Aren't you glad we did?" Was there a hint of laughter in Susannah's voice?

Before Dan could answer a voice sounded behind us.

"He looks wonderful, Irma. He's going to show his socks off."

I turned around to see Neil surveying Susannah, not the horses in the ring. She softly smiled back.

"Why Neil, I didn't know you were coming." I acted surprised, but really wasn't. I should have known.

"Managed to get the day off, so I thought I'd come down and drive Susannah home. And watch the class, of course."

The class clearly was of secondary importance. There was a whole lot of testosterone on the loose around here, not all of it in the ring.

I murmured, "How nice."

Dan chuckled. I wasn't amused.

"Look. He's next. Oh, please God, let him show." Irma unclenched her hands and took another bite out of an already ruined cuticle.

We held our breath as horse and handler took up their stance against the rail. Silhouetted only for a moment, it was long enough to capture center stage. They turned together, walked toward the first judge and stopped. Bryce stood back and slowly raised his whip. Just as slowly Challenge raised his neck and arched it, then pricked his ears forward as he tightened his body. As I watched, images of wild horses framed against desert skies, of soaring hawks and windblown trees, of will untamed, obedience a slender thread given, not demanded, swept through my mind. Then horse and handler floated off to the next judge and the moment was gone.

Bryce and Challenge repeated their performance twice more, then retired to the rail where Bryce accepted the congratulations of Challenge's fans, laughing, patting the horse on the neck and ignoring the scowls of the supporters of other horses. The horses were directly opposite us so we got the full effect of their final presentation as the judges made their last walk down the line. Each stopped in front of Challenge, glanced at the card they held and walked on. They paused by other horses, not always the same one, and barely glanced at others. The crowd screamed, whistled and yelled for their favorites, and the tension mounted. After what seemed like hours all three judges handed their cards to the young lady who'd been trailing them. She bounded toward the announcer's stand.

"All horses will be excused," the announcer instructed. "The top five will be called back in numerical order."

"Do you think we have a chance?" Irma got out.

"Twenty-four horses," she almost moaned, "good ones. We don't have a chance. What's his number?"

"Seven sixty-two," Susannah answered.

"Number twenty-seven," the announcer called. The gate opened and a steel-gray horse led by a blond woman dashed in, helped along by screams of triumph from his owners.

"Number one hundred fifty-one," and in came the chestnut Irma had talked about, followed by Number three thirty-three and five seventy-four.

Challenge was the last of the top five to return to the ring. I didn't think Irma was going to make it.

"Oh my God, oh my God," she kept saying. "Top five. In a class like this one. Oh, if only Bud was here to see."

"It's not over yet." Susannah squeezed Irma's arm. "They're going to announce the Champion."

"It can't be us." Irma shook her head emphatically, but hope underlay denial. "Oh, that chestnut is Reserve Champion. Good choice."

She stopped, waiting, not breathing. I knew because I wasn't, either. At last it came. Number 762 "Last Challenge." Unanimous. Bryce leaped into the air, screaming. The horse, startled, reared a little and joined Bryce in the fun by racing him to the trophy.

The stands exploded. At least our area did. Neil let out a piercing whistle that almost ruptured my eardrum. People around us rushed to congratulate Irma, pausing only to clap and cheer as Bryce and Challenge made one last pass around the ring and out the gate, Championship ribbon flying from the horse's halter.

Irma didn't move. She sat staring at the now empty ring saying over and over, "I don't believe it."

"Come on." Susannah tugged at her. "Let's go back to the barn."

It took a while. Every few feet someone else wanted to congratulate her. Those that hadn't stopped us already were waiting back in the barn aisle.

Bryce was in the middle of the crowd, Stephanie hanging from his arm, accepting accolades as gracefully as glee and ego would allow. Palo, looking not scared but petrified, held on to the horse, who didn't seem to share Bryce's feelings about limelight. Even I knew the arched neck and the pawing front foot meant he was running out of patience.

Chovalo appeared and took the lead, patted the horse, whispered something in his ear and started to lead him off.

"Bring that horse back here." Bryce's voice cracked whiplike through the crowd.

"He is finished and he is tired. It is enough for one day." Chovalo's tone was mild, but his eyes weren't.

"The Bracketts want to see him close up. They have a mare they may want to breed. Bring him here so I can stand him up for them."

The crowd got quiet. Everyone within hearing distance was as shocked at Bryce's rudeness as I was. Chovalo hesitated, looked at Irma, who looked back at him imploringly but said nothing. He slowly turned the horse and led him through the murmuring crowd toward Bryce. There was a stillness about Chovalo, about the way he walked, how he handed the lead to Bryce, how he took the horse away when Bryce had finished showing him, that was chilling. Evidently I wasn't the only one who felt it.

"One of these days Bryce is going to go too far. He'll push someone over the edge."

The voice, speaking ominous words in a thoughtful, matter-of-fact tone, belonged to a pleasant-faced young man with sand-colored, thinning hair, wire-rimmed sunglasses, a designer sports shirt and a very expensive watch.

"What?" I looked at him, startled.

"I know Chovalo. Well, I know who he is, and one of these days he'll have Bryce for lunch. If he doesn't, I will."

"Why? How do you know Bryce?" I wondered if bizarre conversations with strangers were normal at horse shows.

"I'm a charter member of the *I Hate Bryce Ellis Club*. See that man there, the one in the plaid shirt, who thinks he's flirting?"

It was impossible to miss him. He was one of several young men surrounding Bryce, the more conservative middle-aged owners and trainers having moved over to group themselves around Irma. The plaid-shirted man wore jeans that left nothing to the imagination and was almost hanging around Bryce's neck, as were the others. Stephanie was trying to work her way back to Bryce's side from outside the circle where somehow she'd been pushed. Bryce wasn't giving her any help.

The man standing next to me looked nothing like the group around Bryce, but now he sighed.

"I guess I'd better go retrieve Tommy before Bryce has him behind the barn doing a couple of lines and enjoying a few other more, shall we say, athletic activities."

"Bryce? Doing what?" I couldn't keep the shock out of my voice.

"You didn't know? I thought everyone did. Boys or girls. As long as they want to play, it's all the same to our Bryce."

"Oh. My." I couldn't immediately think of anything to say. I looked at my companion with sympathy. "Is Tommy your brother?"

"He's my lover. More's the pity," he added grimly, as he left me standing open mouthed and speechless.

"We're going to lunch," Dan said.

I was so intent on watching the little drama play itself out—my nice young man was now tugging at Tommy's arm with little visible success—that I hadn't seen Dan come up beside me and I jumped.

"What's wrong with you?"

"Look." Bryce and his groupies were starting to leave without Stephanie. She stood, arms hanging by her sides, and watched them go, the expression on her face a mixture of despair and confusion. I felt an involuntary moment of pity. Stephanie hadn't known, either. I watched the expression on her face change and harden. Now any pity I had was for Bryce. I hoped no one ever looked after me with the same mix of rage and venom. Stephanie whirled and walked off, almost bumping into the tall blond man I had seen in the stands with Bryce, who was talking to Chovalo. I hadn't noticed him before.

"I know I've seen that man before. What do you suppose he's doing?"

"Talking." Dan barely glanced at him. "They seem to do a lot of that around here."

"They look pretty intense. There." I grabbed his arm. "Chovalo's going off with him. Where do you suppose they're going? Where do you think Stephanie went?"

"To lunch." Dan removed my hand from my elbow and slipped it into his own. "Which is where we'd like to go. We're starved. You coming?"

"All you ever think about is food." I grumbled but let him pull me along.

"You said that before. I only think about food some- times. Other times…"

I was sure there was a faint smile under that damn mustache.

"Yeah." I barely suppressed a laugh. "Other times."

"Maybe we'll have 'other times' tonight, if we get home early enough." Dan glanced down at me.

I could feel a flush start, but before I could say more we had reached Irma, Susannah and Neil, and I was hurried along to the parking lot.

TWENTY-ONE

WE WENT TO a place called LeRoy's. It was tucked into a corner of a shopping center between a lamp store and a resale children's shop. Both closed.

"Why are we going here?" I looked at the dark narrow doorway with trepidation.

"You'll love it," Susannah said.

LeRoy's was huge. It was filled with tables draped with starched white clothes, booths with old red leather benches, a long wooden bar complete with brass rail and people. Lots of people. Most seemed to know Irma and called congratulations as we wound our way to one of the few empty tables. Almost immediately a tired-looking waitress appeared.

"Anything to drink?" She eyed Susannah.

"Mimosas," said Dan.

For a moment Susannah looked hopeful, glanced at me and sighed. "And one orange juice."

Neil already had his driver's license out.

"You having the buffet or you want menus?" the waitress asked, scribbling rapidly on her pad.

"Buffet," Dan answered for us all.

"When you're ready." She jerked her head toward the main room, moved away and was swallowed up by the crowd.

We were ready, but our progress was slow. The buffet was huge, the line long, and I thought Irma knew everyone in it.

Finally, we were back at our table where four mimosas and one orange juice waited.

"A toast." Dan raised his glass high.

"To Last Challenge." Irma raised hers also.

"And to his perceptive breeder." Neil bowed in Irma's direction with a gallantry I hadn't known he possessed. Hmm.

"May this be the first celebration of many," put in Susannah.

"Amen," I said, not to be left out. I noticed as we drank none of us had mentioned Bryce.

"Irma. Good to see you." A tall, imposing-looking man with closely cut black hair heavily threaded with gray stood beside us. Friendly brown eyes covered with plastic-framed glasses sat on a beaklike nose. His light blue polo shirt was tucked into clean, pressed, but not new jeans, a Timex watch was on the wrist of one mahogany-colored arm.

"Hello, Roland. It's been a while."

"It has," the man agreed. "Nice colt you had out there this morning. Is that the one Bud had me come look at a couple of years ago?"

Irma nodded.

"He grew up even better than I thought. Mind if I have a closer look?"

Irma looked awestruck. "Be pleased if you would, Roland."

"I'm on my way back now, and I've got classes later. Is Chovalo at the barn?"

"Far as I know. He never leaves during a show."

"All right if Chovalo pulls him out for me?"

Irma nodded again and swallowed. I couldn't figure out the expression on her face.

"Great. I'll call you, Irma." He patted her lightly on the shoulder, nodded politely to the rest of us and left.

"Was that Roland Moss?" Neil said in reverential tones.

Irma nodded a third time.

"Wow," breathed Susannah.

Dan and I looked at each other. He raised one eyebrow and I shrugged. They were acting like we'd had a visit from God.

"Who is Roland Moss?" voiced Dan.

"And why do we care?" I added.

"He's the best trainer in the business," Susannah said.

"He's the best horseman anywhere." High praise from idealistic Neil. "He knows more about horses than some vets and he never, ever, takes shortcuts. The horse comes first with him."

"He's got the most successful horse business in the country," Irma told us. "He shows and sells horses all over the world. The stallions he stands are the best anywhere, and his band of mares, and the ones he buys for his clients, is the cream. He's made himself a rich man by only dealing in quality. And he wants to see my horse."

Maybe we really had just seen God.

Irma's mood was catching. She chuckled at her omelet, grinned at her shrimp and had another mimosa. Soon we were all making bad jokes, laughing uproariously at them and everything else. The next step was to burst into song. Luckily we finished and left before that happened.

Still wisecracking, we rounded the corner of the barn. Smack in the middle of the aisle stood Irma's big van, side open and ramp down. Beside it was an angry-looking Wes, a dour-looking Chovalo and a terrified-looking Palo.

Wes and Chovalo both turned toward us. Palo scuttled back to the stalls and immediately a tack drape came down.

"Irma, God damn it," Wes blasted, "I've got to get out of here. That kid, Palo, has almost everything packed but those last few panels. Now tell Chovalo to get the horses on here so I can go."

"The equipment is one thing. And the other horses can go." There was no compromise in Chovalo's tone. "But Challenge will not be loaded until Mr. Moss returns."

"Returns? What do you mean, returns?" Alarm bells rang clearly in Irma's voice.

"He came an hour or more ago," Chovalo explained, "to see Challenge. Bryce would not allow me to show him the horse. He made a bad scene, accusing Señor Moss of wanting to show the horse, of wanting the horse for his barn, of trying to steal the horse from him. Señor Moss is a gentleman. He said he would return when Señora Irma was here. But he has classes and his time is short. We will wait."

"No, we won't." Wes's face was almost the same red as his cap. "This Moss guy isn't the only one whose time is valuable. I've got a schedule and I'm already behind."

"Where is Bryce?" Irma was no longer laughing. From the expression on her face Bryce wouldn't be either when she found him.

Chovalo shrugged. Wes declared, "Haven't seen the little creep since I got back."

"Who's that?" Susannah suddenly interrupted. "I've never seen that horse before."

The last curtain had fallen, exposing a row of heads

watching us with interest. Susannah pointed toward a light gray one. The horse looked at us over an open-top stall door. A bright green tack trunk with no initial or farm name sat under it

"She's going to Indiana. If I can ever get out of Santa Barbara," Wes snarled at Susannah.

"That isn't our tack trunk."

"It's hers."

"Since when does a horse have a tack trunk?"

"The people who bought her own the trunk," Wes snarled again at Susannah, seemingly happy to transfer his frustration to someone other than Chovalo. "They wanted a place to put her blankets and halters so they wouldn't get lost during the trip or mixed up with some other horse's stuff. I said it'd be all right to take it on the van. If, of course, that's all right with you?"

The sarcasm was sharp and Susannah looked like she'd been slapped. My reaction was to take a swing at Wes. Evidently Dan felt the same way because his voice was tightly controlled as he stepped a little in front of me.

"There's no need to talk to her that way…"

He never finished. Neil, who none of us had noticed was missing, returned, ashen-faced and stumbling over his words.

"Dan, we, ah, have a problem."

"What kind of problem?" Dan still watched Wes, not ready to let go.

"A, ah, problem. A real problem. You better come right away."

"What's the matter with you?" Susannah looked at him suspiciously, attention temporarily diverted from Wes.

"Nothing. Dan, come on. The rest of you stay here."

"Right." Dan glanced at Wes once more as if reluctant to let him go, but there was something in Neil's tone... Dan started to follow him. "All of you, don't move until I get back."

This seemed to be directed mostly at Susannah and me. So naturally we followed. The sounds of sirens mingled with the resumed argument around the horse van. Susannah and I looked at each other and hurried faster. We rounded a corner in time to see Dan and Neil disappear through a door.

"We can't go in there." Susannah skidded to a halt. "That's the Men's."

"I think we have more here than a call to nature. Shall we?"

Susannah looked up at the sign then at me and smiled a little sheepishly.

"After you."

We entered the bathroom to see Neil and Dan standing close together, looking through the door leading to a shower room. A black-haired boy of about sixteen, clutching a towel and clean clothes, pushed as close to the wall and as far away from the shower door as he could get.

A portly older man hurried in, bumping into me where I had stopped. "Hey, you can't come in here. This is the Men's."

"Are you sure?" Susannah asked him in her most innocent tone. The man rushed out, looked at the sign on the door and stormed back in.

"Yes. You can't come in here." He made little shooing motions at us with his hands.

"Neither can you." Dan straightened up. He gave the two of us a sour look but addressed the man. "There's been an accident. You'll have to leave."

"But I have to, uh, go, uh, now," babbled the man.

"Use the Ladies'," Dan replied heartlessly.

The sirens got closer.

"Use the…I can't do that."

"Then go find a bush," Dan said unkindly. "I'm securing this area."

"How about him?" The man, who just didn't know when to quit, pointed to the kid still trying to melt into the concrete wall.

"He's a witness."

Susannah slipped around Dan and stood beside Neil, who was too late to prevent her seeing into the shower room.

"Oh, God," she gagged. "It's Bryce."

"Get out." Dan pointed at the man. He fled.

"Don't move." He aimed that at the trembling kid, who probably couldn't.

I'd used the moment to grab my daughter and see the body on the shower floor. It was Bryce all right, one eye bloodied, a bruise the size of Nebraska on the same side of his face. But it wasn't the bruises that had killed him. Bryce wore a thin length of chain tightly wound around his neck, the links digging into his tanned throat. Beautiful Bryce was beautiful no longer.

Sirens died and doors slammed.

"Get Susannah out of here," Dan instructed Neil, "and don't touch anything on your way out. Ellie." He stopped, sighed and shook his head. "How you get me into these things I'll never figure out."

"Me!" I started indignantly, but now was clearly not the time. The first of a parade of men entered the bathroom and Dan resumed his cop exterior.

"Who are these people?" the uniformed officer asked, studying Dan's ID.

"Sightseers," Dan returned. "They'll be over at Barn D when we need them." He pointed to the door. "Get!"

We got.

I followed Neil and Susannah back toward Barn D. I'd only been to two horse shows and had stumbled over a dead body each time. That made my average for involvement in murder one hundred percent. I wondered how I went about trading it in for a minus zero.

TWENTY-TWO

CHOVALO LED THE gray mare up the ramp into the van as we approached the barn. Palo stood beside the open door, determinedly holding on to the skittish colt Bryce had shown early in the morning. Susannah looked at it, shuddered and headed for a deck chair.

"What happened?" Irma appeared in front of us, anxiety deepening the wrinkles around her eyes. "Where's Dan? What are those sirens?" Then a small pause. "Where's Bryce?"

"Shit." Susannah flung back her head against the chair and closed her eyes.

Neil and I both glanced at her, him with surprise, me with sympathy. We turned back to Irma.

"Here, sit here." Neil gently pulled Irma toward the chair next to Susannah.

"Oh, God." She moaned as she sunk into it. "Something has happened. What? Where's Bryce? Is he hurt?"

Chovalo came out of the van and walked toward us. Wes also suddenly appeared.

"What's going on here?" Wes demanded. "Look, I've got to get going. Irma, if you want your colt to get home without hitch-hiking, then tell this fellow here," he stuck his finger almost in Chovalo's chest, "to get him loaded."

"Something's happened to Bryce," Irma moaned.

"Yeah? Well, it couldn't happen to a nicer guy."

Wes's sarcasm went unremarked. "Come on, Irma, make up your mind 'cause I'm pulling out of here."

"What has happened?" Chovalo's tone was soft, but his eyes were wary.

"He's dead," Neil stated.

"Oh, oh no," Irma cried.

"Dead," repeated Chovalo.

"So the kid finally took too much," Wes commented coldly. "Figured it was just a matter of time."

"Is that how he died?" Chovalo had the taut look of an animal that scented danger.

"No." Neil looked at Wes with obvious distaste. "Someone beat him up, then strangled him with a chain. I think it's a cross tie chain." He looked over at Chovalo, who looked quickly toward the curtains that hid the grooming room. He looked back just as quickly.

"Dear God." Irma's face took on a gray tinge, which was better than Susannah's light green one.

"That's too bad, but the little…" Wes paused and left out a word after glancing down at Irma, "kept asking for it. Irma, it doesn't change things. I've got to get out of here."

Susannah's color, I was happy to see, had returned to normal although she still hadn't opened her eyes, even at Wes's insensitive remark. Neil looked at him horrified, and Chovalo studied him with an expression I couldn't read. Before anyone could respond to him, Roland Moss joined us. He nodded politely to all of us as he addressed Irma. "What's going on over by the Men's? Has there been an accident? No horses hurt I hope."

"Worse. Much worse," Neil said. He hadn't taken his eyes off Susannah.

"It's Bryce." Irma's eyes were finally starting to tear. I found a clean tissue and handed it to her.

"Bryce? He didn't take an overdose!"

Bryce's habit seemed to be common knowledge.

"That woulda been no surprise." Wes's acknowledging the fact somehow made it even more tragic.

"Someone murdered him." Neil's voice sounded slightly faint. "Beat him to a pulp, then strangled him."

"With a chain." Susannah's didn't. Her eyes were open again, but still registered the aftermath of shock. Not grief. The beginnings of anger, but not grief. Bryce hadn't left much of a legacy.

"Dead? Murdered?" Moss involuntarily turned to look up the barn aisle although the bathroom and the police cars weren't visible. What could be seen was the white van of the local TV station headed that way, followed by the curious, on foot and on horseback.

Chovalo's tone was urgent. "Irma. Señor Moss must take Last Challenge."

"What?" Irma dabbed her eyes with the tissue.

"You wish him in your barn, no?" Chovalo's eyes were like lasers on Moss's face. Moss stared back at Chovalo with, what? Consternation? Confusion? Sympathy?

"Yes, I'll take the colt if Irma wants to send him."

"You will take him now? Here? From the show?" Chovalo pressed.

"If that is what Irma wants." Moss studied Chovalo with an odd expression.

"Señora Irma. He must go." Chovalo's voice was soft, but there was iron in it.

"If Roland really wants him, of course." Irma was in no shape to make a decision and neither man really waited for it.

"Have your boy bring him to my barn," Moss instructed. "I'll make the arrangements. Irma, I'll call you tomorrow and we'll get the details sorted out." He turned to go, paused, turned back. "I'm sorry." Irma nodded, but I could have sworn he was speaking to Chovalo.

I watched him leave, wondering if I was right and what Moss could have meant, when I caught sight of a tall, blond man. He stood at the end of the barn aisle watching us, not the sideshow going on the other way. It was the same blond man I'd seen talking to Bryce, the same man who had been talking to Chovalo. If he was just another curiosity seeker, why wasn't he gathered with the others behind the yellow crime scene tape, trading theories and gossip? He moved aside to let Moss pass and the bright afternoon sun poured over him, obscuring his features, leaving only an outline and instantly I knew. It was my pirate.

I looked again, not believing my own senses. It was undeniably my pirate. Without a mustache, boots or a pistol and mercifully, without parrots. But still, my pirate. Why? What was he doing here?

The roar of a diesel engine made me whirl back toward our little group. Wes was in the cab; Neil tested the latch on the side door. Chovalo was nowhere to be seen.

"What are you doing?" I was under Wes's open window, pounding on his cab door.

"Leaving." He fiddled with something and barely acknowledged me.

"You can't leave. The police will need to talk to you."

"They know where to find me. Besides, I got nothing to tell them."

"Of course you do. You were one of the last ones to see Bryce alive."

"Not me. The little shit had already stomped off

before I got back here. Now get back. I got a schedule and I'm keeping it."

The engine roared, the van slowly moved down the barn aisle and maneuvered the corner. We all watched it go, including the pirate. He moved over into the shadow of the neighboring barn where he stayed until the van disappeared, then slipped around the corner and was gone.

I was still standing in the middle of the aisle, seething with frustration, when Dan charged up.

"Where the hell does he think he's going?"

Why were those kinds of remarks always addressed to me?

"Back to Santa Louisa. He's got a schedule." I made a huge effort to unclench my fists and keep my voice neutral.

"Why didn't you stop him?"

"Short of throwing myself in front of the van, there didn't seem to be a way."

"God damn it. There's a whole raft of questions he needs to answer."

Dan glared at me. I glared back. He transferred his glare to the others, who were not paying any attention and finally favored Chovalo, who appeared leading Last Challenge.

"Where are you going with that horse?"

"Señor Roland Moss is taking him. I am delivering him to his barn." It amused me that Chovalo could match Dan's curtness.

"Where's the kid?"

"On the van. With the horses." Chovalo hadn't even broken stride.

"What!" yelped Dan. "Don't you people understand there's been a murder here? That the police need to ask questions?" He glared at Chovalo, rage reaching the boiling point. "Material witnesses are supposed to stick around!"

Chovalo shrugged. "Palo will be needed at home. Horses do not care for themselves." He purposefully rounded the corner of the barn.

"For heaven's sake, Dan." I was getting a little tired of the whole scene and my head had started to throb. "Just call one of your people and have them meet the van and ask all your questions there."

"I don't think you understand, Ellie." Dan's voice had quieted, but I could tell he was still seething. "This isn't my case. This isn't my town. This isn't even my county. I can't do anything until I'm invited and so far that hasn't happened."

Frustration as well as fury saturated every word. I could hardly blame him. This might not be Dan's town, but it was still very much his case. Bryce Ellis had been talented at bringing out the best in horses, but he'd been even more talented in bringing out the worst in people. There seemed little doubt that his murder was connected to Rusty's. The same cast was assembled. Or was it? Where was Stephanie? I started to ask, but anyone who might know was gone. Poor Stephanie, this was going to be a terrible shock. Only, I couldn't erase the memory of her face as she'd watched Bryce leave with his groupies. Maybe Stephanie already knew.

I started to say something to Dan when Irma walked up.

"I'm going home. I don't think I can stand any more of this. Susannah, are you coming with me or going home with Neil?" She was looking around somewhat uncertainly, opened her purse and rummaged in the bottom.

"I can't seem to find my keys." Irma's voice trailed away. She looked up to find Dan looking down at her.

"No, Irma, I don't think so," Dan told her gently. "Not you, not Susannah, not Neil, not any of us. Someone will be here any minute to start asking questions. I told the Santa Barbara police we'd all be here to answer them. I intend to keep what I can of that promise."

Stillness settled over us. Irma stared at Dan, Susannah and Neil glanced at me, then at each other. The sounds of the fairgrounds became very loud. "Class One Forty-four, Native Costume, the class in front of you is lining up," screamed the loudspeaker. Cheers went up in the arena. Across the barn aisle someone wailed, "Where's my number? Hurry, I'm going to miss my class." A dog barked, a horse snorted, a hose squirted into an empty bucket. Several people passed us, their voices hushed, curious glances quickly averted, feet kicked up dust and straw as they hurried away. None of us said a word, but we all watched as two men rounded the end of the barn, two men in suits, not jeans, who looked slightly nervous as they skirted moving horses. They pulled out notebooks as they approached us, offered badges for inspection and obviously expected answers to their questions. It would be a while before home saw any of us.

I looked past them to the end of the barn aisle, trying to see if Chovalo had returned. He hadn't. But my pirate had. He stood in the shadow, intently watching the suited police descend on us. Then, as they stopped in front of Irma, he turned and quietly melted away.

TWENTY-THREE

THE TWO SANTA Barbara policemen were polite, asking only general questions. They cautioned us to stay put, as they would need us again. Dan did a creditable job of holding his frustration in check.

They had been gone just a few minutes when Stephanie showed up. She reacted stony-faced to the news. Her only comment was "good riddance to bad rubbish."

Had she seen Bryce after he returned from lunch? Dan asked.

"Yes. I blasted him. He was a hateful, deceitful, lying person. I'm not sorry he's dead."

Dan looked at her a moment, a little taken aback by the venom in her voice. "Was Chovalo here?"

"No. No one was. If you think I did it, you're wrong. Not that I wouldn't have if I'd thought of it. I told him what a piece of shit he was, said I was moving my horses and left. Wes saw me go."

"Wes?" Susannah asked. She looked at Stephanie as if she was something she didn't want to touch.

"He was pulling his rig up." Stephanie sounded impatient, but I saw a shiver run through her. "How long do we have to stay here? I don't feel like answering a bunch of stupid questions."

"Questions about murder are rarely stupid." Dan was having a hard time keeping his temper.

"I'd better call my parents to come get me," Stephanie said. Her defiance looked like it might crack for a second, but she tightened her jaw, raised her chin and went on. "I came down with Bryce. Obviously, I'm not going home that way."

"Tell them to meet you at the Santa Barbara police station." I was sure Dan noted the tiny break the comment made in her determined stride, but she kept going toward the bank of pay phones. "Tell them not to hurry," Dan called after her. "You'll be a while."

Dan and I took her to the police station. The entire time in the car, and later, while we waited to answer more questions and give statements, she alternated between sullen silence and loud diatribes against Bryce. We were grateful when her grim-faced father and tearful mother arrived. We had all been sitting on hard chairs, waiting our turns, for what seemed like a lifetime. Stephanie wasn't helping already ragged nervous systems to remain calm.

Mr. and Mrs. Knudsen acknowledged our existence with the briefest of nods and then dragged Stephanie as far across the room as possible. Her father appeared to be giving her a more thorough third degree than the police, while her mother cried, silently but continuously.

Finally, she was allowed to go home. Her expression hadn't changed in the hours we'd spent. If I'd been her mother I would have been frantic with worry. The iron emotional grip Stephanie had on herself wouldn't last and when it cracked, Stephanie, and everyone around her, was in for an even worse time. I had to wonder if learning of Bryce's expanded sexual tastes was responsible, or if she wrestled with guilt of her own. Had Stephanie murdered Bryce because he betrayed and humiliated her? Had she murdered Rusty because she thought she was protecting Bryce? I would have given a lot to know the questions the police asked her and what answers she'd offered. Dan had finally been invited to sit in. I'd do a little questioning of my own on the way home.

It was only minutes after Stephanie and her parents left that Dan appeared with the news that the police had arrested Chovalo.

Irma almost collapsed. "That's not possible" was all she said. Then she seemed to crumple in her chair, exhausted.

"Did he confess?" Neil asked anxiously.

"No. As a matter of fact he keeps saying he never saw Bryce again after he left the barn."

"When did Chovalo leave the barn?" Susannah looked as wrung out as Irma. I probably didn't look any better, but I had no desire to check.

"Right after Roland Moss left the first time. Bryce made his big scene about Moss wanting the colt in his barn because he knew the horse could be a National Champion. That was when Moss told Chovalo he'd come back when Irma," Dan nodded toward her, "returned, and he left again. Bryce started screaming Chovalo was trying to undermine him. By then Chovalo'd had a belly full and told Bryce what he thought of him, which was not very flattering. He walked away, leaving Bryce standing there."

"What happened then?" Neil asked.

"According to Chovalo, nothing. He never saw Bryce again."

"So they had an argument. It seems to me Bryce fought with half the people on the show grounds and kissed up the other half. Why pick on Chovalo?" It seemed to me pretty thin evidence for an arrest.

"Because Moss saw Chovalo coming out of the men's

bathroom about fifteen minutes or so before we got back from lunch. It fits with the time Bryce died."

There was nothing more to say. Finally, a gray-faced Irma, choking back tears, asked, "Now what?"

"I know you'll want to do everything you can to help Chovalo, Irma, so I've called an attorney friend of mine." Dan squatted down beside her chair so he could look directly at her. His voice was calm and low. "He'll be down in the morning for the arraignment and he'll try to get bail set. The DA wants to go for murder one, but they're going to need a lot more than they've got now to make it stick."

Irma gasped and Susannah, looking not much less stricken, was by her side. Neil watched, grim-faced. "Irma's in no shape to drive home."

"Right," agreed Dan. He got to his feet. "Home is where she needs to be, though. It's where we all need to be. Irma, give me your keys. Which one is the car key?" Dan fumbled with the ring Irma obediently handed him, extracted one and handed the ring back to her.

"You kids take her home. I'll make arrangements to get her car back tomorrow. Get going. Ellie and I will be right behind you. Or, would you rather go with them?" He touched me on the arm. "It'll be another few minutes before I start, and you look pretty beat."

"I'll go with you." I didn't think he looked so great himself, and there was no way I was letting him make the drive home alone. Besides, I had some questions I wanted to ask Police Chief Dan Dunham. Where better than in a nice closed car with no interruptions.

TWENTY-FOUR

We were in the car, finally headed north. We had made a quick detour through McDonald's and neither of us spoke while we'd devoured Big Macs and fries. I stuffed the last greasy paper into the sack and began.

"OK. Chovalo went to the bathroom. People do. Wasn't there someone in there, someone who saw him come in? Or leave?"

I snapped back the lip on the plastic lid of Dan's coffee and watched the steam rise. "You can't drink this yet. How do you suppose they get this stuff so hot?"

"They boil it. At least it tastes that way. Stick it in that tray thing until it cools."

"About Chovalo." I deposited both coffees in the tray and turned as much toward him as my seat belt would allow.

"He says no one was in there, that he was only in there a couple of minutes and never went near the shower room door, which was closed."

"He could be telling the truth."

"He could. On the other hand, the chain around Bryce's neck was the twin of the one in that—what do they call it—the room where they get the horses fixed up."

"The grooming room."

"Whatever." Dan plainly didn't care what you called the room. "Anyway, there should have been two chains in there, but there wasn't. Another thing…"

I groaned and let my head drop back against the seat.

"Well, if you don't want to hear."

"Of course I want to hear." I sat up again. "I don't expect to like it, but I want to hear."

"We found a plastic bag of meth. The late Mr. Ellis had about a half ounce, unopened, which is quite a lot. From the way he'd been acting, his tantrum in front of Moss, his paranoia about how everyone was out to get him, his hyper-activity, he probably needed it bad. The shower fits. Nice and private."

"What else?"

"I told you we think meth is being pipelined somehow through these horse shows. Most likely theory is that Chovalo's an important part of that pipeline and agreed to sell to Bryce because he was afraid of pretty boy's mouth. Got him in the shower and either lost his temper, or because of the chain, had already decided it was time for the unlamented Mr. Ellis to leave, permanently."

"Why didn't he take back the drugs?"

"Good question. Maybe he heard someone coming."

"All this is theory, right? Can't you test for finger-prints or something?"

"Every lab test known to man and the Santa Barbara police department is currently being done, never fear."

Dan yawned and I handed him his coffee.

"Yipes." He handed it right back. "This stuff is still too hot. We'll be home before it cools off."

"It woke you up."

"And left blisters."

I tested my own, which, for some reason, was per-fect, and handed it to him. "Here. Dan, something strange happened."

"The whole damn day was strange. Ellie, do you mind if I take the pass? It'll cut off a half hour at least."

I did. The San Marcos Pass was famous for accidents. At least during the day you could see who was running into you, but I gulped a little and said, "Of course not."

I waited until we had started up the first steep grade before I continued.

"Dan, I saw the pirate again."

"What pirate? Look at that idiot. Wouldn't you think he could turn his brights off?"

"Dan, listen. The pirate from the fair. The one who was snooping around Irma's barn. Remember?"

"I remember." He gripped the wheel, staring intently into the darkness. "Can you take this?" He handed me his empty cup.

"Sure. Dan, the pirate was there today. Hanging around the barn again. I saw him."

"I didn't, and he'd be hard to miss."

"He didn't have his pirate stuff on." I tried not to be miffed. "Remember the blond man talking to Bryce in the stands this morning? That was him. He was also the man talking to Chovalo. Remember? They walked off together, right before you dragged me off to lunch. And listen to this. He was there when the police arrived!"

"Where?"

"Right by the Men's. Well, standing, watching the bathroom."

"So were several hundred others. What else was he doing?"

"Watching Wes leave."

"Did you see him go into the bathroom? Or into any of the stalls? Or into the—what did you call it?—grooming room?" Dan briefly took his eyes off the road to look at me.

"No, but..."

"Ellie, you saw a man who was doing the same thing everyone else on the grounds was doing. Looking at horses, talking to trainers and gawking at the police."

"It was the pirate. Listen, Dan. There's more." I took a deep breath. I didn't think Dan was going to like the fact I had been doing a little investigating on my own, but he needed to know about the pirate, and he needed to know now. "I talked to Becky Monahan. She's on the fair board."

"I know that." Dan's tone was guarded.

"She says the pirate wasn't hired by the fair. They don't know anything about him, where he came from, who he is, nothing. Coupled with the fact he was hanging around Irma's barn all day today, don't you think that means something?"

"Why didn't you recognize him this morning? If it really was the same guy, where was his mustache? That was quite a mustache." Dan ran his finger over his short, tidy one.

"Oh."

"Oh, what?"

"The mustache. It was gone."

"A mustache like that takes a long time." Dan said that with what sounded like a touch of envy. "Ellie, I don't think he was your pirate. I know you don't want to cast Chovalo as a murderer, but I don't think this guy is going to make it as a substitute."

I didn't say any more, but I knew the man was my pirate and he fit somewhere. I was afraid I knew where. He'd been talking to Chovalo, they'd walked off together and I'd be willing to bet they hadn't gone to lunch. He'd been talking to Bryce too. My theory about the pirate being some kind of contact was starting to make even more sense. But if I convinced Dan, it would only look worse for Chovalo, wouldn't it? Unless, of course, the pirate killed Bryce.

This was one maze I wasn't going to work my way out of tonight. I was too tired, but there was one more question I had to ask.

"What about Stephanie?"

"What about her?"

"What did she say? I've never seen anyone look like she did when Bryce walked off and left her. I don't think Stephanie takes kindly to rejection or humiliation. Why isn't she a suspect?"

Dan glanced over at me. "There's no evidence. Plenty of motive, but no one saw her anywhere near the men's bathroom. That is something you would notice."

"Then the Santa Barbara police did ask?"

"They're probably still asking. Right now everything points to Chovalo and nothing away from him."

We were both quiet the rest of the way. I was asleep when we pulled up in front of my house.

"Wake up, Ellie," Dan said. "We're here."

The porch light was on, so were the lights in the front room, but there was no sign of Neil's truck.

"Don't let Susannah go to the barn tomorrow." Dan spoke quietly, looking at the lighted windows. "I think she's stretched loyalty to its limits." He reached for me and gently, but definitely, kissed me. I was just getting into kissing him back when he let me go, reached over and opened my door and gave me a small shove.

"Aren't you coming in?" I asked with marginal enthusiasm.

"No." He smiled faintly. "You're beat and so am I. I'll call you tomorrow."

I watched his car until it turned the corner, then headed for the front door, thinking you should only have mixed emotions when you weren't too tired to untangle them.

Susannah stood in the living room, freshly showered, in my best long nightgown. There was a mug of tea in her hand. "You look beat." She waved her mug toward me. "Want some?"

I looked at the nightgown, started to say something, thought about the old tee shirts she usually slept in, decided this was something symbolic that was way over my exhausted head and nodded yes.

"Tea sounds wonderful. Only, I'm adding a little something." I headed for the kitchen.

She trailed along behind me, watched as I added brandy to my mug, looked down at her own and sighed.

"I don't suppose…" She sighed again.

I looked at her and did a little sighing of my own. I motioned toward her mug, she held it out and I poured.

Somewhere around three o'clock I turned over, pushed Jake off my legs and woke up just enough to realize I had thoughts. I sat straight up in bed. Someone had said something. Who? What? I couldn't remember. But sometime yesterday, during that horrible ordeal, someone said something that didn't make sense. Or didn't—what? It was important. I knew that. Whatever it was, it was buried under exhaustion. I flopped back down on my pillow. I'd remember it in the morning, I assured myself. When I was fresh, rested and back to normal. Only, I didn't.

TWENTY-FIVE

THE CLOCK RADIO clicked on at seven the next morning, ready to regale me with the latest in national disasters. There are plenty of local ones, I thought, I don't need more. I turned it off, thought about pulling the covers back over my head, but climbed out of bed instead. I had a nine o'clock appointment and hoped I'd be awake enough to listen to my clients.

Susannah informed me, as she sat on the closed toilet seat watching me struggle with eye makeup, that she had already called Irma.

"Irma says don't bother to come. She's not going near the barn. The office phone is on the answering machine. Palo will feed and clean, along with the rest of her guys, and she's going to stay in bed with a large brandy and a headache. Actually, she's waiting to hear from the attorney Dan called. I heard Maria Rosa's voice in the background. I'm sure Irma is doing whatever it is you do about bail."

"What are you planning to do?" I watched her in the mirror. The thought of Susannah on the loose all day in this restless mood was, to say the least, unsettling.

"Iron," she said morosely.

I couldn't help it. I burst out laughing, which caused me to apply a large swatch of green eye shadow exactly where it was not supposed to go.

"Damn. Look what you made me do." I reached for the Q-tips.

"You shouldn't laugh. I might, you know."

When pigs fly, I thought, but said instead, "There's plenty in the basket. Any other thoughts?"

"Maybe I'll go visit Aunt Mary. Or go see Dr. Bennington. See what that job is all about."

I heaved a sigh of relief, but silently, of course, and hurried off to work, leaving Susannah thumbing thoughtfully through cookbooks. I had just enough time to hope she wouldn't try anything too elaborate, actually that she wouldn't try anything at all, before I was plunged into the usual Monday chaos.

The day passed quickly with only brief breaks. My young couple's offer had been accepted. I had inspections to order, escrow to open and the lender to talk with. There was an offer on another of my listings sitting on my desk, my client lived out of town, and I had a terrible time tracking him down to present it. Between phone calls I wondered if Chovalo had made bail, if Stephanie still maintained that frightening composure and if the police continued to question her. While I stood in line for a takeout salad I wondered if Wes had started his cross-country run on time, if Linda had pulled the financial information for purchasing the business off her miraculous computer and if Irma was in any shape to care. I spent valuable minutes I should have used preparing for a listing appointment wondering if I should call Becky about that blasted pirate, as well as trying to remember whatever it was I thought I forgot last night. Maybe it wasn't important after all. The phone did not stay silent, but it answered none of my questions.

It was after six before I finally made it home. The kitchen looked undamaged, I noted with relief, as I headed upstairs to shed my panty hose for something less barbaric.

"Hi." Susannah's voice was muffled by the tee shirt I pulled over my head, but I still picked up the slight tone of depression. "I brought you this."

She held a glass of white wine in one hand, a can of Coke in the other. I reached for the wine.

"Thanks. It's been quite a day. How was yours?" I asked cautiously.

"So, so. Let's go sit on the porch."

"Good thinking." Wicker rockers, the mild early summer twilight and not starting dinner right away sounded great.

"Busy day?" Susannah started.

"Hmm. Hectic. Mondays always are. Every weekend holds at least one crisis." How true it had been for this past one. "What did you do?"

"I spent most of the morning with Aunt Mary. She's wonderful, isn't she? You can tell her anything. How come we never came here when I was growing up? Grandma and Grandpa always came to us, and not that often."

"Because your father wasn't—isn't a fan of small towns. Or large family gatherings. They give him claustrophobia. What else did you do?"

"Decided I don't want to be a small-animal vet."

"I didn't know it was on the list," I replied, startled.

Susannah had a "there's lots of things you don't know" look on her face, so I hastily abandoned that line and instead asked, "Have you talked to Irma?"

"No." Her voice radiated gloom. "I tried a couple of times but I got the machine. I haven't talked to Neil, either. Bryce was all over the afternoon news, but there was nothing we don't already know."

I took a sip of wine. Susannah contemplated her Coke.

"Have you heard how Stephanie's doing?"

"No. And I don't care. Bryce was pretty bad, but the way she behaved yesterday made him look like a saint."

She raised her Coke can, paused and put it back down. "Mom, even if Chovalo gets to come home, what happens now? What does Dan say?"

"I haven't heard from Dan. I don't know any more than you do." Gloom colored my tone also. I could hear it, but couldn't seem to erase it.

"Can I ask you something?" Susannah said. There was a hesitation in her voice that surprised me.

"Of course. Ask away."

"Are you and Dan going to get married?"

Now there was a conversation stopper. When I could speak again, I said, "Whatever gave you that idea?"

"He's crazy about you. I think you love him too." She paused, stole a look at me, rocked a little harder and studied the oak tree across the street. "I don't mind." She paused and stole a look at me out of the corner of her eye. "I know what Dad was like and Dan, well, Dan's a good guy."

I had to say something but I had no idea what. "He hasn't asked me."

"He will."

She was probably right, but there hadn't been time for the serious conversation I had planned to have with myself, so what my answer would be, how I wanted my happy ending to read, I had no clue.

"Yeah," I finally said, hoping to close the subject. "Guess I should see about getting us some dinner." I twirled my empty glass, but didn't move.

"You know what I feel like?" Susannah slowed her rocker down almost to a stop.

"No. What?" After that last bombshell, it could be almost anything.

"Barbecue. Chicken. Or maybe pork ribs. Cole slaw. Deep-fried onion rings. And mud pie."

An idea I wasn't expecting. But she was right. Absolutely right. A good dose of well-cooked comfort was what we both needed.

"Smitty's?" I ventured.

She looked over at me and a slow smile formed, probably the first one all day.

"Smitty's."

TWENTY-SIX

I WAS PRETTY sure I waddled as we left Smitty's. Even though I had ordered the small chicken plate, the beans, corn on the cob, garlic bread and bites of Susannah's mud pie had severely damaged the diet I kept meaning to start. Maybe I'd walk home. It was only a few blocks and Susannah could bring the car. Her jeans didn't look tight.

I stood on the sidewalk, breathing in the jasmine-scented night air, watching the stars tune up for their nightly performance, and thought about walking home, when I saw him.

"Susannah, look."

"At what?"

"At the man getting into that blue car. That's the pirate."

"Pirate? The one you think…"

"The same. What's he doing here?"

"I don't know." She stared at him. "Having dinner somewhere? Do you think Dan saw him?"

Smitty's was on the street behind the police station, but I didn't think that mattered.

"Dan could have sat next to him and he wouldn't have noticed," I said, a little bitterly. "He's convinced that pirate has nothing to do with any of this mess. But he does."

The driver's door closed behind the pirate, his engine started, his lights flashed on.

"Come on, hurry." I grabbed Susannah by the arm and pushed her toward our car. "Get in. Hurry up."

I had the car started and had pulled out onto Main Street when Susannah asked, "Are we doing what I think we're doing?"

"If you mean are we following him, yes."

"Why?"

"Because."

"That makes sense."

"Look. Every time something happens that man is there, every time there's been a murder, he's there. That's a little too much coincidence for me even if Dan doesn't think so. Or pretends not to. Somehow he's right in the middle of all this, and absolutely nobody is paying any attention."

"You think this guy is some kind of arch-criminal, maybe masterminding a drug ring, and we're going to play Nancy Drew and follow him. What happens if we catch him?"

"Don't be so melodramatic. We're only going to see where he goes. Then we'll tell Dan."

"Uh huh. Well, it beats re-runs. Do you see him?"

By now we were out of town and on dark country roads. I could see the bright beams ahead of me and dropped back as much as I dared.

"This is the way to Irma's." Susannah sat up straighter. "If he makes that turn coming up...he turned. Speed up."

"No. I don't want him to know we're following. We'll see his headlights if he turns into Irma's driveway. But why would he go there?"

"I don't know. I don't like this. Did he turn? I can't see any lights."

Neither could I. We were at the mouth of Irma's long

driveway, the large trailer barn a black shadow, Irma's house and horse barns invisible. The only light was a faint blue glow behind the drawn shade in Wes and Linda's mobile home.

"Where did he go?" whispered Susannah.

"I've no idea." I stared down the drive, mystified. "Do you see any light?"

"No," Susannah whispered again, leaning against the dash to peer out the front window. "He has to be somewhere."

"Why are you whispering? He's not lurking outside our window."

She gave a little nervous laugh and resumed her normal voice. "I wouldn't count on it. Now what?"

"I don't know. Maybe we should go back to town and…"

Susannah grabbed my arm. "Look. There. Aren't those headlights?"

The soft glow that suddenly appeared could have been headlights flickering in the direction of Irma's barn.

"No one should be back there now. Come on, Mom. Drive down there."

I hesitated. We really had no business here, but I wanted to know where the car had gone. Besides, Irma was a friend.

"Lock your door." I turned down the drive.

We approached Irma's barn when a pickup truck with two men appeared briefly in our lights, startling me so much I almost ran off the road.

"Oh!" Susannah twisted around to watch their taillights rapidly disappear. "Who was that?"

"I don't know, but I'll bet they were the source of the headlights we saw."

I kept going. Only my lights pierced the darkness, picking out the closed barn doors and the by now familiar shape of a large horse van parked in front of it. I came to a stop by the barn, but left the engine running.

"Where do you suppose the pirate went?"

I shrugged. "Who do you think those men who almost ran us off the road were?"

"Beats me." Uncertainty was in her voice as she peered out the window. She turned toward Irma's house, but like everything else it showed no light.

"Now what?" I asked.

Before she could reply a hand tapped on my window and someone tried the door. Susannah screamed. My breath caught in my throat, my foot jerked, the engine roared, coughed and died.

"Hey. What are you doing here?"

"It's Wes." Susannah slumped with relief. "Roll down your window."

I did, but not with enthusiasm.

"What are you two doing here?"

"I, ah, left something. Mom drove me out to get it," Susannah lied. "Who was that just drove out of here? Where are the yard lights?"

"Those guys? They came to talk to me. About a job."

"A little late for a job interview," I commented. I wasn't feeling too charitable about being startled.

"When you work days, nights are all you got left," Wes said, oh so patronizingly. I could have slugged him.

"Why aren't the yard lights on?" repeated Susannah.

Wes shrugged. "No idea. They weren't on when I got down here. What difference does it make?"

"They're supposed to be on," Susannah insisted stubbornly.

The only lights were my headlights shining directly

on the large van, making the red letters of the Long logo glow dully against the silver sides. The van. There. In front of the horse barn. That wasn't right. What had happened to the cross-country run?

"I thought you would be halfway to Denver by now."

"I'm not going to Denver. Going to Indiana, then Lexington."

"Wherever. But you were in such a hurry yesterday. What happened?"

Susannah stared at the van as if she was seeing it for the first time.

"What's wrong? Did one of the horses get sick?"

"No. The schedule just got changed," Wes said impatiently. "What is this anyway? Some kind of third degree? Look, why don't you get whatever it was you said you forgot?"

"My purse," Susannah put in quickly.

"Yeah. Well, I got a flashlight and I'll help you find it." His hand was on my door handle, ready to open it. "Where'd you leave it?"

"In the tack room." Susannah talked rapidly. "We'll be fine. I know right where it is. I know where the lights are. We'll just get it. I'll close the barn for you."

"You will, huh."

"Yes. We will."

"Uh huh. If that's the way you want it." Wes continued to hold on to the door handle for another moment as though he was trying to make up his mind, then he shrugged and headed back up the drive.

"Can you believe the arrogance of that man?" Susannah muttered as she rummaged through my glove compartment. "I thought you kept a flashlight in here."

"Why does Irma put up with him?" I handed over

the small light I kept tucked in the map compartment on the driver's door.

"Because they're good at what they do. What's this?" She snapped it on.

"A flashlight."

"Barely. Come on."

"Come on where?"

"To the barn. I want to check on the horses. Besides, I'm supposed to be looking for my purse. Remember?"

I shouldn't have agreed. I knew it. But it seemed safe enough. The pirate couldn't have come down Irma's drive or we would have seen him. There was no one around but the horses. I switched off my headlights and opened the door.

"Should I take my purse?" For some reason now I was whispering.

"Why?"

I couldn't think of a reason, so I threw the keys on the seat beside my purse and started after my daughter, who was already at the barn doors, pulling on one of them. It slid open with only a small protest.

It felt like walking into a cave. I knew Susannah was moving because I could see the weak light dancing down the barn aisle, but for a moment, while my eyes adjusted, that was all. I could hear the rustle of straw, the soft snort of a horse, the brush of Susannah's feet. I could smell the alfalfa, the molasses-orange smell of the grain and the distinctive odor of horse. Gradually, I could make out shapes moving behind the bars of the wide stall doors and I ventured past the closed door of the tack room as far as the first stall. Its door was open. I had only enough time to wonder why before Susannah was beside me. The flashlight was off. I almost screamed when she grabbed my arm.

"Don't make a sound. There's someone outside. Quick, get in here."

Screams are hard to swallow, but I managed. We darted behind the open stall door and she pulled me down on the floor. The barn seemed unnaturally still with only my heart making noise as it tried to climb out of my chest through my throat.

"Who is it?" I whispered in her ear.

She shook her head and put her finger against her lips.

The soft sound of footsteps and the glow of a stronger flashlight came down the barn aisle. It had to be the pirate, I thought wildly. How could I protect Susannah from this terrible peril? Exactly what it was I didn't know, but I was sure it was peril.

The footsteps went slowly down the aisle, starting, stopping, starting, stopping. I could feel a scream getting ready for another try.

The flashlight beam illuminated the horse in the stall next to the one where we crouched. The footsteps started again. There was no place to hide. We were trapped. All the old war movies I'd ever seen flashed back, prison camp escapees caught under the cruel glare of the spot light. I could almost hear the machine gun fire. Only the footsteps didn't stop and the light didn't flash.

I took a deep breath and hiccupped. Susannah looked at me aghast, then started to giggle. I pinched her and she glared at me instead.

"Where did he go?" I mouthed at her.

"I don't know," she whispered back.

She rolled carefully over on her hands and knees and started to pull herself up on the stall wall.

"No." I wanted to shout. Tugging at her did nothing,

but after what seemed like an eternity she squatted back down. Her eyes were wide as she whispered in my ear, "It's Chovalo. Irma must have gotten him bailed out."

Chovalo. So Dan was right. "What's he doing?"

"He went into the tack room." She grabbed my arm as a door quietly snapped open. A quick flash of light, the soft footstep again, the rattle of the barn door on its track and the barn was once more dark.

Susannah was moving. She crawled to the open stall door, looked around it and rapidly crawled back to me.

"It was Chovalo all right."

"But why?" I said in an almost normal tone. "Why would he want to roam around his own barn in the dark with only a flashlight?"

"I don't know." The distress in her voice made me want to reach out and hug her, but it would have to wait. We had to figure out what to do. If Chovalo really was a murderer and a drug runner, we were in serious trouble.

"We've got a problem," I told Susannah.

"Another one?"

"No. Same one. Chovalo knows we're here."

"How could he? We never made a sound. Unless we count your hiccup."

"You're forgetting something."

"What?"

"Our car."

She didn't say anything, but her eyes got a lot bigger. "Damn," she finally said. My sentiments exactly.

"Stay here." I reached for the flashlight. She gave it up reluctantly. I stood up slowly and edged out of the stall into the barn aisle, toward the slight opening in the big barn doors. The faint glow that entered made my weak flashlight unnecessary.

"Where are you going?" Her whisper echoed loudly in the quiet barn.

"To see if I can spot Chovalo. Or that blasted pirate. Or anybody. If no one's near our car, we'll make a run for it."

"You sound like a bad movie." Her voice came right on my heels.

"I told you to stay in the stall."

I didn't say it with much force. I motioned to her to help me. As silently as possible we pushed the big door back enough so we could see the whole yard. I could just see my car, still there.

"Look." Susannah plucked at my sleeve. There was the flashlight beam again, but somehow muted. I didn't think we could be seen against the unlit backdrop of the barn but wasn't in the mood to take chances, so we huddled tightly against the doors. Someone was coming out of the horse van. I pushed Susannah back and carefully took another look. The flashlight beam lit up his face like an angel in a Christmas play. It was Chovalo. He closed the van door, swung the light around the yard, letting it pause on my car. He walked over to it, studied it for a moment before letting the light play once more around the yard.

We were doomed.

The light swung our way. I gestured madly to Susannah but she'd already jumped back. We looked silently across the aisle at each other as the beam of light lingered on the open doorway.

Suddenly it went out. We waited. It must have been only minutes but it seemed like hours before Susannah crept across that small expanse and stood beside me. "Will you please tell me what's going on?"

"Chovalo was in the van." I spoke in a whisper even

though I didn't think anyone was in earshot. "Looking for something, I think. Then he left."

"Looking for what?"

"I'm not sure." Something was nagging at me. Chovalo. The van. Tack trunks. "Susannah, that's the same van Wes drove yesterday, isn't it?"

"Sure."

"Oh, oh."

"Oh, oh, what?"

"I just remembered what someone said and it's given me an idea."

"What kind of idea?"

"Wait. Let me think about this. Yes, that's it. I think. How could we have been so blind?"

"What are you talking about? Mom, I don't like the look on your face. I don't like the way this place feels. Let's get out of here."

"In a minute. Susannah, how many of these big vans does Irma have?"

"Mother, this isn't the time to take an inventory. Let's go."

"Wait. How many?"

"Two." Susannah stood still, watching me, but ready to sprint. "Why?"

"You're positive that's the one that was in Santa Barbara yesterday. The one Wes used?"

Susannah turned and stared at the van waiting quietly under the stars.

"It has to be. The other one's back on the East Coast somewhere."

"Wes was supposed to start his run last night. He made a terrible fuss about that."

"He had a schedule change. He said so." She stared

at the van some more. "Maybe he sent the horses some other way."

"Let's find out. Would you recognize the gray horse that was supposed to leave?"

"Won't be hard. We don't have a gray horse."

She took the flashlight, and we started down the barn aisle, checking each horse, making them blink as we shone the light on them.

"Here she is." Susannah's tone was a mixture of confusion and anger. "What's going on here?"

"Isn't this the horse with the tack trunk?"

Susannah looked from me to the horse, more confused all the time. "Yes."

"When was the last time you knew a horse that needed a trunk?"

"Wes said this is a special favor for the people who bought her. It's not a big deal, Mom."

"It might be."

"What are you talking about?" Susannah finished scratching the gray horse's nose and followed me down the aisle. "Where are we going?"

"To find the trunk."

"You can't possibly think...can you?"

She was right behind me as I pushed open the tack room door.

"Don't switch on the overhead light."

She was already flashing the light around the room, letting it bounce off saddles, bridles, blankets, tack trunks. Two red and silver ones and right beside them, a green one.

"Open it."

Susannah knelt beside it, pushing at its lid. "It's locked." She got up and stood beside me. We both stared down at the trunk, daring it to give up its secret.

"Do you keep Irma's locked?"

"Couldn't. No one ever trusted Bryce with the keys."

"Chovalo was looking for something in here, but he was also in the van." I thought about that. "If we're right and these trunks contain what we think, Chovalo must know it. So what's he looking for?"

"Does that mean you think he's innocent?" Susannah stared at the trunk as though it would sit up and answer all our questions any minute.

"I don't know. But if I'm right, he's sure not alone in all this."

"Are you talking about the pirate?" She looked around as if he might appear at any moment. "Where is he, anyway?"

"I don't know that, either."

"Let's go get Dan." It was the best idea I'd heard all night.

TWENTY-SEVEN

THE MOON WAS out, the yard bright under its light. It would be easy to cross to the waiting van. Chovalo had been in there, and I'd be willing to bet the farm he'd found something. I had to know for sure. Dan would be willing to listen to me if I had a few facts, not vague suspicions. The van might harbor some of those facts. My car was also waiting, inviting me to get the hell out of here and go home. I was tempted.

"Susannah, go get in the car and lock the doors. If anything happens, go for help."

"Oh sure, Mom. No problem." That clearly meant she wasn't leaving me. She followed me up the ramp and through the van door back into darkness.

"Turn on the damn light," I hissed. "I can't see a thing."

But I could hear. There was a terrible crash. Then a moan.

"Oh my God. Where are you? Are you all right?"

The flashlight came on to show Susannah sitting in a corner, her back against a hay bale.

"I tripped over some buckets."

"Maybe you can find some firecrackers to set off next. They wouldn't make much more noise. What's all this stuff?"

My light traveled slowly around the inside of the van, showing us we were in the empty middle, empty except for the hay bales Susannah was sitting on. A few plastic sacks that said "wood shavings" were shoved in a corner along with the pails and some long plastic things that looked like fish net hung on the wall.

"What are those things?" Curiosity momentarily won over the need to hurry.

"Hay nets." Susannah waved at them vaguely then pointed at what looked like padded pipe. "These are stalls. You back the horse into this space here and swing this thing against it and secure it with this pin. These chains go in front of the horse's chest."

There were metal arms on each side of us, suspended from the ceiling. They looked very efficient and at some other time I'd be fascinated to see how it all worked, but not now.

"I don't need a lesson in horse transporting," I snapped. "I want to know what Chovalo was looking for. Flash the light around."

It came to rest on two blue tack trunks.

"Where did those come from?" Susannah walked over to examine them better.

"I've got a pretty good idea. Keep the light on them."

This time the lid was unlocked. Not a good idea, for neatly stacked on the upper tray were little plastic sacks filled with coarse white granules. Lots of little sacks. Lots of money. Lots of trouble.

"Oh, dear God," breathed Susannah, the light glued on the trunk. "Is that…?"

"I'm pretty sure." I could feel myself start to shake. I'd never been so sorry to be right in my life. "Now we really have something to tell Dan. Come on. We're getting out of here."

I was a little late. The lights came on, flooding the inside of the van, momentarily blinding us. I gasped.

Susannah screamed, but neither of us slammed down the trunk lid.

"I wondered what was going on down here." Linda stood in the doorway, a few stray hairs straggling out from her normally severe ponytail, legs still encased in those tight jeans.

"Oh, Linda. Thank God, it's only you," gasped Susannah.

"Only me," Linda repeated. "Who were you afraid it might be?" Her slightly nasal voice was expressionless, but the look in those pale brown eyes wasn't.

"Chovalo, I guess. I can't believe it, but it must be true."

"What's true?" Linda filled the doorway, her tone only mildly curious, but she'd spotted the open lid on the tack trunk.

"Chovalo's selling drugs. Or, helping sell them. Look what we found." Susannah gestured toward the open trunk.

Linda took a half step forward. "You found something in that trunk? What do you suppose it is?" She took another step forward and I took one backward. I aimed a kick at Susannah, trying to shut her up, but missed. Too bad.

"Drugs." Susannah waved at the open trunk in her most dramatic manner. "That's what. We're sure that's what they are, aren't we, Mom."

I tried to get between Linda and Susannah while I figured out how to maneuver Susannah closer to the door. Linda took another couple of steps into the van, which made me happy, but she hadn't taken her hands out of her jacket pockets, which didn't.

"So," she said, her voice still mild. "What do you plan to do now?"

Run like hell, I thought.

"Why, go get Dan, of course," Susannah told her, "and I think you should find Wes. Don't you think so, Mom?"

I didn't, not that it mattered. Linda had only come inside enough to clear the doorway for him.

"Wes is right here. Aren't you. Honey!"

"Lay off, Linda. None of this is my fault." Wes slouched in, looking from us to the trunk and back. "You two just can't keep your noses clean, can you."

Susannah looked bewildered. Unfortunately, I wasn't. What I remembered, what I had begun to suspect was true, was. The only question left was, what did I do now?

"The two men in the pickup truck, they brought those two blue trunks, didn't they?" I blurted out before I could stop myself. "That's why you didn't leave. You were waiting for them."

Linda sighed. "Too smart by half, but it won't do you much good." She pulled a small, black, horrible looking gun out of her pocket and pointed it at me, then at Susannah.

"OK, Wesley Leon Fowler. Since you're getting so good at killing folks, figure out how you're going to get rid of these two."

"What?" squeaked Susannah. "What are you talking about? Mom?"

Amazing how you always turn to your mother when you need help. Only this time, Mom felt pretty helpless.

"How come I have to do it?" Wes looked at us belligerently. "Why don't you just shoot 'em?"

"You are an idiot," she told him, her tone dripping with contempt.

"Linda, I told you. Don't start."

"Biggest mistake I ever made, starting with you. You and your stupid temper." Her voice got tighter and angrier as she raged at him.

"I told you, Linda…" Wes took a step toward her and raised his fist.

"Don't threaten me, you red neck. This whole operation is a mess, and it's all your fault."

"My fault?" sputtered Wes. He'd taken a good look at the gun and dropped his fist. "You're crazy. I'm the one who keeps saving us."

"Oh?" Linda sneered. "First you tried to bully the old lady into not selling the business, then you thought you could bully Bryce into keeping his mouth shut. That's saving us? Push people around, that's the only thing you know how to do, besides drive a truck. If you'd kept your stupid hands off the little creep's neck, I could have made this gig last us another year."

This was another Linda. What happened to the quiet, obedient one? I hadn't much liked her, but she was a bunch better than the one in front of us.

"Neck?" Susannah's mouth was wide open. "You killed Bryce?"

I really wished she didn't feel the need to enter this conversation. I was pretty sure the more they fought, the longer we would stay healthy. Besides, ever since I'd seen what was in the blue tack trunks, I'd been certain who'd done the killing and why. Linda, however, I hadn't figured on.

"What have you been doing to Irma?"

"Not a damn thing," Linda snapped. "The old lady's never been so well off. She wouldn't have sold, either. Not after her buyer got a load of the books I was planning to give him. It woulda' worked too, if you'd kept your nose out and hadn't dragged her off to get 'professional advice.'"

The look she shot made me want to hide behind the hay bales. Susannah seemed oblivious. She kept staring at Wes's hands and repeated, "You killed Bryce? And Rusty?"

"Of course he killed Bryce. Killing people in a rage is one of the few things he knows how to do. And as soon as these local yokels get tired of trying to match up the prints from the bathroom and the fingerprints on the pitchfork with something on their computers and send them off to the FBI, we're finished here. I've been expecting the feds to come visiting for a week."

"Pitchfork? No." Susannah shook her head. "Wes wasn't even there when Rusty was killed. Bryce was gone when Wes got back. He couldn't have killed either of them. There's some mistake."

"You're right about that," Linda said bitterly. "But the mistake was mine."

"Shut up, Linda," Wes snarled. "You know as well as I do no one threatens me with blackmail. And Bryce was too fond of the stuff for us to trust his mouth." He turned to Susannah and laughed. "Nice to know I fooled you all though."

"You didn't." I shouldn't have spoken but that last statement was just a little too patronizing. "Stephanie said she'd seen you, that you pulled up before Bryce had left. But you told us you hadn't seen Bryce. Dan was right there when Stephanie told us. He knows you were lying, so you'd better leave us alone."

Wes looked a little uncertain. Unfortunately, Linda didn't. "We'll have to think what to do about that little bitch, but first things first." She smiled. Not a pretty sight. "If Dan hasn't come calling, then it's certain he didn't make that connection. Too bad you did."

My weak bluff hadn't worked. I'd better come up with something else and fast. But what?

"Move over there." Linda waved the gun toward the hay and waited none too patiently while Susannah and I backed up. "Sit down and don't move."

I pulled Susannah down beside me and whispered, "Keep quiet. I'll try and think of something." She looked at me with huge eyes filled with fear, bewilderment, but unfortunately not confidence. I could hardly blame her.

"Get the trunks stored before we get more company," Linda told Wes, who was still grumbling. He moved over to the stall area and started to pull back a rough black rubber mat. Then he lifted up several floorboards.

"Oh my God," said Susannah.

"Sure you want them to see this?" Wes glanced up at Linda.

"Who are they going to tell?"

"You're the one always bitching that things keep going wrong. At least no one's ever caught on to this before. And it was my idea."

"No one but Chovalo's nephew."

"I took care of him real neat. You're not the only smart one. Just the one with the biggest mouth."

"And we've had Chovalo sniffing around ever since."

"He hasn't found anything, has he? All you do is bitch, but I'm the one gets things done."

Wes finished lifting the blue trunks into the hole left by the removed boards. I thought for a moment he was going to occupy it. Linda raised the gun toward his bent back and the expression on her face wasn't a loving one. But she lowered the gun, leveling it instead on us, and hissed at Wes. "Get that other trunk and hurry."

Both trunks were stored, the floorboards, the mats back in place before anyone said another word. Linda gave one more instruction. "Go get the horse."

"What horse?"

"The one you're supposed to be delivering."

"Why? I thought you said we need to get out of here."

"We do. It would be nice if we didn't have anyone on our tail for a while. That horse is your cover. Just like always, she's going to stand right on top of those trunks and no one's going to think to ask you to move her. You're going to pick up the other horses in Fresno and head for LA, drop the stuff off and drive to Lexington. Just like your schedule says."

"How about them?" He jerked his head at us.

"You're going out Highway 41. Right? It gets pretty desolate out there. It won't be light for hours. There're plenty of canals and ditches out that way. Be sure you pick a good spot."

Wes nodded and left the van, returning moments later leading the gray mare. He backed her up over the spot where he'd stored the trunks and swung the stanchion against her side, securing it with a large pin. He pulled a bar in place across her chest, then pulled down one of the nets and snapped it onto rings so that it made a hammock in easy reach of the mare's head. She could move enough to balance herself but she wasn't going anywhere. It didn't seem to bother the horse. She just looked expectantly from the net to Wes. He walked over to us, said "Move," tore off a large flake of hay and dumped it into the net.

"You ready?" Linda shifted her weight and her gun, impatiently.

"Yep. All I need is my paperwork. If this is going to look like a real trip, let's make it good. I need to know where to meet up with you."

"Then come on."

Wes left the van and Linda backed toward the door, keeping the gun on us. "Hate to leave you in the dark, ladies, but you know how it is. Too bad I can't wish you a pleasant trip."

The lights went out and the door slammed. The loud clang that followed was the sound of a bar dropped into place. Neither of us moved or said anything for a moment. Then Susannah said softly, "Mom, you brought your cell phone, didn't you?"

"Sure."

"See if you can call Dan. Or nine-one-one."

"Good idea, but hard to do. It's in my purse. Which I left in the car."

Her "Oh" was pretty deflated.

"Do you still have the flashlight?"

"I think so. Why?"

"Seems better than sitting here in the dark. Turn it on. Maybe it'll help us think of a way out of here."

"Like what? We're locked in and we can't call for help. This doesn't look promising. The only good part is we know Chovalo's innocent. Of everything."

"He must have been looking for evidence, either that someone was running drugs or that his nephew was murdered. Or both."

"But now we can help him. If we ever get out of here."

I was trying to think of something to say when we

heard a whisper. Someone was at one of the small barred windows, softly calling.

"Susannah. Can you hear me? Susannah. Come to this window quickly. Susannah."

"It's Chovalo."

TWENTY-EIGHT

SUSANNAH SWITCHED ON the light and shone it at each window. "Chovalo. Where are you?"

"Here. On this side. Be quiet. They will be back any moment. I will try to open the van door and let you out, but I am afraid they have locked it. I will try now."

"No." Suddenly, I had a brainstorm. "Chovalo, we need help. Is my car still there?"

"Yes. They have not been near it."

"They will soon. Listen. In my purse is a phone. Go get it and call the police. Tell them what's happened and get them out here, fast. Then see if you can get the door opened."

"Si. I will do that. Do not worry. You will be free in no time."

We both held our breaths while we listened. I was sure I could hear the crunch of footsteps going away and the soft click of a door opening. Then there was no sound but the munching of hay and the contented blowing of the horse. Moments passed. We found ourselves huddled close against the van door, trying to hear something, anything. There! A vague murmur that had to be voices. Why was Chovalo talking so loud? He didn't need to shout into the phone like that, he needed to keep his voice down. Only, it wasn't Chovalo. It was Wes doing the shouting. A shot echoed. Just one. And silence. A terrible silence, broken by a soft sob from Susannah, followed by the sound of the bar being removed from the door. It opened, but the light didn't go back on, the moon did the job. Wes staggered in carrying a large bundle and dumped it at our feet.

"You people are a hell of a lot more trouble than you're worth. It'll be a real pleasure gettin' rid of you."

He was gone again. The door swung into place, followed by a rasping noise and a loud angry clank as the bar crashed down.

"What was that?" I could feel the jolt of the crash all through me. It wasn't a pleasant feeling.

"Wes slipped the ramp in place. We're ready to move."

"Oh" was all I could think of to say. I didn't have time for any more. The bundle moaned, to our relief.

"Shine the light down here," I told Susannah. "Maybe we can see how badly he's hurt."

The left side of Chovalo's shirt and down his arm was sticky and wet. The puny light made the blood a dull rust color. It didn't matter. The only question was how much damage the bullet had done. Neither of us knew how to find out.

"What do we do now?" Susannah knelt beside him, tears rolling down her face. "I'm afraid to touch him."

"I know, but I think we have to. Hold the flashlight closer. Here. Oh, God."

I'd been trying desperately to think what people did in the mystery books I read, but only old Western movies came to mind, the kind where the heroine pulls off her petticoat, tears it apart and uses it to stop the hero from bleeding to death. I didn't have a petticoat, but that didn't stop me from tearing open Chovalo's shirt. He'd never miss the buttons. Below his left shoulder was a large nasty-looking hole, oozing blood each time he took another ragged breath.

"Do you have a handkerchief?" I already knew the answer.

"Only one dirty Kleenex," she answered. "What're we going to do?"

"He's still alive, but we need to stop the bleeding. Anyway, that's what they do in the movies. Do you have on a bra?"

She shook her head. I spent a precious second pining for the lost modesty of the younger generation. I pulled my tee shirt up, slipped off my own and used it the best I could as a bandage.

The expression on Susannah's face was a wonder to see. I might have enjoyed it more, but just then the engine roared. We started to move.

Chovalo groaned again, from the movement or from my ministrations, I didn't know. Either way, it seemed a good sign. His eyelids flickered, he tried to say something, but only another groan came out.

I had to know. "Chovalo, did you find the phone? Did you make the call?"

It was only a faint whisper, but it was enough. No. We were on our own, heading toward a desolate highway, locked in a moving horse van with no way out until the man who was driving decided it was time to open the door. I hoped he'd keep driving a long time.

Chovalo coughed up some blood, then tried to say something. It sounded like "sit up." He struggled a little, then collapsed, making an ominous gurgling sound.

"Oh, dear God. Mom, what do we do? Should we prop him up a little?"

I had no idea, but working on the theory that doing

something was better than standing around wringing our hands, I said, "I think just a little. What are those things over there?"

"Horse blankets. They aren't clean."

I didn't think that counted. "They're soft and they'll keep him from rolling around every time this damn van jolts. Here. Help me."

Watched curiously by the gray mare as she methodically consumed her dinner, we made a bed of sorts. It seemed to help, for Chovalo started to breathe a little more normally and opened his eyes. He looked like he was trying to say something when the van gave another hard jolt; he gave a gasp and passed out.

"Do you think he'll live?"

"Probably. Until Wes stops this thing. Then none of us will, unless we think of something quick."

"I can't believe this is happening." Susannah ran her hands through her hair, making it stand on end. She looked from Chovalo to me to the horse. The horse. Standing there in her narrow stall, eating out of a net.

"Susannah, flash your light over the back wall." I had a vague idea that was beginning to take shape. I hoped.

"Why?"

"This is not the time for a discussion. I want to see those hay nets."

"Hay nets? What on earth... Hay nets! Mom, you're brilliant."

Finally, confidence. If I could only muster up some of my own, I thought, as she flashed the light around. The nets hung on the wall, three or four of them. Nice flat, strong nylon nets with three snaps on each side for attaching onto a stall wall, a safe and efficient way of holding hay. Only, it wasn't hay I was thinking of holding.

Susannah was way ahead of me, reaching up to lift one down, then another.

"How are we going to do this?" She handed one to me.

Old movies once again replayed through my mind.

"We'll let him open the door, you flash the light in his eyes and I'll throw the net over his head. You run out of the van and get the phone in the truck cab and call nine-one-one."

It sounded simple. It could have worked. It almost did. We'd been anxious for Wes not to stop, but now that we were ready, it seemed he was determined to drive forever. Susannah and I discussed over and over how she would hold the light, how I would throw one net over his head, then the next one. While he was fighting to free himself she would run to the cab. It was flawless. At one point I thought Chovalo was awake and listening. He seemed to be trying to lift his hand, but when we knelt by his side, he was again unconscious.

"I wish we had some water to give him." Susannah started to touch the wound, then drew her hand away. "I wish we had something besides your bra."

"Be grateful I wear one."

That was when the van slowed down, the gears changed and we felt the bump as we pulled off the road. It was black outside and since we immediately snapped off the flashlight, it was black inside also.

"Get ready." I gathered up my nets and crawled over behind the door. "Don't be scared."

"Why would I be scared?" I could hear Susannah's voice coming from somewhere near the middle of the van but I didn't bother to answer. Let her bolster courage any way she wanted.

The footsteps were faint but the scrape of the ramp

and the removal of the bar wasn't. The lock squeaked and the door rasped as Wes pulled it open.

"Sittin' in the dark won't help, ladies. Won't even buy you any more time then...hey!"

Susannah shone the light directly on him and I started to throw the net. I hadn't counted on Wes's flashlight, whose beam swung wildly around the van, landing directly in the eyes of the up-to-now calm gray horse. No longer. As soon as the light hit her she went ballistic, throwing herself against her chest bar, trying to rear. Her wild whinnying echoed against all sides of the van. That set her off even more. The flash that was supposed to stay on Wes suddenly shone on the horse.

"No, no. Shine it back. I can't see," I screamed.

"What the hell are you doin'?" Wes hollered. I had the first net on him but had no idea if his arms were pinned. They weren't. I could feel them flail around. He still had his light. It landed on Susannah, who shone hers back on us.

"Quick, Mom. The other net. Oh, I can't see."

I tried, but I only had his head covered and he was jumping and heaving like he'd been stuck with a spur. He dropped his light as I jumped on his back and tried to throw the other net over him, but not being experienced in rodeo, it didn't work. The net fell. I stayed on. For a moment.

"Watch out. He's got a gun," Susannah hollered and dropped her flashlight. I could see the light roll toward the horse, who was doing some serious rearing and noise making of her own. The horse came down on the flashlight and the van was plunged into darkness. Until the gunshot. A brilliant flash told me where Wes stood, followed by the sound of a bullet hitting the side of the van and what must have been a ricochet as it hit another side. For a second, all was still. Then I heard a groan. A loud one, accompanied with a sob. Susannah. The son of a bitch had shot Susannah. I used his hair to climb higher on his back. I clawed at his eyes with my fingernails. I roared in his ear that I was going to kill him, alternating with pleas for Susannah to speak to me. She didn't. Wes did. He bellowed like a bull and swung around with me still clinging. He plucked me off effortlessly and flung me across the van. I could feel myself hit the wall, could feel the back of my head split open, could taste the blood that started to pour down my face just as the lights came on. There was a figure in the doorway. I stayed conscious only long enough to recognize him. The missing pirate.

TWENTY-NINE

A VOICE CALLED my name.

"Mom, Mom? Wake up, please."

"Ellen. For God's sake, will one of you look at her? Ellen?"

Susannah. I knew that other voice too. Didn't I? My eyes weren't focusing and I wasn't sure what had happened, only that wherever we were I didn't like it. Susannah. She shouldn't be in this nightmare.

"Lift her up, there, gently. Um, quite a mess."

I didn't know that voice at all and immediately decided whoever it belonged to needed to go away. Movement had set off fireworks inside my head and I wanted to be left alone.

"Go away," I groaned.

"Oh, Mom. You're alive."

I could just make out Susannah, who seemed to be crying.

"Of course I'm alive," I managed. Memories slowly returned. It was my turn to panic. I struggled to sit up more in spite of the roman candles that refused to stop exploding in my brain. "Are you all right? Are you shot?"

"Not even a scratch. But I thought he'd killed you."

Another face came into focus and the relief on it was obvious. Only seeing it didn't relieve me. It was the damn pirate again.

"What are you doing here?" The van seemed to be

full of people, some in dark jackets with "police" in yellow letters on their backs, others in the navy blue of the paramedics. I saw a stretcher being carefully lifted through the van door and heard someone crooning gently to the mare. She evidently wasn't totally convinced life had returned to normal and kept pawing the floor. Each bang felt like a cherry bomb going off in my skull.

"Fine thanks for saving your life." He grinned down at me.

"You? Saved our lives?"

The man who had pronounced my head a mess was back, along with someone else and a stretcher.

"This one gets a ride to the hospital too. OK, Jack, on my count of three."

"Where's Wes?" I gasped as they started strapping me down. "I'm not going to the hospital. I'm fine." Only things were getting a little fuzzy around the edges again and I wasn't quite up to arguing.

I felt Susannah's hand in mine as the stretcher was lifted and just made out her face. She kept saying something, but I couldn't understand. I wanted to ask her if the pirate really had saved us, wanted to tell her not to trust him, but I was getting cold and felt myself slipping, slipping. I tried to squeeze her hand, tried to make the words come out, tried to take one more look at her, only she wasn't who I saw. It was my blasted pirate, grinning down on me as I passed out cold.

THIRTY

THE SUN WAS shining. I could feel it trying to get under my eyelids, but I didn't want it there. A voice called my name, softly, insisting. A voice I didn't know. I opened one eye just a slit, found it didn't hurt too much and opened the other one. I had no idea where I was or the identity of the man who smiled down on me.

"Nice to have you back." He proceeded to shine a light in my eyes, lifted my head up slightly, nodded and said, "You'll do. Head still hurts? We'll give you something. Don't worry. Your hair will grow back."

Before I could protest, croak out a question or even reach for my hair, a nurse I hadn't even seen injected something into an IV I hadn't known I was hooked to. I was gone again.

This time there was no sun, and I knew the voice calling me. Susannah.

"Mom? Are you all right? Are you awake?"

"I think so." I tested my eyelids. They slid open. There was Susannah, Dan right behind her.

"You gave us quite a scare." Another familiar voice.

I turned my head with surprisingly little pain. There was Aunt Mary. I grinned at her.

"Sorry. Can you crank this bed up, someone? I feel like I've been lying down for a month."

"Only two days," said Susannah.

"You're kidding," I said, incredulous. "That long?"

"Well, at first you were just out, but after they found

you didn't have a skull fracture, they gave you something. You've been sleeping. Lots."

"How's your head?" Dan hovered close. "Are you in pain?"

"I've felt better," I admitted, "but it feels good to sit up. Wow."

Memories flooded back. The van, Wes, Chovalo, Susannah.

"Chovalo. Is he all right?" I asked anxiously.

"He's going to be fine," Aunt Mary answered. "We all gave blood. He'd lost a lot but he should be able to go home in a couple of days."

"Thanks to a very inventive bandage," Dan said with a straight face.

I could feel myself blush. "What happened to Wes? How did you find us?"

"He didn't. I did." A familiar face appeared around Dan's shoulder, gray eyes smiling, soft blond curls gone, but it didn't matter. I knew who he was.

"The pirate!"

"Meet Robert 'Bobbie' Thomas, Special Agent with the Bureau of Alcohol, Tobacco and Firearms." Dan grinned down at me.

"I understand my parrots upset you a bit." Special Agent Thomas's face was grave but there was a little crinkle around the corners of his eyes.

"Your parrots were only part of it. What's going on here? I missed the whole thing."

"You'd better tell her everything, Dan," Aunt Mary said. "She'll drive us all crazy until she knows. Besides, after what she went through, she deserves to know."

"You're darn right." I sat up straighter and winced. I put my hand up to touch my bandage and cringed as I felt a shaved spot.

"Don't worry, Mom. It doesn't look too bad. Maybe we can fix it later."

How reassuring, I thought, but let any concern for my hair go. I felt as if I'd come into the movie in the middle. I wanted the beginning and the end. "Tell me. Everything."

Susannah perched on the end of my bed. Dan pulled up another chair. Special Agent Thomas, my pirate, leaned against the doorframe.

"If you're all cozy." I said that as sarcastically as I could manage.

"OK." Dan laughed. "You first." He gestured at Thomas, who nodded.

"About a month ago the Sheriff's Department called us, asking for help. They'd located a couple of sites where they thought methamphetamine was being manufactured. They had a couple of hot suspects, but nothing they could take to court. They knew the stuff was being moved in large quantities, but couldn't figure out how. They'd traced it, through that Rusty kid who got killed, to the horse shows, but they still didn't know who his contact was or how it was being transported. That's where I came in. The pirate outfit is one I use for my kids' birthday parties. Raising parrots is my hobby. I have six of them. Kids. I have more parrots. Anyway, I was supposed to wander around and see if I could spot Rusty's contact."

"So you did know him." I turned to Dan accusingly.

"Not exactly." Dan shook his head. "I'd been tipped off by the Sheriff, but we didn't actually meet." Dan and Special Agent Thomas gave each other that "all good buddies together" look. "That is, until after he grabbed you out of the horse trailer."

"What about Chovalo," I asked, "and his nephew?"

"Let's start a little earlier." Dan reached down and pulled my blanket a little higher up on my lap. While he was there, he patted my hand. I smiled at him but wiggled my fingers for him to go on. "Wes and Linda have a record that goes back quite a way."

That didn't surprise me one bit.

"That's why she was so worried about Wes's fingerprints," put in Susannah.

"They really know about the horse hauling business, but Wes's been in jail half a dozen times and couldn't get a respectable job. When they heard about Bud's death, they faked some references, which Irma was in no shape to properly check, then moved in and took over. They started moving drugs almost immediately, let all Irma's old drivers do the runs that were clean. Wes took the important ones. Linda used the books to launder the money. It all worked fine until the day Miguel found the hole in the floor of the van. He wanted to know about it. Wes gave him some excuse and later gave the kid a Coke laced with enough meth to kill an elephant."

"You OK?" Dan looked at me anxiously. I felt sick. Partly because my head hurt and partly because of the story. What a waste of a promising young life.

"I'm fine. Go on. I want to hear it all."

"Chovalo never believed Miguel would have taken drugs on his own. He thought Bryce was somehow responsible. He kept nosing around looking for some kind of proof. Only, he was making Wes nervous. In the meantime, Rusty managed to get a job for the horse show with Bryce. He was one of Wes's contacts, a not very reliable one, so when he tried a little blackmail, Wes lost his temper and skewered him on the pitchfork."

Susannah shivered a little. Aunt Mary reached over and patted her hand. "Such a tragedy. All of it."

I silently agreed. "Why Bryce?"

"Bryce had quite a habit. Rusty had kept him supplied, at a price, of course." Special Agent Thomas took up the story again. "The Sheriff's Department and Dan," he nodded toward him, "were looking hard at Gutierrez. I was leaning more toward Ellis. He was all over the country with the horses and his habit needed a lot of feeding. Which meant more money than I thought he was making showing horses."

"How about Stephanie? Speaking of another waste."

"She kept getting in the way. She knew about Bryce's habit and evidently thought she could get him to stop. It wasn't until she found out about his, uh, other tastes that she backed off. I don't think she ever knew about Wes."

"Bryce did?" I asked.

"Rusty told him. Or, told him enough. He tried to make a buy off of Wes Sunday afternoon, after Stephanie reamed him out. It was Wes who took him into the shower room under the pretext of supplying him with more meth."

"That's something I should have picked up on sooner." I sighed. "Stephanie told us that night that Wes pulled up while Bryce was there. But Wes said he never saw Bryce. It didn't hit me until Susannah and I were in that barn, staring at the tack trunks."

"I should have picked up on it sooner too," said Dan. "When I did it was almost too late. You and Susannah were already at the ranch, getting yourselves locked in the horse van. That's something we are going to talk about." His grim face softened and he squeezed my hand. Too hard, but somehow I didn't care.

"Later?"

"Later," he replied.

"Where did you disappear to?" I asked Thomas. "And, how did you find us?" It was hard to think of him as Agent Thomas. He was still the pirate to me.

"I turned my lights off when I saw you following me, drove on past Irma's driveway and parked. When you turned down Irma's driveway, I figured I better find out what was going on. I have this aversion to getting shot, so left my car where it was and walked through the fields toward the barn. Do you know how many gopher holes are in those fields?" He grimaced, but I didn't feel sorry for him. I would have traded him his gopher holes for my head any day.

"I arrived in time to see Wes shoot Chovalo," Pirate Thomas went on. "I got the license number off the van, alerted the Sheriff on my cellular and followed. The Sheriff caught up about the time Wes pulled over. Great timing, don't you think?"

He smiled, knowing there was only one answer.

"Two minutes earlier would have been nice." I put my hand carefully where hair used to be. "What happened to Linda?"

"The Sheriff sent out a couple of deputies to the ranch to pick her up. She'd already converted everything she could get her hands on into cash, including all of Irma's money. She wasn't planning on joining back up with Wes. Great gal, Linda. Guess she gave the Sheriff's boys quite a time."

He stopped for a second and then grinned. "The hardest part was keeping Dan from attacking Wes. He appeared right as you were being lifted into the ambulance, and if he'd had his way, Wes would have been riding on a stretcher right beside you."

"Not in Ellie's ambulance," Dan stated. "He'd have had to find one of his own."

What a shame I missed all that.

The pirate, or Agent Thomas, looked around the room, then down at me and winked. "That's about it. Any time you need a pirate, whistle. I'll come running. Speaking of which, I've got to catch a plane. Good luck." He was gone.

"He sure is good at fading away," I muttered, but I was looking up at Dan, savoring the idea of his coming to my rescue, even if a little late.

"Hmm. Yes." Aunt Mary also looked at Dan, who still had hold of my hand. "Susannah, what do you say we do a little fading of our own."

"No, I want to tell Mom...oh." She looked at Dan, at me, at Dan's hand holding mine. "I guess it can wait. I think you get to come home later today, Mom. I'll tell you then. Maybe."

She dropped a quick kiss on my forehead, grinned at Dan and left with Aunt Mary.

"Well," Dan began. He sounded uncertain. Trying to decide whether to kiss or scold me? "You gave me quite a scare. I'd just as soon you didn't do, ah, something so, ah, damn it, Ellie. You almost got yourself killed."

A warm glow filled me. Dan cared. Really cared. And, would wonders never cease, I cared that he cared. "Does that mean you haven't given up on me?"

"I thought about it, but I seem to have gotten used to you. Think you could get used to me?"

"I might. We could talk about it."

"I'm probably not going to change much. But, I'll make you one promise."

"Only one?"

"The only one that counts. I love you, Ellen Page

McKenzie. I don't know why. I'm pretty sure there'll be times I'll regret it. But I won't stop. I promise."

He leaned over and kissed me, gently at first, then with the same passion, the same intensity as last Saturday night.

"Ellie, I thought I'd lost you. A thought I don't like. Just as soon as you're better I'm going to show you how much."

He loved me. I loved him too. So he would be a little overprotective. I'd struggle against it, I'd scold him, watch his calories, do a little protecting of my own. I had a pretty good idea that it all might feel just right. Live to regret it, huh? We'd see about that. I glanced at the door. Susannah had thoughtfully closed it.

"I think there's too much talking going on." I reached out my arms to kiss him back.

* * * * *

REQUEST YOUR FREE BOOKS!

2 FREE NOVELS
PLUS 2 FREE GIFTS!

WORLDWIDE LIBRARY®
Your Partner in Crime

YES! Please send me 2 FREE novels from the Worldwide Library® series and my 2 FREE gifts (gifts are worth about $10). After receiving them, if I don't wish to receive any more books, I can return the shipping statement marked "cancel." If I don't cancel, I will receive 4 brand-new novels every month and be billed just $5.24 per book in the U.S. or $6.24 per book in Canada. That's a saving of at least 34% off the cover price. It's quite a bargain! Shipping and handling is just 50¢ per book in the U.S. and 75¢ per book in Canada.* I understand that accepting the 2 free books and gifts places me under no obligation to buy anything. I can always return a shipment and cancel at any time. Even if I never buy another book, the two free books and gifts are mine to keep forever.

414/424 WDN FEJ3

Name	(PLEASE PRINT)	

Address		Apt. #

City	State/Prov.	Zip/Postal Code

Signature (if under 18, a parent or guardian must sign)

Mail to the **Reader Service:**
IN U.S.A.: P.O. Box 1867, Buffalo, NY 14240-1867
IN CANADA: P.O. Box 609, Fort Erie, Ontario L2A 5X3

Not valid for current subscribers to the Worldwide Library series.

Want to try two free books from another line?
Call 1-800-873-8635 or visit www.ReaderService.com.

* Terms and prices subject to change without notice. Prices do not include applicable taxes. Sales tax applicable in N.Y. Canadian residents will be charged applicable taxes. Offer not valid in Quebec. This offer is limited to one order per household. All orders subject to credit approval. Credit or debit balances in a customer's account(s) may be offset by any other outstanding balance owed by or to the customer. Please allow 4 to 6 weeks for delivery. Offer available while quantities last.

Your Privacy—The Reader Service is committed to protecting your privacy. Our Privacy Policy is available online at www.ReaderService.com or upon request from the Reader Service.

We make a portion of our mailing list available to reputable third parties that offer products we believe may interest you. If you prefer that we not exchange your name with third parties, or if you wish to clarify or modify your communication preferences, please visit us at www.ReaderService.com/consumerschoice or write to us at Reader Service Preference Service, P.O. Box 9062, Buffalo, NY 14269. Include your complete name and address.

WWLI1B

FAMOUS FAMILIES

YES! Please send me the *Famous Families* collection featuring the Fortunes, the Bravos, the McCabes and the Cavanaughs. This collection will begin with 3 FREE BOOKS and 2 FREE GIFTS in my very first shipment— and more valuable free gifts will follow! My books will arrive in 8 monthly shipments until I have the entire 51-book *Famous Families* collection. I will receive 2-3 free books in each shipment and I will pay just $4.49 U.S./$5.39 CDN for each of the other 4 books in each shipment, plus $2.99 for shipping and handling.* If I decide to keep the entire collection, I'll only have paid for 32 books because 19 books are free. I understand that accepting the 3 free books and gifts places me under no obligation to buy anything. I can always return a shipment and cancel at any time. My free books and gifts are mine to keep no matter what I decide.

268 HCN 0387   468 HCN 0387

Name	(PLEASE PRINT)	
Address		Apt. #
City	State/Prov.	Zip/Postal Code

Signature (if under 18, a parent or guardian must sign)

Mail to the **Reader Service:**

IN U.S.A.: P.O. Box 1867, Buffalo, NY 14240-1867
IN CANADA: P.O. Box 609, Fort Erie, Ontario L2A 5X3

ReaderService.com

Manage your account online!

- Review your order history
- Manage your payments
- Update your address

We've designed the Reader Service website just for you.

Enjoy all the features!

- Reader excerpts from any series
- Respond to mailings and special monthly offers
- Discover new series available to you
- Browse the Bonus Bucks catalogue
- Share your feedback

Visit us at:

ReaderService.com